JACK HIGGINS

COLD HARBOUR

A SIGNET BOOK

And this one for my daughter Sarah

SIGNET

Published by the Penguin Group
Penguin Books Ltd, 27 Wrights Lane, London W8 5TZ, England
Penguin Books USA Inc., 375 Hudson Street, New York, New York 10014, USA
Penguin Books Australia Ltd, Ringwood, Victoria, Australia
Penguin Books Canada Ltd, 10 Alcorn Avenue, Toronto, Ontario, Canada M4V 3B2
Penguin Books (NZ) Ltd, 182–190 Wairau Road, Auckland 10, New Zealand

Penguin Books Ltd, Registered Offices: Harmondsworth, Middlesex, England

First published by William Heinemann Ltd 1990
Published in Signet 1997
1 3 5 7 9 10 8 6 4 2

Foreword

My reputation for novels of the Second World War since the unprecedented success of *The Eagle Has Landed* means that fans constantly write asking for more. *Cold Harbour* was firmly based in fact. Both British and German forces during the war assumed the identity of the enemy. Many German planes flew for the RAF and many British planes were operated by the Luftwaffe. At least two U boats were operated by the Royal Navy. So the idea of *Cold Harbour*, the secret base in Cornwall where the planes were Luftwaffe and the ships were Kriegsmarine, took shape. I've been asked again and again to produce a sequel – who knows?

JACK HIGGINS
October 1996

One

There were bodies all around, clear in the moonlight, some in lifejackets, some not. Way beyond, the sea was on fire with burning oil and as Martin Hare lifted on the crest of a wave, he saw what was left of the destroyer, her prow already under the water. There was a dull explosion, her stern lifted and she started to go. He skidded down the other side of the wave, buoyant in his lifejacket, and then another washed over him and he choked, half-fainting as he struggled for breath, aware of the intense pain from the shrapnel in his chest.

The sea was running very fast in the slot between the islands, six or seven knots at least. It seemed to take hold of him, carrying him along at an incredible rate, the cries of the dying faded into the night behind. Again he was lifted higher on a wave, paused for a moment, half blind from the salt, then swept down very fast and cannoned into a liferaft.

He grabbed at one of the rope handles and looked up. A man crouched there, a Japanese officer in uniform. His feet were bare; Hare noticed that. They stared at each other for a long moment and then Hare tried to pull himself up. But he had no strength left.

The Japanese crawled forward without a word, reached down, caught him by the lifejacket and hauled him on to the raft. At the same moment the raft spun like a top, caught by an eddy, and the Japanese pitched headfirst into the sea.

Within seconds he was ten yards away, his face clear in the moonlight. He started to swim back towards the raft and then behind him, cutting through the white froth between the waves, Hare saw a shark's fin. The Japanese didn't even cry out, simply threw up his arms and disappeared. And it was Hare who screamed, as he always did, coming bolt upright in the bed, his body soaked in sweat.

The duty nurse was McPherson, a tough, no-nonsense lady of fifty, a widow with two sons in the Marines fighting their way through the islands. She came in now and stood looking at him, hands on hips.

'The dream again?'

Hare swung his legs to the floor and reached for his robe. 'That's it. Who's the doctor tonight?'

'Commander Lawrence, but he won't do you any good. Another couple of pills so you'll sleep some more like you've slept all afternoon already.'

'What time is it?'

'Seven o'clock. Why don't you have a shower and I'll lay out that nice new uniform for you. You can come down to dinner. It'll do you good.'

'I don't think so.'

He looked in the mirror and ran his fingers through the unruly black hair that was streaked with grey, although at forty-six you had to expect that. The face was handsome enough, pale from months of hospitalisation. But it was in the eyes that the lack of hope showed, no expression there at all.

He opened a drawer in the bedside locker, found his lighter and a pack of cigarettes and lit one. He was already coughing as he walked to the open window and looked out over the balcony to the garden.

'Wonderful,' she said. 'One good lung left, so now you're

trying to finish what the Japs started.' There was a Thermos flask filled with coffee by the bed. She poured some into a cup and brought it over. 'Time to start living again, Commander. As they say in those Hollywood movies, for you the war is over. You should never have started in the first place. It's a young man's game.'

He sipped his coffee. 'So what do I do?'

'Back to Harvard, Professor.' She smiled. 'The students will love you. All those medals. Don't forget to wear your uniform the first day.'

He smiled in spite of himself, but only briefly. 'God help me, Maddie, but I don't think I could go back. I've had the war, I know that.'

'And it's had you, angel.'

'I know. The butcher's shop at Tulugu finished me off. It also seems to have finished me for anything else.'

'Well, you're a grown man. You want to sit around this room and quietly decay that's your business.' She walked to the door, opened it and turned. 'Only I would suggest you comb your hair and make yourself respectable. You've got a visitor.'

He frowned. 'A visitor?'

'Yes, he's with Commander Lawrence now. I didn't know you had any British connection.'

'What are you talking about?' Hare asked, bewildered.

'Your visitor. Very top brass. A Brigadier Munro of the British Army, though you'd never think so. Doesn't even wear a uniform.'

She went out, closing the door. Hare stood there for a moment, frowning, then hurried into the bathroom and turned on the shower.

Brigadier Dougal Munro was sixty-five and white-haired, an engagingly ugly man in an ill-fitting suit of Donegal tweed.

He wore a pair of steel-rimmed spectacles of the type issued to other ranks in the British Army.

'But is he fit, that's what I need to know, Doctor?' Munro was saying.

Lawrence wore a white surgical coat over his uniform. 'You mean physically?' He opened the file in front of him. 'He's forty-six years of age, Brigadier. He took three pieces of shrapnel in his left lung and spent six days on a liferaft. It's a miracle he's still around.'

'Yes, I take your point,' Munro said.

'Here's a man who was a professor at Harvard. A naval reserve officer, admittedly, because he was a famous yachtsman with connections in all the right places who gets himself in PT boats at the age of forty-three when the war starts.' He leafed through the pages. 'Every damned battle area in the Pacific. Lieutenant Commander, and medals.' He shrugged. 'Everything there is, including two Navy Crosses and then that final business at Tulugu. That Japanese destroyer blew him half out of the water so he rammed her and set off an explosive charge. He should have died.'

'As I heard it, nearly everyone else did,' Munro observed.

Lawrence closed the file. 'You know why he didn't get the Medal of Honor? Because it was General MacArthur who recommended him and the Navy doesn't like the Army interfering.'

'You're not regular Navy, I take it?' Munro said.

'Am I hell.'

'Good. I'm not regular Army, so plain speaking. Is he fit?'

'Physically – yes. Mind you, I should think it's taken ten years off the other end of his life. The medical board has indicated no further seagoing duty. In view of his age, he has the option of taking a medical discharge now.'

'I see.' Munro tapped his forehead. 'And what about up here?'

'In the head?' Lawrence shrugged. 'Who knows? He's certainly suffered from depression of the reactive kind, but that passes. He sleeps badly, seldom leaves his room and gives the distinct impression of not knowing what the hell to do with himself.'

'So he's fit to leave?'

'Oh, sure. He's been fit enough for weeks. With the proper authorisation, of course.'

'I've got that.'

Munro took a letter from his inside pocket, opened it and passed it across. Lawrence read it and whistled softly. 'Jesus, it's that important?'

'Yes.' Munro put the letter back in his pocket, picked up his Burberry raincoat and umbrella.

Lawrence said, 'My God, you want to send him back in.'

Munro smiled gently and opened the door. 'I'll see him now, Commander, if you please.'

Munro looked out on to the balcony across the garden to the lights of the city in the falling dusk. 'Very pleasant, Washington, at this time of year.' He turned and held out his hand. 'Munro – Dougal Munro.'

'Brigadier?' Hare said.

'That's right.'

Hare was wearing slacks and an open-necked shirt, his face still damp from the shower. 'You'll forgive me for saying so, Brigadier, but you are the most unmilitary man I ever saw.'

'Thank God for that,' Munro said. 'Until 1939, I was an Egyptologist by profession, a Fellow of All Souls, Oxford. My rank was to give me, shall we say, authority in certain quarters.'

Hare frowned. 'Wait a minute. Do I smell intelligence here?'

'You certainly do. Have you heard of SOE, Commander?'

'Special Operations Executive,' Hare said. 'Don't you handle agents into occupied France and so on?'

'Exactly. We were the forerunners of your own OSS who, I'm happy to say, are now working closely with us. I'm in charge of Section D at SOE, more commonly known as the dirty tricks department.'

'And what in the hell would you want with me?' Hare demanded.

'You were a Professor of German Literature at Harvard, am I right?'

'So what?'

'Your mother was German. You spent a great deal of time with her parents in that country as a boy. Even did a degree at Dresden University.'

'So?'

'You speak the language fluently, I understand, or so your Naval intelligence service tells me and your French is quite reasonable.'

Hare frowned. 'What are you trying to say? Are you trying to recruit me as a spy or something?'

'Not at all,' Munro told him. 'You see, you're really quite unique, Commander. It's not just that you speak fluent German. It's the fact that you're a naval officer with a vast experience in torpedo boats who also speaks fluent German that makes you interesting.'

'I think you'd better explain.'

'All right.' Munro sat down. 'You served on PT boats with Squadron Two in the Solomons, am I right?'

'Yes.'

'Well, this is classified, but I can tell you that at the urgent request of the Office of Strategic Services your men are to be transferred to the English Channel to land and pick up agents on the French coast.'

'And you want me for that?' Hare said in amazement. 'You're crazy. I'm all washed up. Christ, they want me to take a medical discharge.'

'Hear me out,' Munro said. 'In the English Channel, British

MTB's have had a very rough time with their German counterparts.'

'What the Germans call a *Schnellboot*.' Hare said. 'A fast boat. An apt title.'

'Yes. Well, for some contrary reason we call them E-boats. As you say, they're fast, too damn fast. We've been trying to get hold of one ever since the war started and I'm happy to say we finally succeeded last month.'

'You're kidding,' Hare said in astonishment.

'I think you'll find I never do, Commander,' Munro told him. 'One of the S.80 series. Had some engine problem on a night patrol off the Devon coast. When one of our destroyers turned up at dawn, the crew abandoned ship. Naturally, her captain primed a charge before leaving to blow the bottom out of her. Unfortunately for him, it failed to explode. Interrogation of his radio operator indicated that their final message to their base at Cherbourg was that they were sinking her, which means we have their boat and the Kriegsmarine don't know.' He smiled. 'You see the point?'

'I'm not sure.'

'Commander Hare, there is in Cornwall a tiny fishing port called Cold Harbour. No more than two or three dozen cottages and a manor house. It's in a defence area so the inhabitants have long since moved out. My department uses it for, shall we say, special purposes. I operate a couple of planes from there, German planes. A Stork and a Ju88S night fighter. They still carry Luftwaffe insignia and the man who flies them, gallant RAF pilot though he is, wears Luftwaffe uniform.'

'And you want to do the same thing with this E-boat?' Hare said.

'Exactly, which is where you come in. After all, a Kriegsmarine boat needs a Kriegsmarine crew.'

'Which is contrary to the rules of war enough to put the same crew in front of a firing squad if caught,' Hare pointed out.

'I know. War, as your General Sherman once said, is hell.' Munro stood up, rubbing his hands. 'God, the possibilities are limitless. I should tell you, and this again is classified, that all German military and naval intelligence traffic is encoded on Enigma machines, a gadget the Germans are convinced is absolutely foolproof. Unfortunately for them we have a project called Ultra which has succeeded in penetrating the system. Think of the information that would give you from the Kriegsmarine. Recognition signals, codes of the day for entry into ports.'

'Crazy,' Hare said. 'You'd need a crew.'

'The S.80 usually carries a complement of sixteen. My friends at the Admiralty think you could manage with ten, including yourself. As it's a joint venture, both our people and yours are searching out the right personnel. I've already got you the perfect engineer. A Jewish German refugee who worked at the Daimler-Benz factory. They manufacture the engines for all E-boats.'

There was a long pause. Hare turned and looked out across the garden to the city. It was quite dark now and he shivered, for no accountable reason remembering Tulugu. When he reached for a cigarette, his hand shook and he turned and extended it to Munro.

'Look at that and you know why? Because I'm scared.'

'So was I in the belly of that damned bomber flying over,' Munro said. 'I'll be just as bad when we fly back tonight though this time it's a Flying Fortress. I understand they have a little more room.'

'No,' Hare said hoarsely. 'I won't do it.'

'Oh, but you will, Commander,' Munro said. 'And shall I tell you why? Because there's nothing else you can do. You certainly can't go back to Harvard. Back to the classroom after all you've been through? I'll tell you something about yourself because we're both in the same boat. We're men who've spent most of our lives living in the head. Other men's stories. All in the book and then the war came and do you know what, my friend? You've enjoyed every golden moment.'

'You go to hell,' Martin Hare told him.

'Very probably.'

'What if I say no?'

'Oh, dear.' Munro extracted the letter from his inside pocket. 'I think you'll recognise the signature at the bottom there as being that of the Commander-in-Chief of the American Armed Forces.'

Hare looked at it in stupefaction. 'Good God!'

'Yes, well he'd like a word before we go. What you might call a command performance so be a good lad and get into your uniform. We haven't got much time.'

At the White House, the limousine stopped at the West Basement entrance where Munro showed his pass to the Secret Service agents on the night shift. There was a pause while an aide was sent for. He appeared after a few moments, a young naval lieutenant in impeccable uniform.

'Brigadier,' he said to Munro, turned to Hare and saluted him as only an Annapolis man could. 'It's a great honour to meet you, sir.'

Hare acknowledged the salute, faintly embarrassed.

The boy said, 'Follow me, gentlemen. The President's waiting.'

The Oval Office was shadowed, the lamp on the desk which was littered with papers the only light. President Roosevelt was in his wheelchair at the window staring out, a cigarette in his usual long holder glowing in the darkness.

He swivelled round in the chair. 'There you are, Brigadier.'

'Mr President.'

'And this is Lieutenant Commander Hare?' He held out his

hand. 'You're a credit to your country, sir. As your President, I thank you. That Tulugu business was quite something.'

'Better men than me died sinking that destroyer, Mr President.'

'I know, son.' Roosevelt held Hare's hand in both of his. 'Better men than you or me are dying every day, but we just have to press on and do our best.' He reached for a fresh cigarette and put it in his holder. 'The Brigadier's filled you in on this Cold Harbour business? You like the sound of it?'

Hare glanced at Munro, hesitated, then said, 'An interesting proposition, Mr President.'

Roosevelt tilted back his head and laughed. 'A neat way of putting it.' He wheeled himself to the desk and turned. 'To wear the enemy uniform is totally against the terms of the Geneva Convention, you understand that?'

'Yes, Mr President.'

Roosevelt stared up at the ceiling. 'Correct me if I get my history wrong, Brigadier, but isn't it a fact that during the Napoleonic Wars, ships of the British Navy occasionally attacked under the French flag?'

'Indeed it is, Mr President, and usually when sailing French ships taken as prizes of war and recommissioned into the British Navy.'

'So, there is precedence for this type of action as a legitimate *ruse de guerre*?' Roosevelt observed.

'Certainly, Mr President.'

Hare said, 'It's a point worth making that in all such actions, it was customary for the British to hoist their own flag just before battle commenced.'

'I like that.' Roosevelt nodded. 'That, I understand. If a man must die, it should be under his own flag.' He looked up at Hare. 'A direct order from your Commander-in-Chief. You will at all times carry the Stars and Stripes on this E-boat of yours and if the day ever dawns that you find yourself sailing into battle, you will hoist it in place of the Kriegsmarine ensign. Understood?'

'Perfectly, Mr President.'

Roosevelt held out his hand again. 'Good. I can only wish you Godspeed.'

They both shook hands with him and, as if by magic, the young lieutenant appeared from the shadows and ushered them out.

As the limousine turned down Constitutional Avenue, Hare said, 'A remarkable man.'

'The understatement of the year,' Munro said. 'What he and Churchill have achieved between them is amazing.' He sighed. 'I wonder how long it will be before the books are written proving how unimportant they really were.'

'Second-rate academics out to make a reputation?' Hare said. 'Just like us?'

'Exactly.' Munro looked out at the lighted streets. 'I'm going to miss this town. You're in for a culture shock when we reach London. Not only the blackout, but the Luftwaffe is trying night bombing again.'

Hare leaned back against the seat, closed his eyes, not tired but aware of a sudden fierce exhilaration. It was as if he'd been asleep for a long time and was awake again.

The Flying Fortress was brand new and on its way to join the American 8th Air Force in Britain. The crew made Munro and Hare as comfortable as possible with Army blankets and pillows and a couple of Thermos flasks. Hare opened one as they crossed the New England coast and moved out to sea.

'Coffee?'

'No thanks.' Munro positioned a pillow behind his head and pulled up a blanket. 'I'm a tea man myself.'

'Well, it takes all kinds,' Hare said.

He sipped some of the scalding coffee and Munro grunted.

'I knew there was something. I forgot to tell you that in view of the peculiar circumstances, your Navy has decided to promote you.'

'To full Commander?' Hare said in astonishment.

'No, to Fregattenkapitän actually,' Munro told him, hitched the blanket over his shoulders and went to sleep.

Two

As Craig Osbourne reached the edge of St Maurice, there was a volley of rifle fire and rooks in the beech trees outside the village church lifted into the air in a dark cloud, calling to each other angrily. He was driving a Kubelwagen, the German Army's equivalent of the jeep, a general purpose vehicle that would go anywhere. He parked it by the lych-gate that gave entrance to the cemetery and got out, immaculate in the grey field uniform of a Standartenführer in the Waffen-SS.

It was raining softly and he took a greatcoat of black leather from the rear seat, slipped it over his shoulders and went forward to where a gendarme stood watching events in the square. There were a handful of villagers down there, no more than that, an SS firing squad and two prisoners waiting hopelessly, hands manacled behind their backs. A third lay face down on the cobbles by the wall. As Osbourne watched, an elderly officer appeared, wearing a long greatcoat with the silver grey lapel facings affected by officers of general rank in the SS. He took a pistol from his holster, leaned down and shot the man on the ground in the back of the head.

'General Dietrich, I suppose?' Osbourne asked in perfect French.

The gendarme, who had not noticed his approach, answered automatically. 'Yes, he likes to finish them off himself, that

13

one.' He half turned, became aware of the uniform and jumped to attention. 'Excuse me, Colonel, I meant no offence.'

'None taken. We are, after all, fellow countrymen.' Craig raised his left sleeve and the gendarme saw at once that he wore the cuff title of the French Charlemagne Brigade of the Waffen-SS. 'Have a cigarette.'

He held out a silver case. The gendarme took one. Whatever his private thoughts concerning a countryman serving the enemy, he kept them to himself, face blank.

'This happens often?' Osbourne asked, giving him a light. The gendarme hesitated and Osbourne nodded encouragingly. 'Go on, man, speak your mind. You may not approve of me, but we're both Frenchmen.'

It surfaced then, the anger, the frustration. 'Two or three times a week and in other places. A butcher, this one.'

One of the two men waiting was positioned against the wall; there was a shouted command, another volley. 'And he denies them the last rites. You see that, Colonel? No priest and yet when it's all over, he comes up here like a good Catholic to confess to Father Paul and then has a hearty lunch in the café across the square.'

'Yes, so I've heard,' Osbourne told him.

He turned away and walked back towards the church. The gendarme watched him go, wondering, then turned to observe events in the square as Dietrich went forward again, pistol in hand.

Craig Osbourne went up the path through the graveyard, opened the great oak door of the church and went inside. It was dark in there, a little light filtering down through ancient windows of stained glass. There was a smell of incense, candles flickering by the altar. As Osbourne approached, the door of the sacristy opened and an old white-haired priest emerged. He wore an alb, a violet stole over his shoulder. He paused, surprise on his face.

'May I help you?'

'Perhaps. Back in the sacristy, Father.'

The old priest frowned. 'Not now, Colonel, now I must hear confession.'

Osbourne glanced across the empty church to the confessional boxes. 'Not much custom, Father, but then there wouldn't be, not with that butcher Dietrich expected.' He put a hand on the priest's chest firmly. 'Inside, please.'

The priest backed into the sacristy, bewildered. 'Who are you?'

Osbourne pushed him down on the wooden chair by the desk, took a length of cord from his greatcoat pocket. 'The less you know, the better, Father. Let's just say all is not what it seems. Now hands behind your back.' He tied the old man's wrists firmly. 'You see, Father, I'm granting you absolution. No connection with what happens here. A clean bill of health with our German friends.'

He took out a handkerchief. The old priest said, 'My son, I don't know what you plan, but this is God's house.'

'Yes, well I like to think I'm on God's business,' Craig Osbourne said and gagged him with the handkerchief.

He left the old man there, closed the sacristy door and crossed to the confessional boxes, switched on the tiny light above the door of the first one and stepped inside. He took out his Walther, screwed a silencer on the barrel and watched, the door open a crack so that he could see down to the entrance.

After a while, Dietrich entered from the porch with a young SS Captain. They stood talking for a moment, the Captain went back outside and Dietrich walked along the aisle between the pews, unbuttoning his greatcoat. He paused, took off his cap and entered the other confessional box and sat down. Osbourne flicked the switch, turned on the small bulb that illuminated the German on the other side of the grille, remaining in darkness himself.

'Good morning, Father,' Dietrich said in bad French. 'Bless me for I have sinned.'

'You certainly have, you bastard,' Craig Osbourne told him, pushed the silenced Walther through the flimsy grille and shot him between the eyes.

Osbourne stepped out of the confessional box and at the same moment the young SS Captain opened the church door and peered in. He saw the General on his face, the back of his skull a sodden mass of blood and brain, Osbourne standing over him. The young officer drew his pistol and fired twice wildly, the sound of the shots deafening between the old walls. Osbourne returned the fire, catching him in the chest, knocking him back over one of the pews, then ran to the door.

He peered out and saw Dietrich's car parked at the gate, his own Kubelwagen beyond. Too late to reach it now for already a squad of SS, rifles at the ready, were running towards the church, attracted by the sound of firing.

Osbourne turned, ran along the aisle and left from the back door by the sacristy, racing through the gravestones of the cemetery at the rear of the church, vaulting the low stone wall, and started up the hill to the wood above.

They began shooting when he was half way up and he ran, zigzagging wildly, was almost there when a bullet plucked at his left sleeve sending him sideways to fall on one knee. He was up again in a second and sprinted over the brow of the hill. A moment later he was into the trees.

He ran on wildly, both arms up to cover his face against the flailing branches and where in the hell was he supposed to be running to? No transport and no way of reaching his rendezvous with that Lysander now. At least Dietrich was dead, but, as they used to say in SOE in the old days, a proper cock-up.

There was a road in the valley below, more woods on the other side. He went sliding down through the trees, landing in a ditch, picked himself up and started to cross and then to his total astonishment, the Rolls-Royce limousine came round the corner and braked to a halt.

René Dissard of the black eye-patch was at the wheel in his chauffeur's uniform. The rear door was opened and Anne-Marie looked out. 'Playing heroes again, Craig? You never change, do you? Come on, get in, for heaven's sake and let's get out of here.'

As the Rolls moved off, she nodded at the blood-soaked sleeve of his uniform. 'Bad?'

'I don't think so.' Osbourne stuffed a handkerchief inside. 'What in the hell are you doing here?'

'Grand Pierre was in touch. As usual, just a voice on the phone. I still haven't met the man.'

'I have,' Craig told her. 'You're in for a shock when you do.'

'Really? He says that Lysander pick-up isn't on. Heavy fog and rain moving in from the Atlantic according to the Met. boys. I was supposed to wait for you at the farm and tell you, but I always had a bad feeling about this one. Decided to come along and see the action. We were on the other side of the village by the station. Heard the shooting and saw you running up the hill.'

'Good thing for me,' Osbourne told her.

'Yes, considering this effort wasn't really any of my business. Anyway, René said you were bound to come this way.'

She lit a cigarette and crossed one silken knee over the other, elegant as always in a black suit, a diamond brooch at the neck of the white silk blouse. The black hair was cut in a fringe across her forehead and curved under on each side, framing high cheekbones and pointed chin.

'What are you staring at?' she demanded petulantly.

'You,' he said. 'Too much lipstick as usual, but otherwise, bloody marvellous.'

'Oh, get under the seat and shut up,' she told him.

She turned her legs to one side as Craig pulled down a flap revealing space beneath the seat. He crawled inside and she pushed the flap back into position. A moment later, they went round a corner and discovered a Kubelwagen across the road, half-a-dozen SS waiting.

'Nice and slow, René,' she said.

'Trouble?' Craig Osbourne asked, his voice muffled.

'Not with any luck,' she said softly. 'I know the officer. He was stationed at the Château for a while.'

René stopped the Rolls and a young SS Lieutenant walked forward, pistol in hand. His face cleared and he holstered his weapon. 'Mademoiselle Trevaunce. What an unexpected pleasure.'

'Lieutenant Schultz.' She opened the door and held out her hand which he kissed gallantly. 'What's all this?'

'A wretched business. A terrorist has just shot General Dietrich in St Maurice.'

'I thought I heard some shooting back there,' she said. 'And how is the General?'

'Dead, Mademoiselle,' Schultz told her. 'I saw the body myself. A terrible thing. Murdered in the church during confession.' He shook his head. 'That there are such people in this world passes belief.'

'I'm so sorry.' She pressed his hand in sympathy. 'You must come and see us again soon. The Countess had rather a fondness for you. We were sorry to see you go.'

Schultz actually blushed. 'Please convey my felicitations, but now I must delay you no longer.'

He shouted an order and one of his men reversed the Kubelwagen. Schultz saluted and René drove away.

'As always Mamselle has the luck of the Devil,' he observed.

Anne-Marie Trevaunce lit another cigarette and Craig

Osbourne said softly, 'Wrong, René, my friend. She *is* the Devil.'

At the farm, they parked the Rolls-Royce in the barn while René went in search of information. Osbourne removed his tunic and ripped away the blood-soaked sleeve of his shirt.

Anne-Marie examined the wound. 'Not too bad. It hasn't gone through, simply ploughed a furrow. Nasty, mind you.'

René returned with a bundle of cloths and a piece of white sheeting which he proceeded to tear into strips.

'Bandage him with this.'

Anne-Marie set about the task at once and Osbourne said, 'What's the score?'

'Only old Jules here and he wants us out fast,' René said. 'Change into this lot and he'll put the uniform in his charcoal burner. There's a message from Grand Pierre. They've been on the radio to London. They're going to pick you up by torpedo boat off Leon tonight. Grand Pierre can't make it himself, but one of his men will be there – Bleriot. I know him well. A good man.'

Osbourne went round to the other side of the Rolls and changed. He returned wearing a tweed cap, corduroy jacket and trousers, both of which had seen better days, and broken boots. He put the Walther in his pocket and gave the uniform to René who went out.

'Will I do?' he asked Anne-Marie.

She laughed out loud. 'With three days growth on your chin perhaps, but to be honest, you still look like a Yale man to me.'

'That's really very comforting.'

René returned and got behind the wheel. 'We'd better get moving, Mamselle. It'll take us an hour to get there.'

She pulled down the flap under the seat. 'In you go like a good boy.'

Craig did as he was told and peered out at her. 'I'm the one who's going to have the last laugh. Dinner at the Savoy tomorrow night. The Orpheans playing, Carroll Gibbons singing, dancing, girls.'

She slammed the flap shut, climbed in and René drove away.

Leon was a fishing village so small that it didn't even have a pier, most of the boats being drawn up on the beach. There was the sound of accordion music from a small bar, the only sign of life, and they drove on, following a rough track past a disused lighthouse to a tiny bay. A heavy mist rolled in from the sea and somewhere in the distance a foghorn sounded forlornly. René led the way down to the beach, a flashlight in his hand.

Craig said to Anne-Marie, 'You don't want to go down there. You'll only spoil your shoes. Stay with the car.'

She took off her shoes and turned, tossing them into the back of the Rolls. 'Quite right, darling. However, thanks to my Nazi friends, I do have an inexhaustible supply of silk stockings. I can afford to ruin one pair for the sake of friendship.'

She took his arm and they went after René. 'Friendship?' Craig said. 'As I recall, in Paris in the old days it was rather more than that?'

'Ancient history, darling. Best forgotten.'

She held his arm tight and Osbourne caught his breath sharply, aware that his wound was really hurting now. Anne-Marie turned her head and looked at him. 'Are you all right?'

'Damned arm hurting a bit, that's all.'

There was a murmur of voices as they approached and found René and another man standing beside a small dinghy, an outboard motor tilted over on its stern.

'This is Bleriot,' René said.

'Mamselle.' Bleriot touched his cap, acknowledging Anne-Marie.

'This is the boat, I presume?' Craig demanded. 'And what exactly am I supposed to do with it?'

'Around the point and you will see the Grosnez light, Monsieur.'

'In this fog?'

'It's very low lying.' Bleriot shrugged. 'I've put a signalling lamp in and there's this.' He took a luminous signal ball from his pocket. 'SOE supply these. They work very well in the water.'

'Which is where I'm likely to end up from the look of the weather,' Craig said as waves lapped in hungrily across the beach.

Bleriot took a lifejacket from the boat and helped him into it. 'You have no choice, Monsieur, you must go. Grand Pierre says they are turning the whole of Brittany upside down in their search for you.'

Craig allowed him to fasten the straps of the lifejacket. 'Have they taken hostages yet?'

'Of course. Ten from St Maurice, including the Mayor and Father Paul. Ten more from farms in the surrounding area.'

'My God!' Craig said softly.

Anne-Marie lit a Gitane and passed it to him. 'The name of the game, lover, you and I both know that. Not your affair.'

'I wish I could believe you,' he told her as René and Bleriot ran the dinghy down into the water. Bleriot got in and started the outboard. He got out again.

Anne-Marie kissed Craig briskly. 'Off you go like a good boy and give my love to Carroll Gibbons.'

Craig got into the dinghy and reached for the rudder. He turned to Bleriot who held the boat on the opposite side from René. 'Pick up by MTB, you say?'

'Or gunboat. British Navy or Free French, one or the other. They'll be there, Monsieur. They've never let us down yet.'

'So long, René, take care of her,' Craig called as they pushed him out through the waves and the tiny outboard motor carried him on.

Rounding the point and facing the open sea, he was soon in trouble. The waves lifted in white caps, the wind freshening, and water slopped over the sides so that he was already ankle-deep. Bleriot was right. He could see the Grosnez light occasionally through gaps in the fog blown by the wind and he was steering towards it when suddenly the outboard motor died on him. He worked at it frantically, pulling the starting cord, but the dinghy drifted helplessly, pulled in by the current.

A heavy wave, long and smooth and much larger than the others swept in, lifting the dinghy high in the air, where it paused in a kind of slow-motion, water pouring in.

It went down like a stone and Craig Osbourne drifted helplessly in the water, buoyed up by his lifejacket.

It was intensely cold, biting into his arms and legs like acid so that even the pain of his wound faded for the time being. Another large wave came over and he drifted down the other side into calmer water.

'Not good, my boy,' he told himself. 'Not good at all,' and then the wind tore another hole in the curtain of the fog and he saw the light of Grosnez, he heard a muted throbbing of engines, saw a dark shape out there.

He raised his voice and called frantically. 'Over here!' and then he remembered the luminous signal ball that Bleriot had given him, got it out of his pocket, fumbling with frozen fingers, and held it up in the palm of his right hand.

The curtain of fog dropped again, the Grosnez light disappeared and the throb of the engines seemed to be swallowed by the night.

'Here, damn you!' Osbourne cried and then the torpedo

boat drifted out of the fog like a ghost ship and bore down on him.

He had never felt such relief in his life as a searchlight was switched on and picked him out in the water. He started to flail towards it, forgetting his arm for the moment and stopped suddenly. There was something about the craft, something wrong. The paintwork for example. Dirty white merging into sea green, a suggestion of striping for camouflage and then the flag on the jackstaff flared out with a sharp crack in a gust of wind and he saw the swastika plainly, the cross of the upper left-hand corner, the scarlet and black of the Kriegsmarine. No MTB this but a German E-boat and as it slid alongside, he saw painted on the prow beside its number the legend *Lili Marlene*.

The E-boat seemed to glide to a halt, the engines only a murmur now. He floated there, sick at heart, looking up at the two Kriegsmarine ratings in sidecaps and peajackets who looked down at him. And then one of them threw a rope ladder over the rail.

'All right, my old son,' he said in ripest Cockney. 'Let's be having you.'

They had to help him over the rail and he crouched, vomiting a little on the deck. He looked up warily as the German sailor with the Cockney accent said cheerfully, 'Major Osbourne, is it?'

'That's right.'

The German leaned down. 'You're losing a lot of blood from the left arm. Better take a look at that for you, sir. I'm the sick berth attendant.'

Osbourne said, 'What goes on here?'

'Not for me to say, sir. That's the skipper's department. Fregattenkapitän Berger, sir. You'll find him on the bridge.'

Craig Osbourne got to his feet wearily, fumbling at the

straps of his lifejacket, taking it off, stumbling to the small ladder and went up. Then he went into the wheelhouse. There was a rating at the wheel, an Obersteuermann from his rank badges, Chief Helmsman. The man in the swivel chair at the small chart table wore a crumpled Kriegsmarine cap. It had a white top to it, usually an affectation of U-boat commanders, but common enough amongst E-boat captains who saw themselves as the elite of the Kriegsmarine. He wore an old white polo neck sweater under a reefer coat and turned to look at Osbourne, his face calm and expressionless.

'Major Osbourne,' he said in good American. 'Glad to have you aboard. Excuse me for a moment. We need to get out of here.'

He turned to the coxswain and said in German, 'All right, Langsdorff. Leave silencers on until we're five miles out. Course two-one-oh. Speed, twenty-five knots until I say different.'

'Course two-one-oh, speed twenty-five knots, Herr Kapitän,' the coxswain replied and took the E-boat away with a surge of power.

'Hare,' Craig Osbourne said. 'Professor Martin Hare.'

Hare took a cigarette from a tin of Benson & Hedges and offered him one. 'You know me? Have we met?'

Osbourne took the cigarette, fingers trembling. 'After Yale, I was a journalist. Worked for *Life* magazine amongst others. Paris, Berlin. I spent a lot of my youth in both of those places. My dad was State Department. A diplomat.'

'But when did we meet?'

'I came home for a vacation. That's Boston, by the way. April, '39. A friend told me about this series of lectures you were giving at Harvard. Supposedly on German Literature, but very political, very anti-Nazi. I went to four of them.'

'Were you there for the riot?'

'When the American Bund tried to break things up? Oh,

sure. I broke a knuckle on some ape's jaw. You were quite something.' Osbourne shivered and the door opened and the Cockney appeared.

'What is it, Schmidt?' Hare asked in German.

Schmidt was holding a blanket. 'I thought the Major might need this. I would also point out to the Herr Kapitän that he is wounded in the left arm and needs medical attention.'

'Then do your job, Schmidt,' Martin Hare told him. 'Get on with it.'

Seated on the narrow chair at the tiny ward room table below, Osbourne watched as Schmidt expertly bandaged the wound. 'A little morphine, guvnor, just to make things more comfortable.' He took an ampoule from his kit and jabbed it on to Osbourne's arm.

Craig said, 'Who are you? No German, that's for sure.'

'Oh, but I am in a manner of speaking, or at least my parents were. Jews who thought London might be more hospitable than Berlin. I was born in Whitechapel myself.'

Martin Hare said from the door in German, 'Schmidt, you have a big mouth.'

Schmidt stood up and sprang to attention. *'Jawohl, Herr Kapitän.'*

'Go on, get out of here.'

'Zu befehl, Herr Kapitän.'

Schmidt grinned and went out taking his medical kit with him. Hare lit a cigarette. 'This is a mixed crew. Americans and Brits, some Jews, but everyone speaks fluent German and they have only one identity when they serve on this ship.'

'Our very own E-boat,' Osbourne said. 'I'm impressed. The best kept secret I've come across in quite a while.'

'I should tell you that we play this game to the hilt. Normally, only German is spoken, only Kriegsmarine uniform worn, even back at base. It's a question of staying in character.

Of course the guys break the language rule sometimes. Schmidt is a good example.'

'And where's base?'

'A little port called Cold Harbour near Lizard Point in Cornwall.'

'How far?'

'From here? A hundred miles. We'll have you there by morning. We take our time on the way back. Our people warn us in advance of the Royal Navy MTB routes each night. We like to keep out of their way.'

'I should imagine you do. A confrontation would be most unfortunate. Whose operation is this?'

'It's run officially by Section D of the SOE, but it's a joint venture. You're OSS, I hear?'

'That's right.'

'A tricky way to make a living.'

'You can say that again.'

Hare grinned. 'Let's see if they've got sandwiches in the galley. You look as if you could do with some nourishment,' and he led the way out.

It was just before dawn when Osbourne went on deck. There was quite a sea running and spray stung his face. When he went up the ladder and entered the wheelhouse, he found Hare on his own, his face dark and brooding in the compass light. Osbourne sat by the chart table and lit a cigarette.

'Can't you sleep?' Hare said.

'The boat's too much for me, but not for you, I think?'

'No, sir,' Hare told him. 'I can't remember when boats didn't figure in my life. I was eight years old when my grandfather put me to sea in my first dinghy.'

'They tell me the English Channel's special?'

'A hell of a lot different from the Solomons, I can tell you that.'

'That's where you were before?'

Hare nodded. 'That's right.'

'I'd always heard torpedo boats were a young man's sport,' Osbourne said, curious.

'Well, when you need someone with the right experience who can also pass as a German, you've got to take what you can get.' Hare laughed.

There was a faint grey light around them now, the sea calmer and land loomed before them.

'Lizard Point,' Hare said.

He was smiling again and Osbourne replied, 'You like it, don't you, all this?'

Hare shrugged. 'I suppose so.'

'No, really like it. You wouldn't want to go back to how it was before. Harvard, I mean.'

'Perhaps.' Hare was solemn. 'Will any of us know what to do when it's over? What about you?'

'Nothing to go back to. You see, I have a special problem,' Osbourne told him. 'It would seem I have a talent for this. I killed a German General yesterday. In a church, just to show how much I lack the finer feelings. He was head of SS intelligence for the whole of Brittany. A butcher who deserved to die.'

'So what's your problem?'

'I kill him so they take twenty hostages and shoot them. Death seems to follow at my heels if you know what I mean.'

Hare didn't answer, simply reduced power and opened a window, allowing rain to drift in. They rounded a promontory and Osbourne saw an inlet in the bay beyond, a wooded valley above.

A small grey harbour nestled at the foot of it, and two dozen cottages around. There was an old manor house in the trees. Below, the crew had come out on deck.

'Cold Harbour, Major Osbourne,' Martin Hare told him and took the *Lili Marlene* in.

Three

The crew busied themselves tying up and Hare and Osbourne went over the side and walked along the cobbled quay.

'The houses all look pretty much the same,' Craig observed.

'I know,' Hare told him. 'The whole place was put together in one go by the lord of the manor, a Sir William Chevely, in the mid-eighteenth century. Cottages, harbour, the quay, everything. According to local legend, most of his money came from smuggling. He was known as Black Bill.'

'I see. He created this model fishing village as a front for other things?' Craig said.

'Exactly. This, by the way, is the pub. The boys use it as their mess.'

It was a low squat building with high gables, timber inserts and mullioned windows which gave it an Elizabethan look.

Craig said, 'Nothing Georgian about that. Tudor, I'd say.'

'The cellars are medieval. There's always been some sort of an inn on this site,' Hare said and clambered into a jeep which stood outside. 'Come on, I'll take you up to the manor.'

Craig looked up at the inn sign over the door. 'The Hanged Man.'

'Rather appropriate,' Hare said as he started the engine. 'Actually, it's a new sign. The old one was falling apart and pretty revolting at that. Some poor sod swinging on the end of a rope, hands tied, tongue popping out.'

As they drove away Craig turned to look at the sign again. It depicted a young man hanging upside-down, suspended by his right ankle from a wooden gibbet. The face was calm, the head surrounded by some kind of halo.

'Did you know that's a Tarot image?' he said.

'Oh, sure, the housekeeper at the manor arranged it, Madame Legrande. She's into that kind of thing.'

'Legrande? Would that be Julie Legrande?' Craig asked.

'That's right.' Hare glanced at him curiously. 'Do you know her?'

'I knew her husband before the war. He lectured in Philosophy at the Sorbonne. Later he was mixed up with the Resistance in Paris. I came across them there in '42. Helped them get out when the Gestapo were on their backs.'

'Well, she's been here since the beginning of the project. Works for SOE.'

'And her husband, Henri?'

'From what I know, he died of a heart attack in London last year.'

'I see.'

They were passing the last of the cottages. Hare said, 'This is a defence area. All civilians moved out. We use the cottages as billets. Besides my crew, we also have a few RAF mechanics to service the planes.'

'You have aircraft here? What for?'

'The usual purpose. To drop agents in or bring them out.'

'I thought Special Duties Squadron at Tempsford handled that?'

'They do or at least they handle the normal cases. Our operation is a little more unusual. I'll show you. We're just coming up to the field.'

The road curved through trees and on the other side was an enormous meadow with a grass runway. A prefabricated hangar stood at one end. Hare turned the jeep in through the gate, bumped across the grass and stopped. He took out a cigarette and lit it.

'What do you think?'

A Fieseler Storch spotter plane taxied out of the hangar, the Luftwaffe insignia plain on its wings and fuselage and the two mechanics who followed it wore black Luftwaffe overalls. Behind, in the hangar there was a Ju88 nightfighter.

'My God,' Craig said softly.

'I told you things were a little unusual here.'

The pilot of the Stork clambered out, exchanged a word with the mechanics and came towards them. He wore flying boots, baggy, comfortable trousers in blue-grey as worn by Luftwaffe fighter pilots, very unusual, with large map pockets. The short *Fliegerbluse* gave him a dashing look. He wore his silver pilot's badge on the left side, an Iron Cross First Class above it and the Luftwaffe National Emblem on the right.

'Everything but the bloody Knight's Cross,' Osbourne observed.

'Yes, he is a bit of a fantasist, this lad,' Hare told him. 'Also something of a psychopath if you want my opinion. Still, he did pull in two DFCs in the Battle of Britain.'

The pilot approached. He was about twenty-five, the hair beneath the cap straw blond, almost white. Although he seemed to smile frequently, there was a touch of cruelty to the mouth and the eyes were cold.

'Flight Lieutenant Joe Edge – Major Craig Osbourne, OSS.'

Edge smiled charmingly enough and held out his hand. 'Brigandage a speciality, eh?'

Craig didn't like him one little bit but tried not to show it. 'You've got quite a set-up here.'

'Yes, well the Stork can land and take off anywhere. Better than the Lysander in my opinion.'

'Rather unusual camouflage, the Luftwaffe insignia.'

Edge laughed. 'Useful on occasions. Had a weather problem the other month so I was running short of juice. I landed at the Luftwaffe Fighter base at Granville. Got them to refuel me. No problem.'

'We have these wonderful forged credentials from Himmler, ...ntersigned by the Führer which indicate that we're on ... ial assignment for SS security. Nobody dares query that,' ... said.

...cy even gave me dinner in the mess,' Edge told Craig. 'Of course, my dear old mum being a Kraut, it does mean I speak the lingo fluently which helps.' He turned to Hare. 'Give me a lift up to the manor will you, old boy? I hear the boss might be coming down from London.'

'I didn't know that,' Hare told him. 'Hop in.'

Edge got in the back. As they drove away, Craig said, 'Your mother? She's over here, presumably?'

'Good God, yes. Widow. Lives in Hampstead. Greatest disappointment of her life was when Hitler didn't manage to drive up the Mall to Buckingham Palace in 1940.'

He laughed hugely. Craig turned away, disliking him even more and said to Hare, 'I've been thinking. You said Section D of SOE was running this thing. Isn't that the good old dirty tricks department?'

'That's right.'

'Would Dougal Munro still be in charge there?'

'You know him, too!'

'Oh, yes,' Craig said. 'I worked for SOE from the beginning. Before we came into the war. We've had dealings, me and Dougal. A ruthless old bastard.'

'Which is how you win wars, old boy,' Edge commented from the rear.

'I see. You're an anything goes man, are you?' Craig asked.

'Thought we all were in our business, old son.'

For a moment, Craig saw General Dietrich's frightened face through the confessional grille. He turned away, uncomfortable.

Hare said, 'He hasn't changed – Munro. The motto really

is anything goes, but I expect you'll see for yourself soon enough.'

He turned in through cross gates and braked to a halt in a flagged courtyard. The house was grey stone, and three storeys high. Very old, very peaceful. Nothing to do with war at all.

'Does it have a name?' Craig asked.

'Grancester Abbey. Rather grand, eh?' Edge told him.

Hare said, 'Here we are then.' He got out of the jeep. 'We'll beard the ogre in his den if he's here.'

But at that precise moment, Brigadier Dougal Munro was being admitted into the library at Hayes Lodge in London, the house which General Dwight D. Eisenhower was using as temporary headquarters. The General was enjoying coffee and toast and an early edition of *The Times* when the young Army Captain ushered Dougal Munro in and closed the door behind him.

'Morning, Brigadier. Coffee, tea – anything you want is on the sideboard.' Munro helped himself to tea. 'How's this Cold Harbour project working out?'

'So far, so good, General.'

'You know war is a little like the magician who fools people into watching his right hand while his left is attending to the real business of the day.' Eisenhower poured more coffee. 'Deception, Major. Deception is the name of the game. I had a report from Intelligence which tells me that Rommel has done incredible things since they put him in charge of the Atlantic Wall.'

'Quite true, sir.'

'This E-boat of yours has taken engineer officers in by night to the French coast to get beach samples on so many occasions that you must have a pretty good idea where we intend to go in?'

'That's right, General,' Munro said calmly. 'All the indications would seem to predict Normandy.'

'All right. So we're back with deception,' Eisenhower said and walked to the wall map. 'I've got Patton heading a phantom army up here in East Anglia. Fake army camps, fake planes – the works.'

'Which would indicate to the Germans our intentions to take the short route and invade in the Pas de Calais area?' Munro observed.

'Which they've always expected because it makes military sense.' Eisenhower nodded. 'We've already got things moving to reinforce that idea. The RAF and 8th Air Force will raid that area frequently, considerably closer to the invasion, of course. That'll make it look as if we're trying to soften things up. Resistance groups in the region will constantly attack the power cables and railways, that sort of thing. Naturally, the double agents we're running will transmit the right, false information to Abwehr headquarters.'

He stood there, staring at the map and Munro said, 'Something worrying you, sir?'

Eisenhower moved to the bow window and lit a cigarette. 'Many people wanted us to invade last year. Let me now be explicit with you, Brigadier, as to why we didn't. SHAEF has always been convinced that we can only succeed with this invasion by having every advantage. More men than the Germans, more tanks, more planes – everything. You want to know why? Because in every engagement fought in this war on equal terms, facing either Russian, British or American troops, the Germans have always won. Unit for unit, they usually inflict fifty per cent more casualties.'

'I'm aware of that unfortunate fact, sir.'

'Intelligence sent me details of a speech Rommel made to his Generals the other day. He said if he didn't beat us on the beaches they'd lost the war.'

'I think he's right, sir.'

Eisenhower turned. 'Brigadier, I've always been sceptical of the exact worth of secret agents in this war. Their material is usually sketchy at the best. I think we get better information from the decoding of cyphers by Ultra.'

'I agree, sir,' Munro hesitated. 'Of course, if major information isn't processed by Enigma in the first place, the facts aren't there to be decoded and they could well be the most important facts.'

'Exactly.' Eisenhower leaned forward. 'You sent me a report last week I hardly dare to believe. You said that there was to be a Staff Conference headed by Rommel himself quite soon now. A conference concerned solely with the question of Atlantic Wall defences.'

'That's right, General. At a place called Château de Voincourt in Brittany.'

'You further stated that you had an agent who could penetrate that conference?'

'Correct, General.' Munro nodded.

Eisenhower said, 'My God, if I was a fly on the wall at that meeting. To know Rommel's thoughts. His intentions.' He put a hand on Munro's shoulder. 'You realise how crucially important this could be? Three million men, thousands of ships, but the right information could make all the difference. You understand?'

'Perfectly, General.'

'Don't let me down, Brigadier.'

He turned and stared up at the map. Munro let himself out of the room quietly, went downstairs, picked up his coat and hat, nodded to the sentries and went to his car. His aide, Captain Jack Carter, sat in the rear, hands folded over his walking stick. Carter had a false leg, courtesy of Dunkirk.

'Everything all right, sir?' he asked as they drove away.

Munro pulled the glass panel across, cutting them off from the driver. 'The de Voincourt conference has assumed crucial importance. I want you to get in touch with Anne-Marie

Trevaunce. She can go on another false trip to Paris. Arrange a Lysander pick-up. I need to talk with her, face-to-face. Say three days from now.'

'Right, sir.'

'Anything else I need to know?'

'Message came in concerning Cold Harbour, sir. Seems the OSS had problems yesterday. One of their agents knocked off General Dietrich, the SD chief in Brittany. Due to bad weather, their Lysander pick-up had to be aborted, so they asked us for help.'

'You know I don't like doing that, Jack.'

'Yes, sir. Anyway, Commander Hare got the message direct, went across to Grosnez and picked up the agent concerned. A Major Osbourne.'

'There was a pause and Munro turned in astonishment. 'Craig Osbourne?'

'Looks like it, sir.'

'My God, is he still around? His luck must be good. The best man I ever had at SOE.'

'What about Harry Martineau, sir?'

'All right, point taken, and he's another bloody Yank. Is Osbourne at Cold Harbour now?'

'Yes, sir.'

'Right. Stop at the nearest phone. Call the CO at RAF Croydon. Tell him I want a Lysander within the next hour. Priority One. You hold the fort here, Jack, and handle the Anne-Marie Trevaunce affair. I'll fly down to Cold Harbour and see Craig Osbourne.'

'You think he could be useful, sir?'

'Oh, yes, Jack, I think you could say that,' and Munro turned and looked out of the window, smiling.

Craig Osbourne sat on a chair by the sink in the large old-fashioned bathroom stripped to the waist; Schmidt, still in his

Kriegsmarine uniform, the medical kit open on the floor, sat beside him and worked on the arm. Julie Legrande leaned on the doorway, watching. She was in her late thirties and wore slacks and a brown sweater, blonde hair tied back rather severely, a contrast with the calm sweet face.

'How does it look?' she asked.

'So-so.' Schmidt shrugged. 'You can't tell with gunshot wounds. I've got some of this new penicillin drug. It's supposed to work wonders with infection.'

He primed a hypodermic and filled it from a small bottle. Julie said, 'Let's hope so. I'll get some coffee.'

She left as Schmidt administered the injection. Osbourne winced slightly and Schmidt put a dressing pad in place and bandaged the arm expertly.

'I think you're going to need a doctor, guv,' he said cheerfully.

'We'll see,' Craig told him.

He stood up and Schmidt helped him into the clean khaki shirt Julie had provided. He managed to button it for himself and went into the other room as Schmidt repacked his medical kit.

The bedroom was very pleasant, a little shabby now and much in need of decorating. There was a bed, mahogany furniture, and a table and two easy chairs in the bow window. Craig went and looked out. There was a terrace with a balustrade below, beyond that an unkempt garden, beech trees, a small lake in a hollow. It was very peaceful.

Schmidt came out of the bathroom, his medical kit in one hand. 'I'll check you out later. It's me for the bacon and eggs.' He grinned, a hand on the door knob. 'And don't bother reminding me I'm Jewish. I was corrupted by the great British breakfast a long time ago.'

As he opened the door, Julie Legrande entered with a tray bearing coffee, toast and marmalade, fresh rolls. Schmidt left and she came and placed the tray on the table at the window. They sat opposite each other.

As she poured coffee she said, 'I can't tell you how good it is to see you again, Craig.'

'Paris seems a long time ago,' he said, taking the coffee cup she handed him.

'A thousand years.'

'I was sorry to hear about Henri,' he went on. 'A heart attack, I understand?'

She nodded. 'He knew nothing. Died in his sleep and at least he had that last eighteen months in London. We have you to thank for that.'

'Nonsense.' He felt strangely embarrassed.

'The simple truth. Would you like some toast or a roll?'

'No thanks. I'm not hungry. Another cup of coffee would go down just fine, though.'

As she poured, she said, 'Without you, we'd never have evaded the Gestapo that night. You were a sick man, Craig. Have you forgotten what those animals did to you? And yet you went back in the truck that night for Henri when others would have left him.' She was suddenly emotional, tears in her eyes. 'You gave him a life, Craig, the gift of those last few months in England. I'll always be in your debt for that.'

He lit a cigarette, stood up and looked out of the window. 'I left SOE after that affair. My own people were starting OSS. They needed my kind of experience and to be honest, I'd had enough of Dougal Munro.'

'I've been working for him down here for four months,' she said. 'We use it as a jumping-off point, safe house, the usual thing.'

'You get on with Munro, then?'

'A hard man.' She shrugged. 'But then it's a hard war.'

He nodded. 'A strange set-up, this place, and even stranger people. The pilot, for example, Edge, swaggering around in his Luftwaffe uniform playing Adolf Galland.'

'Yes, Joe's quite mad, even on a good day,' she said. 'I sometimes think he really imagines he *is* Luftwaffe. He gives the rest of us the willies, but you know Munro — always ready to look the other way if a man is truly excellent at what he does. And Edge's record is extraordinary.'

'And Hare?'

'Martin?' She smiled and put the cups back on the tray. 'Ah, Martin is a different story. I think I'm a little bit in love with Martin.'

The door opened and Edge entered without knocking. 'So there we are. All very tête-à-tête.'

He leaned against the wall and put a cigarette in the corner of his mouth. Julie said wearily, 'You really are a rather unpleasant little rat at heart, aren't you, Joe?'

'Touched a nerve did I, sweetie? Never mind.' He turned to Osbourne. 'The boss has just flown in from Croydon.'

'Munro?'

'Must want to see you bad, old boy. He's waiting in the library now. I'll show you the way.'

He went out. Osbourne turned and smiled at Julie. 'See you later,' he said and followed him.

The library was an imposing room, its walls crammed with books from floor to a ceiling of beautiful Jacobean plasterwork. A log fire burned on the open stone hearth and comfortable couches and leather club chairs were ranged around it. Munro was standing in front of the fire, cleaning his spectacles carefully as Craig Osbourne entered the room. Edge leaned against the wall by the door. Munro adjusted his spectacles and looked at Osbourne calmly.

'You can wait outside, Joe.'

'Oh, dear, so I'm to miss all the fun, am I?' Edge said, but did as he was told.

'Good to see you, Craig,' Munro said.

'I can't say it's mutual,' Craig told him and he moved to one of the chairs and sat down, lighting a cigarette. 'We go back too far.'

'Don't be bitter, dear boy, it doesn't suit.'

'Yes, well I was always just a blunt instrument to you.'

Munro sat opposite. 'Colourfully put, but apt. Now then, what about this arm? I understand Schmidt has had a look at it?'

'He thinks I might need a doctor, just to make sure.'

'No problem. We'll have that taken care of. This Dietrich business, Craig. Really quite something. You exhibited all your usual flair, if I might say so. It's going to give Himmler and the SD severe problems.'

'And how many hostages did they shoot in reprisal?'

Munro shrugged. 'It's that kind of war. Not your affair.'

Craig said, 'Anne-Marie used the same phrase. The exact same.'

'Ah, yes, I was delighted to hear that she was of assistance to you. She works for me, you know.'

'Then God help her,' Craig said forcefully.

'And you, dear boy. You see, you're on the strength as of right now.'

Craig leaned forward, tossing his cigarette into the fire. 'Like hell I am. I'm an American officer, a Major in the OSS. You can't touch me.'

'Oh, yes I can. I operate under the direct authority of General Eisenhower himself. The Cold Harbour project is a joint venture. Hare and four of his men are American citizens. You'll join me, Craig, for three reasons. First, because you now know too much about the entire Cold Harbour project. Second, because I need you here. There's a lot happening with the invasion coming up and you can make a very positive contribution.'

'And the third reason?' Craig asked.

'Simple. You're an officer in the armed forces of your

country just like me and you'll obey orders, just like me.' Munro stood up.

'No more nonsense, Craig. We'll go down to the pub, see Hare and tell him and his boys you're now a member of the club.'

He turned and walked to the door and Craig followed him feeling curiously light-headed, despair in his heart.

The Hanged Man was exactly what one would have expected, a typical English village pub. The floor was stone flagged, there was a log fire on an open hearth, iron-work tables which had seen years of use, high-backed wooden benches. The ceiling was beamed and the old mahogany bar was conventional enough, bottles ranged on the shelves behind it. The one incongruous thing was Julie pulling pints behind the bar and the Kriegsmarine uniforms of the men who leaned against it.

As the Brigadier entered followed by Osbourne and Edge, Hare was sitting by the fire drinking coffee and reading a newspaper. He stood up and called, in German. 'Attention. General officer present.'

The men clicked heels. Brigadier Munro waved a hand and said in fair German. 'At ease. Carry on drinking.' He held out a hand and said to Hare, 'No need for the usual formalities, Martin. We'll use English. Congratulations. Good job last night.'

'Thank you, sir.'

Munro warmed his backside at the fire. 'Yes, you used your initiative, which is fine, but do try to clear things with me in future.'

Edge said to Hare, 'Good point, old boy. For all you knew, the gallant Major might have been expendable.'

Something flared in Hare's eyes and he took a step towards Edge who backed off, laughing. 'All right, old boy, no violence if you please.' He turned to the bar. 'Julie, my blossom. A very large gin and tonic, *s'il vous plaît.*'

'Calm down, Martin,' Munro said. 'An unpleasant young sod, but a flyer of genius. Let's all have a drink.' He turned to Craig. 'It's not that we're alcoholics here, but as the lads work by night, they do their drinking in the morning.' He raised his voice. 'Listen, everybody. As you all know by now this is Major Craig Osbourne of the Office of Strategic Services. What you don't know is that as of right now, he will be one of us here at Cold Harbour.'

There was a moment's silence. Julie, at the bar, paused in the act of pulling a pint, face grave, then Schmidt raised his glass of ale. 'Gawd help you, guvnor.'

There was a general laugh and Munro said to Hare, 'Introduce them, Martin.' He turned to Osbourne. 'Under their assumed identities, of course.'

The Chief Petty Officer, Langsdorff, who had been at the wheel, was American. So were Hardt, Wagner and Bauer. Schneider, the engineer, was obviously German and as he discovered latter, Wittig and Brauch, like Schmidt, were English Jews.

Craig was feeling more than light-headed now. He was sweating, he knew that, and his forehead was hot. 'It's warm in here,' he said, 'damn warm.'

Hare looked at him curiously, 'Actually I thought it rather chilly this morning. Are you okay?'

Edge approached with two glasses. He gave one to Munro and the other to Craig. 'You look like a gin man to me, Major. Get it down. It'll set the old pulses roaring. Julie will like that.'

'Screw you!' Craig told him but he took the glass and drank it.

'No, the general idea is screw her, old boy.' Edge squeezed on to the bench beside him. 'Though she does seem to keep it to herself.'

'You're an unpleasant little swine, aren't you, Joe?' Martin Hare said.

Edge glanced at him, managing to look injured. 'Intrepid bird man, old boy, that's me. Gallant knight of the air.'

'So was Hermann Goering,' Craig said.

'Quite right. Brilliant pilot. Took over the Flying Circus after von Richthofen was killed.'

Craig's voice sounded to him as if it came from some-one else. 'An interesting idea, the war hero as psychopath. You must feel right at home in that Ju88 you've got up at the airfield.'

'Ju88S, old boy, let's be accurate. Its engine boosting system takes me up around four hundred.'

'He forgets to tell you that his boosting system depends on three cylinders of nitrous oxide. One hit in those tanks and he ends up in a variety of very small pieces,' Martin Hare said.

'Don't be like that, old boy,' Edge moved closer to Craig. 'This kite is a real honey. Usually has a crew of three. Pilot, navigator and a rear-gunner. We've done a few improvements so I can manage on my own. For instance, the Lichtenstein radar set which actually enables one to see in the dark – they've repositioned that in the cockpit so I can see for myself and . . .'

His voice faded as Craig Osbourne plunged into darkness and rolled on to the floor. Schmidt ran across from the bar and crouched down as the room went silent. He looked up at Munro.

'Christ, sir, he's got a raging fever. That's bloody quick. I only checked him out an hour ago.'

'Right,' Munro said grimly and turned to Hare. 'I'll take him back to London in the Lysander. Get him into hospital.'

Hare nodded. 'Okay, sir.' He stood back as Schmidt and two others picked Osbourne up and carried him out.

Munro turned to Edge. 'Joe, get through to Jack Carter at my office. Tell him to arrange for Osbourne to be admitted to the Hampstead Nursing Home as soon as we get in,' and he turned and followed the others out.

Craig Osbourne came awake from a deep sleep feeling fresh and alert. No sign of any fever at all. He struggled up on one elbow and found himself in what seemed to be a small hospital bedroom with white painted walls. He swung his legs to the floor and sat there for a moment as the door opened and a young nurse came in.

'You shouldn't be up, sir.'

She pushed him back into bed and Craig said, 'Where am I?'

She went out. A couple of minutes passed. The door opened again and a doctor in a white coat, a stethoscope around his neck, entered.

He smiled. 'So, how are we, Major?' and took Craig's pulse. He had a German accent.

'Who are you?'

'Dr Baum is my name.'

'And where am I?'

'A small nursing home in north London. Hampstead to be precise.' He put a thermometer in Craig's mouth, then checked it. 'Very good. Very nice. No fever at all. This penicillin is a miracle. Of course the chap who treated you gave you a shot, but I gave you more. Lots more. That's the secret.'

'How long have I been here?'

'This is the third day. You were quite bad. Frankly, without the drug,' Baum shrugged. 'Still, now you have some tea and I'll ring Brigadier Munro. Tell him you are all right.'

He went out. Craig stayed there, then got up, found a robe and went and sat by the window looking out at the high-walled garden. The nurse came back with a pot of tea on a tray.

'I hope you don't mind, Major. We don't have any coffee.'

'That's okay,' he told her. 'Do you have any cigarettes?'

'You shouldn't really, sir,' she hesitated then took a packet of Player's from her pocket and some matches. 'Don't tell Dr Baum where they came from.'

'You're a honey,' Craig kissed her hand. 'First night out I'll take you to Rainbow Corner in Piccadilly. Best cup of coffee in London and great swing to dance to.'

She blushed and went out, laughing. He sat there, smoking, staring into the garden, and after a while there was a knock at the door and Jack Carter limped in, a stick in one hand, a briefcase in the other.

'Hello, Craig.'

Craig, truly delighted to see him, stood up. 'Jack – how bloody marvellous after all this time. So, you still work for that old sod.'

'Oh, yes.' Carter sat down and opened the briefcase. 'Dr Baum says you're much better?'

'So I hear.'

'Good. The Brigadier would like you to do a job for him, if you feel up to it, that is.'

'Already? What's he trying to do? Kill me off?'

Carter raised a hand. 'Please, Craig, hear me out. It's not good, this one. This friend of yours, Anne-Marie Trevaunce?'

Craig paused, a cigarette to his lips. 'What about her?'

'The Brigadier needed to see her face-to-face. Something very big is coming up. Very big.'

Craig lit his cigarette. 'Isn't it always?'

'No, this time, it really is of supreme importance, Craig. Anyway, a Lysander pick-up was arranged to bring her out and I'm afraid things went very badly wrong.' He passed a file across. 'See for yourself.'

Craig went to the window seat, opened the file and started to read. After a while, he closed it, great pain on his face.

Carter said, 'I'm sorry. It's pretty bad, isn't it?'

'About as bad as it could be. A horror story.'

He sat there thinking of Anne-Marie, the lipsticked mouth,

the arrogance, the good legs in the dark stockings, the constant cigarette. So damned irritating and so bloody marvellous and now . . . ?

Carter said, 'Did you know of the existence of this twin sister, this Genevieve Trevaunce in England?'

'No.' Craig handed back the file. 'She was never mentioned in all the time I knew Anne-Marie, even in the old days. I knew there was an English father. She once told me Trevaunce was a Cornish name, but I always thought he was dead.'

'Not at all. He's a doctor. Lives in Cornwall. North Cornwall. A village called St Martin.'

'And the daughter? This Genevieve?'

'She's a Staff Nurse here in London at St Bartholomew's Hospital. She was recently rather ill with influenza. She's on extended sick leave staying with her father at St Martin.'

'So?' Craig said.

'The Brigadier would like you to go and see her.' Carter took a large white envelope from his briefcase and passed it across. 'This will explain just how important it is that you help us out on this one.'

Craig opened the envelope, took out the typed letter and began to read it slowly.

Four

Just behind the village of St Martin there was a hill, a strange place with no name that was marked on the maps as probably having been some kind of Roman-British fort in ancient times. It was Genevieve Trevaunce's favourite place. From its crest she could sit and look out across the estuary to where the surf washed in over treacherous shoals, only the seabirds to keep her company.

She had climbed up there after breakfast for what was to be the last time. On the previous evening, she had reluctantly faced up to the fact that she was well again and those raids on London, according to the BBC news, had intensified. They would need everyone they could get on the casualty wards at Bart's now.

It was a fine, soft day of a kind peculiar to North Cornwall and nowhere else, the sky very blue, white water breaking across the bar. She felt at peace with herself for the first time in months, relaxed and happy, turned and looked down at the village below, her father working in the garden of the old rectory. And then she noticed a car some distance away. At that stage of the war with severe petrol rationing it usually meant either the doctor or the police, but as it drew nearer, she saw that it was painted with the drab olive green colour used by the military.

It stopped outside the rectory gate and a man in some sort

of uniform got out. Genevieve started down the hill at once. She saw her father straighten, put down his spade and go to the gate. A few words were exchanged and then he and the other man went up the path together and went inside the house.

It took her no more than three or four minutes to reach the bottom of the hill. As she did so, the front door opened and her father came out and started down the path. They met at the gate.

His face was working terribly, a glazed look in his eyes. She put a hand on his arm. 'What is it? What's happened?'

His eyes focused on her for a moment and he recoiled, as if in horror. 'Anne-Marie,' he said hoarsely. 'She's dead. Anne-Marie is dead.'

He pushed past her, making for the church. He went through the graveyard in a grotesque, limping, half-run and entered the porch. The great oak door closed with a hollow boom.

The sky was still blue, the rooks in the trees beyond the church tower called harshly to each other. Nothing had changed, yet everything was different. She stood there, suddenly ice-cold. No emotion at all, only an emptiness.

Footsteps approached behind. 'Miss Trevaunce?'

She turned slowly. The uniform was American, a trenchcoat open over an olive drab battledress. A Major and with several medal ribbons. A surprising number for such a young man. The forage cap was tilted across gold hair with lights in it. A smooth, blank face gave nothing away, eyes the same cold grey as the Atlantic in winter. He opened his mouth slightly, then closed it again as if unable to speak.

She said, 'You bring us bad news, I believe, Major?'

'Osbourne.' He cleared his throat. 'Craig Osbourne. Dear God, Miss Trevaunce, but for a moment there it was like seeing a ghost.'

*

She took his trenchcoat in the hall and opened the parlour door. 'If you'll just go through, I'll ask the housekeeper to make some tea. No coffee, I'm afraid.'

'That's very kind of you.'

She put her head round the kitchen door. 'Could we have some tea, Mrs Trembath? I have a visitor. My father's in the church. I'm afraid we've had bad news.'

She turned from the sink, wiping her hands on her apron, a tall gaunt woman, the strong Cornish face very still, blue eyes watchful. 'Anne-Marie, is it?'

'She's dead,' Genevieve said simply and closed the door.

When she went into the parlour, Craig was standing at the mantelpiece looking at an old photo of Anne-Marie and her as children.

'Not much difference, even then,' he said. 'It's remarkable.'

'You knew my sister, I take it?'

'Yes. I met her in Paris in 1940. I was a journalist then. We became friends. I knew she had an English father, but to be honest, she never mentioned you. Not even a hint that you existed.'

Genevieve Trevaunce made no comment. She sat down in one of the wing-back chairs by the fire and said calmly, 'Have you come far, Major?'

'London.'

'A long drive.'

'Easy enough. Not much traffic on the roads these days.'

There was an awkward pause, but it could be put off no longer. 'How exactly did my sister die?'

'In a plane crash,' Craig told her.

'In France?'

'That's right.'

'How would you know that?' Genevieve asked. 'France is occupied territory.'

'We have our channels of communication,' he said. 'The people I work for.'

'And who would they be?'

The door opened and Mrs Trembath came in with a tray which she placed carefully on the side table. She glanced at Osbourne briefly and departed. Genevieve poured the tea.

'I must say you're taking this remarkably well,' he said.

'And you've just managed to avoid answering my question, but never mind.' She handed him a cup of tea. 'My sister and I were never close.'

'Isn't that unusual for twins?'

'She went to live in France when my mother died in 1935. I stayed with my father. It was as simple as that. Now, let me try again. Who do you work for?'

'Office of Strategic Services,' he said. 'It's a rather special-ised organisation.'

She noticed a strange feature of his uniform. On his right sleeve he wore wings with the letters SF in the centre which, as she learned later, stood for Special Forces, but underneath he also wore British paratrooper's wings.

'Commandos?'

'Not really. Most of the time our people wouldn't tend to go in wearing uniform at all.'

She said, 'Are you trying to tell me that my sister was involved in that sort of thing?'

He produced a pack of cigarettes and offered her one. She shook her head. 'I don't smoke.'

'Mind if I do?'

'Not at all.'

He lit one, got up and walked to the window. 'It was in the spring of 1940 that I met your sister. I was working for *Life* magazine. She was quite big on the social scene, but then you'd know that.'

'Yes.'

He peered out at the garden. 'I did a feature on the de Voincourts which, for various reasons, never saw press, but it meant I had to interview the Countess . . .'

'Hortense?'

He turned, a wry smile on his face. 'Quite a lady, that one. She'd just lost her fourth husband when I saw her. An infantry Colonel, killed at the front.'

'Yes. And my sister?'

'Oh, we became,' Craig paused, 'good friends.' He came back to the fireplace and sat down. 'And then the Germans took Paris. Being a neutral, they didn't bother me at first, but then I got involved with entirely the wrong people from their point of view and I had to exit stage left rather quickly. I came to England.'

'Which was when you joined this OSS of yours?'

'No, America wasn't at war with Germany at that time. I worked for a British outfit at first – SOE. Same kind of work, you might say. I transferred to my own people later.'

'And how did my sister come to be involved?'

'The German High Command started to use your aunt's château. Generals, those sort of people, putting up there for a few days' rest, a conference or two.'

'And Anne-Marie and my aunt?'

'Allowed to stay on as long as they behaved, and it was good for propaganda purposes to have the Countess de Voincourt and her niece acting as hostesses.'

Genevieve was angry then. 'You expect me to believe this? That Hortense de Voincourt would allow herself to be used in this way?'

'Hold on a minute and let me explain,' Craig said. 'Your sister was allowed to travel backwards and forwards to Paris whenever she wished. She got in touch with people in the Resistance there. Offered to work for us and she was in a unique position to do that.'

'So, she became an agent?' she said calmly.

'You don't seem very surprised?'

'I'm not. She probably thought your kind of work rather glamorous.'

'War,' Craig Osbourne said quietly, 'is not in the least glamorous. What your sister was doing even less so, considering what they'd have done to her if she'd been caught.'

'I think I should tell you that I'm a Staff Nurse at St Bartholomew's Hospital in London, Major,' Genevieve said. 'Military Ward 10. We had one of your boys in during my last week of duty. An air gunner on a Flying Fortress and we had to amputate what was left of his hands. You don't need to tell me much about the glamour of war. I meant something rather different. If you knew my sister as well as you say, I'm sure you'll understand me.'

He didn't answer, simply stood up and paced restlessly around the room. 'We got information about a special conference the Nazis were going to hold. Something very important. So important that it was necessary for our people to talk to Anne-Marie face-to-face. She arranged a holiday in Paris and a Lysander aircraft was sent to pick her up. The idea was that she would be brought to England for a briefing then flown back.'

'Is that usual?'

'Happens all the time. A regular shuttle service. I've done it myself. She was supposed to be driving to St Maurice to catch the Paris train. But in fact, the car was looked after for her and she was taken by truck to the field where the Lysander was to put down.'

'What went wrong?'

'According to our Resistance sources, they were shot down by a German nightfighter as they took off. It seems the plane blew up instantly.'

'I see,' Genevieve said.

He stopped pacing and said to her angrily, 'Don't you care? Do you even give a damn?'

'When I was thirteen, Major Osbourne,' she told him, 'Anne-Marie broke my right thumb in two places.' She held it up. 'See, it's still a little crooked. She told me she wanted to see how much pain I could stand. She used one of those old-fashioned walnut crackers – the kind you screw very tight. She told me I must not cry out, however much it hurt, because I was a de Voincourt.'

'My God!' he whispered.

'And I didn't. I simply fainted when the pain became unbearable, but by then, the damage had been done.'

'What happened?'

'Nothing. A playful prank turned sour, that's all. Where my father was concerned she could do no wrong.' She poured herself another cup of tea. 'How much of all this have you told him, by the way?'

'I simply said that we'd learned through our Intelligence sources that your sister had been killed in a bad car accident.'

'But why tell me and not him?'

'Because you looked as if you could take it, he didn't.'

He was lying, she knew that instantly, but at that moment, her father walked past the window. She stood up. 'I must see how he is.'

As she got the door open, Craig said, 'None of my business, but I'd say you're the last person he'd want to see right now.' And that hurt, really hurt, because in her heart, she knew that it was true. 'Having you around will only make it worse for him,' he said gently. 'Every time he sees you he'll think it's her for just a split second.'

'Hope it's her, Major Osbourne,' Genevieve corrected him. 'But what would you suggest?'

'I'm driving back to London now, if that would be of any help.'

And then she saw, knew beyond any shadow of doubt. 'That's why you're here, isn't it? I'm what you came for.'

'That's right, Miss Trevaunce.'

She turned and left him there by the fire and went out, closing the door behind her.

Her father was gardening again, pulling weeds and throwing them into a barrow. The sun was shining, the sky was blue. It was still a fine soft day as if nothing had happened.

He straightened and said, 'You'll be off on the afternoon train from Padstow?'

'I thought you might want me to stay on for a while. I could phone the hospital. Explain. Ask for an extension of leave.'

'Would it alter anything?' He was lighting his pipe, his hands shaking slightly.

'No,' Genevieve said wearily. 'I suppose not.'

'Then why stay?' He returned to his weeding.

She moved round her tiny bedroom making sure she hadn't forgotten anything and paused at the window watching her father working down there. Had he loved Anne-Marie more because he couldn't have her? Was that it? She'd never felt there were any similarities between herself and the rest of the family. The only one on either side for whom she'd had any genuine feeling was her Aunt Hortense, but she, of course, was something special.

She opened the window and called to her father, 'Major Osbourne is going back to London now. He's offered me a lift.'

He glanced up. 'Kind of him, I'd take it if I were you.'

He returned to his digging, looking at least twenty years older than he had an hour earlier. As if he had already crawled into the grave with his beloved Anne-Marie. She closed the window, took a last look around the room, picked up her case and went out. Craig Osbourne was sitting on a chair at the door. He stood up and took the case from her without a word as Mrs Trembath came in from the kitchen, wiping her hands on her apron again.

'I'm going now,' Genevieve said. 'Look after him.'

'Haven't I always?' She kissed Genevieve on the cheek. 'On your way, girl. This is no place for you and never was.'

Craig went to the car and put her case on the rear seat. She took a deep breath and approached her father. He looked up, and she kissed him on the cheek. 'I'm not sure when I'll be back. I'll write.'

He hugged her hard and then turned away quickly. 'Go back to your hospital, Genevieve. Do some good for those that can still be helped.'

She went to the car, then, without another word, aware of the strangest sense of release in his rejection of her. Craig handed her in, closed the door, stepped behind the wheel and drove away.

After a while he said, 'Are you okay?'

'Would you think I was crazy if I told you I felt free for the first time in years?' she said.

'No, knowing your sister as I did and after what I've seen here this morning, I'd say that makes a certain wild sense.'

'And just how well did you know her?' Genevieve asked him. 'Were you lovers?'

Craig smiled wryly. 'You don't really expect me to answer that, do you?'

'Why not?'

'Hell, I don't know. Lovers would be entirely the wrong term. Anne-Marie never loved anyone but herself in her life.'

'True, but we're not talking about that. We're discussing the flesh, Major.'

He was angry for a moment then a muscle twitched in his cheek. 'Okay, lady, so I slept with your sister a time or two. Does that make you feel better?'

She sat face averted and for ten miles they didn't exchange a word. Finally, he produced the pack of cigarettes, one-handed. 'They have their uses, these things.'

'No thanks.'

He lit one himself and wound the window down a little. 'Your father – quite a guy. A country doctor, yet according to that plate on the gate back there he's a Fellow of the Royal College of Surgeons.'

'Are you trying to tell me you didn't know that before you came down here?'

'Some,' he said. 'Not all. Neither you nor he figured much in Anne-Marie's vocabulary when I knew her.'

She leaned back, arms folded, head against the seat. 'The Trevaunces have lived in this part of Cornwall past memory. My father broke a family tradition of centuries by going to medical school instead of to sea. He came out of Edinburgh University in the summer of 1914 with a talent for surgery which he was able to put to good use in the field hospitals of the Western Front in France.'

'I imagine that must have been one hell of a postgraduate course,' Craig said.

'During the spring of 1918 he was wounded. Shrapnel in his right leg. You probably noticed that he still limps. Château de Voincourt was used as a convalescent home for officers. You see how much of a fairy story it's beginning to sound?'

'You could say that,' he said. 'But go on. It's interesting.'

'My grandmother, holder of one of the oldest titles in France in her own right and proud as Lucifer; the elder sister, Hortense, sardonic, witty, always in control; and then there was Hélène, young and wilful and very, very beautiful.'

'Who fell in love with the doctor from Cornwall?' Craig nodded. 'I shouldn't imagine the old girl would have liked that.'

'She didn't, so the lovers fled away by night. My father was established in London and all was silent from the French connection . . .'

'Until la belle Hélène produced twins?'

'Exactly.' Genevieve nodded. 'And blood, they say, is thicker than water.'

'So you started to visit the old homestead?'

'My mother, Anne-Marie and me. It worked very well. We fitted in. My mother raised us to speak only French in the house, you see.'

'And your father?'

'Oh, he was never made welcome. He did very well over the years. A Senior Surgeon at Guy's Hospital, rooms in Harley Street.'

'And then your mother died?'

'That's right. Pneumonia. 1935. We were thirteen at the time. The year of the thumb, I call it.'

'And Anne-Marie chose France while you stayed with your father? What was all that about?'

'Simple.' Genevieve shrugged, looking suddenly all French. 'Grandmère was dead and Hortense was the new Countess de Voincourt, a title held in her own right by the eldest in the female line in our family since the days of Charlemagne, and the one thing which had become clear to Hortense after several marriages was that she couldn't have children.'

'And Anne-Marie was next in line?' Craig asked.

'By eleven minutes. Oh, Hortense had no legal claim, but my father gave Anne-Marie free choice in the matter, in spite of the fact that she was only thirteen.'

'He hoped she'd choose him – right?'

'Poor Daddy.' Genevieve nodded. 'And Anne-Marie knew exactly what she wanted. For him, it was the final straw. He sold up in London, moved back to St Martin and bought the old rectory.'

'It's good enough for the movies,' Craig said. 'Bette Davis as Anne-Marie.'

'And who for me?' Genevieve demanded.

'Why, Bette Davis, of course.' He laughed. 'Who else? When did you last see Anne-Marie?'

'Easter of 1940. My father and I visited Voincourt together. That was before Dunkirk. He tried to persuade her to return with us to England. She thought he was quite mad. Charmed him right out of the idea.'

'Yes, that I can imagine,' Craig wound down the window and flicked his cigarette out. 'So, you're the new heir?'

Genevieve Trevaunce turned to him, her face suddenly drained of colour. 'God help me, but I hadn't thought of that – not for a moment.'

He put an arm around her. 'Hey, come on, soldier, it's okay. I understand.'

She suddenly looked very tired. 'When do we get to London?'

'Early evening, with any luck.'

'And then you'll tell me the truth? The whole truth?'

He didn't even glance at her, but kept his attention on the road. 'Yes,' he said briefly. 'I think I can promise you that.'

'Good.'

It started to rain. She closed her eyes as he turned on the wipers and after a while she slept, turning on the seat, arms folded under her breasts, her head pillowed on his shoulder.

The perfume was different. Anne-Marie, yet not Anne-Marie. Craig Osbourne had never felt so bewildered in his life and drove onwards to London glumly.

As they approached London it was dark, and there were the first hints of fire on the horizon, the crunch of bombs as the Ju88S pathfinders operating out of Chartres and Rennes in France laid the flares that would lead in the heavy bombers following.

As they drove into the city, there were signs of bomb damage everywhere from the previous night's raid. On several occasions, Craig had to divert where streets were blocked off. When Genevieve wound down the window she could smell smoke on the damp air and people were crowding into the tube stations, whole families carrying blankets, suitcases and personal belongings ready for another night underground. Nineteen-forty all over again.

'I thought we'd finished with all this,' she said bitterly. 'I thought the RAF was supposed to have dealt with it.'

'Somebody must have forgotten to tell the Luftwaffe,' Craig said. 'The Little Blitz, that's what they're calling it. Nothing like as bad as the first time around.'

'Unless you happen to be underneath the next bomb they drop,' she said.

There were flames over to the right of them and a stick of bombs fell close enough for Craig to swerve from one side of the street to the other. He pulled in at the kerb and a policeman in a tin hat emerged from the gloom.

'You'll have to park here and take shelter in the tube. Entrance at the other end of the street.'

'I'm on military business,' Craig protested.

'You could be Churchill himself, old son, you still go down the bleeding tube,' the policeman said.

'Okay, I surrender,' Craig told him.

They got out and he locked the car, and they followed a motley crowd streaming along the street to the entrance to the tube station. They joined the queue and went down two escalators, finally walking along a tunnel until they emerged into the tunnel itself beside the track.

The platforms were crowded, people sitting everywhere, wrapped in blankets, their belongings around them. WVS ladies were dispensing refreshments from a trolley. Craig queued and managed to secure two cups of tea and a corned beef sandwich which he and Genevieve shared.

'People are marvellous,' she said. 'Look at them. If Hitler could see this right now, he'd call off the war.'

'Very probably,' Craig agreed.

At that moment, a warden in a boiler suit and tin hat, his face covered in dust, appeared in the entrance. 'I need half-a-dozen volunteers. We got someone trapped in a cellar up on the street.'

There was a certain hesitation, then a couple of middle-aged men sitting near by got up. 'We'll go.'

Craig hesitated, touching his wounded arm. 'Count me in.'

Genevieve followed him and the air raid warden said, 'Not you, love.'

'I'm a nurse,' she said crisply. 'You might need me more than the others.'

He shrugged wearily, turned and led the way out, and they all followed, back up the escalators and into the street. The bombs were falling further away now, but fires blazed over to the left and there was the stench of acrid smoke on the air.

About fifty yards from the entrance to the tube, a row of shops had been blasted into rubble. The warden said, 'We should wait for the heavy rescue boys, but I heard someone crying out over here. Used to be a café called Sam's. I think there's someone in the cellar.'

They crowded forward, listening. The warden called out and almost immediately there was a faint answering cry.

'Right, let's get this lot cleared,' the warden said.

They attacked the pile of bricks with their hands, burrowing deep, until after fifteen or twenty minutes, the top of the area steps appeared. There was barely room for a man to enter headfirst. While they crouched to inspect it, someone cried out in alarm and they scattered as a wall crumbled into the street.

The dust cleared and they stood up. 'Madness to go down there,' one of the men said.

There was a pause then Craig put his cap in his trenchcoat pocket, took the coat off and handed it to Genevieve. 'Jesus,

I only got his damn uniform two days ago,' he said, dropped on his belly and slithered into the slot above the steps.

Everyone waited. After a while they could hear a child crying. His hands appeared holding a baby. Genevieve ran forward to take it from him and retreated into the centre of the street. A little later, a boy of about five years of age crawled out, covered in filth. He stood there, bewildered, and Craig emerged behind him. He took the boy's hand and crossed to join Genevieve and the warden in the middle of the street. Someone cried a warning and another wall cascaded down in a shower of bricks, completely covering the entrance.

'Blimey, guvnor, your luck is good,' the warden said and he dropped on one knee to comfort the crying child. 'Anyone else down there?'

'A woman. Dead, I'm afraid.' Craig managed to find a cigarette. He lit it and gave Genevieve a tired grin. 'There's nothing like a really great war, that's what I always say, Miss Trevaunce. What do you always say?'

She held the baby close. 'The uniform,' she said. 'It's not so bad. It should clean up very well.'

'Did anyone ever tell you you're a great comfort?' he enquired.

Later, driving on, she felt tired again. The bombing was well into the distance now, but even this area had seen action, glass crunching under the tyres. She saw a street sign – Haston Place – and Craig stopped outside number ten, a pleasant Georgian terrace house.

'Where are we?' she asked.

'About ten minutes' walk from SOE Headquarters in Baker Street. My boss has the top floor flat here. He thought it would be more private.'

'And who might this boss be?'

'Brigadier Dougal Munro.'

'Now that doesn't sound very American,' she observed.

He opened the door for her. 'We'll take anything that comes to hand, Miss Trevaunce. Now, if you'd follow me please.'

He led the way up the steps and pressed one of the buzzers at the front door.

Five

Jack Carter was waiting on the landing as they went up the stairs, leaning on his stick. He held out his hand. 'Miss Trevaunce. A great pleasure. My name's Carter. Brigadier Munro is expecting you.'

The door stood open. As she went in Carter said to Craig, 'Everything all right?'

'I'm not sure,' Craig told him. 'I wouldn't expect too much at this stage.'

The sitting room was very pleasant. A coal fire burning in a Georgian grate, a great many antiques on display, all of them an indication of Munro's original career as an Egyptologist. The room was shadowed, the main light coming from a table lamp of brass on the desk by the window. Munro sat behind it reading some papers. Now he stood up and came round the desk.

'Miss Trevaunce.' He nodded. 'Quite remarkable. I wouldn't have believed it unless I'd seen it with my own eyes. My name is Munro – Dougal Munro.'

'Brigadier.' She nodded in acknowledgement.

He turned to Craig, 'Good God, you are in a state. What on earth have you been up to?'

'A little tricky getting through town tonight with the bombing,' Craig told him.

Genevieve said, 'He saved the lives of two children trapped in a cellar. Crawled in and got them out himself.'

'Dear me,' Munro observed. 'I wish you wouldn't indulge in heroics, Craig. You really are too valuable to lose at this stage and it can hardly have done that damned arm any good. Please sit down, Miss Trevaunce, or may I call you Genevieve? Your sister was always Anne-Marie to me.'

'If you like.'

'A drink, perhaps. We've limited supplies, but Scotch would be a possibility.'

'No thanks. It's been a long day. Do you think we could get down to business?'

'A little difficult to know where to begin.' He sat behind the desk and Genevieve stood up.

'Some other time perhaps, when you've made up your mind.'

'Genevieve – please.' He raised a hand. 'At least listen to me.'

'The trouble with listening is that one so often ends up by being persuaded.' But she did sit down again. 'All right. Get on with it.'

Jack Carter and Craig sat by the fire opposite each other. Munro said, 'I imagine Major Osbourne has explained the situation regarding your sister?'

'Yes.'

He opened a silver box and held it across the desk. 'Cigarette?'

'No thanks. I don't smoke.'

'Your sister did – incessantly and this brand. Gitanes. Try one.'

There was a persistence to him now that she didn't like. She said impatiently, 'No – why should I?'

'Because we'd like you to take her place,' he said simply.

He held the cigarette box open and she stared at him, stomach suddenly empty as everything fell into place. 'You're mad,' she said. 'Quite mad. You must be.'

'It's been said before.' He snapped the box shut with a sharp click.

'You want me to go to France in my sister's place, is that what you're saying?'

'Yes, on Thursday of this week.' He turned to Craig. 'The moon is right that night for a Lysander drop?'

'Yes, if everything the Met. boys promise about the weather holds true.'

She turned to look at him. He sprawled in the chair, smoking a cigarette, face calm as ever. No help there and she turned back to Munro. 'This is nonsense. You must have any number of trained agents far better qualified than I to take on this job.'

'No one else who can be Anne-Marie Trevaunce, niece of the Countess de Voincourt at whose château, this coming weekend, some very important members of the High Command of the German Army will be holding a conference to discuss the Atlantic Wall defence system against the coming Allied invasion. We'd like to hear what they have to say. It could save thousands of lives.'

'I'm disappointed in you, Brigadier,' she said. 'That one went out years ago.'

He leaned back in his chair, fingertips pressed together, a slight frown on his face as he considered her. 'You know, it occurs to me that perhaps you don't really have any choice in the matter.'

'What do you mean?'

'Your aunt – you have something of a fondness for her, I understand?'

'To ask that question means you know the answer already.'

'She'll be in a difficult position when Anne-Marie fails to materialise from that trip to Paris on Friday.' He shrugged, 'German Intelligence hasn't the slightest idea who was in that Lysander, you see.'

And now she really was afraid. 'Did my aunt know about Anne-Marie's activities?'

'No, but if she vanishes from the face of the earth completely the Germans will start to dig. They're very thorough. It would only be a question of time before they knew something of the truth at least. Then, I think, they'd turn to your aunt and she's not exactly up to the kind of pressure they'd put on her.'

'What are you saying?' she said. 'Is she ill?'

'I understand her heart's not been too good for some time now. She's leading a normal enough life on the surface, but that's about all.'

Genevieve took a deep breath and squared her shoulders. 'No,' she said, 'I think you're quite wrong. As Major Osbourne said earlier, she's valuable to the Germans for propaganda reasons. They wouldn't touch her, not Hortense de Voincourt. She's too important.'

'I think you might find that things have altered a little since you were last in France,' he said. 'No one is safe any more, believe me.'

'What would they do?'

It was Craig who answered. 'They have camps for people like her. Very unpleasant places.'

'Major Osbourne, I should tell you, has had personal experience of such a situation,' Munro said. 'He knows what he's talking about.' She sat there staring at him, throat dry. 'As I've said, we would put you in by Lysander,' he told her gently. 'No parachute training necessary. No time. We have only three days to prepare you.'

'That's ridiculous.' She could feel a rising panic. 'I can't play Anne-Marie. It's been four years. You know more about her than I do.'

'She was your twin sister,' he said remorselessly. 'Same face, same voice. None of those things have changed. We can handle the rest. Her hairstyle, her taste in clothes, make-up, perfume. We'll show you photographs, tell you how she handled herself at the Château. We *will* make it work.'

'But it wouldn't be enough, can't you see?' Genevieve said.

'Except for a few familiar faces, it would be a house of strangers. New servants since I was last there, plus the Germans. I wouldn't know who was who.' Suddenly, the nonsense of the whole business made her laugh. 'I'd need a still small voice whispering in my ear every step of the way, and that isn't possible.'

'Isn't it?' He opened a drawer, took out a cigar and clipped the end carefully with a penknife. 'Your aunt had a chauffeur. A man called Dissard.'

'René Dissard,' she said. 'Of course. He's served the family all his life.'

'He worked with Anne-Marie. He was her right hand. He's in the next room now.'

She stared at him in astonishment. 'René? Here? But I don't understand.'

'He was supposed to drive your sister to St Maurice, then accompany her to Paris by train. In reality, he was to go to ground with the local Resistance unit in that area while she was flown out to wait for her return. When they radioed the news of what had happened, we sent in another plane to pick him up on the following night.'

'May I see him?'

'Of course.'

Craig Osbourne opened the far door and she stood up and crossed to join him. It was a small study lined with books, blackout curtains drawn. There were a couple of armchairs on either side of a gas fire and not much else – except René Dissard.

He stood up slowly, the same old René, totally unchanged, one of the eternal figures from childhood that always seemed to have been there. Small, broad-shouldered under the cord jacket, iron-grey hair and beard, the scar on the right cheek disappearing under the black patch, evidence of the wound that had cost him an eye as a young soldier at Verdun.

'René? Is it you?'

He recoiled, for a moment the same fear there that she had seen in her father's, as if the dead walked, but he recovered quickly.

'Mademoiselle Geneviève. It is so wonderful to see you.'

His hands were shaking and she held them tight. 'My aunt is well?'

'As may be expected in the circumstances.' He shrugged. 'The Boche. You must understand that things are very different at the Château these days.' He hesitated. 'This is very terrible, this thing which has taken place.'

It was as if something clicked inside her head, a reality to things now, because of him. 'You know what they want me to do, René?'

'Oui, Mamselle.'

'You think I should do it?'

'It would complete what she started,' he said gravely. 'There would be less sense of waste.'

She nodded, turned, brushed past Craig Osbourne and went back into the other room.

'All right?' Munro said.

And then a sudden revulsion hit her. It wasn't that she was afraid; simply that something in her protested totally at being manipulated in this way.

'No, it damn well isn't,' she said. 'I've already got a job, thank you very much, Brigadier. I'm in the business of saving lives when I can.'

'Strangely enough, so are we, but if that's how you feel.' He shrugged and turned to Osbourne. 'You'd better take her to Hampstead and get this whole thing wrapped up.'

She said, 'Hampstead? What nonsense are you trying to pull now?'

He looked up, a mild surprise on his face. 'Your sister's personal effects. There are a few in our possession which will be handed over to you. A document or two to sign, just for the records, and you can forget this whole sorry business.

Naturally, the Official Secrets Act will apply in full to all or any part of the conversation we've had here this evening.'

He opened a file, picked up a pen as if dismissing her. She turned, thoroughly angry now, walked past Osbourne and went out.

The house in Hampstead was a late Georgian affair in a couple of acres of ground with high walls and a metal gate which was opened by a man in a peaked cap and some sort of blue uniform. A board on the gate said Rosedene Nursing Home. She couldn't see much of the garden because of the dark. When Craig led the way up the steps to the front door, he carried a flashlight in his hand. He pulled on an old-fashioned bell chain and they waited.

She heard footsteps approaching. There was the rattle of a chain, the sound of a bolt being withdrawn. The door opened, to reveal a young, fair-haired man in a white dust coat. He stood back and Craig led the way inside without a word.

The hall was dimly lit with cream-painted walls and a floor of polished wood blocks. There was a strangely antiseptic smell that reminded her of a hospital ward. The young man bolted and chained the door carefully behind them and when he turned to speak, his voice was as colourless as his appearance.

'Herr Doktor Baum will be with you in a moment. If you'll come this way, please.'

He opened a door at the end of the hall, let them pass in and closed it again without a word. It was like a dentist's waiting room, shabby chairs, a few magazines, and was rather cold in spite of the electric fire. There was something different about Craig Osbourne now, she could sense that, a restlessness, an air of tension as he lit a cigarette and moved across to the blackout curtains which were slightly open. He pulled them together.

'Herr Baum,' she said. 'German, I presume?'

'No – Austrian.'

The door opened. The man who entered was small, balding and wore a white doctor's jacket, a stethoscope around his neck. His clothes hung on him as if he had lost weight.

'Hello, Baum,' Craig Osbourne said. 'This is Miss Trevaunce.'

The eyes were small and anxious and suddenly, there was the same touch of fear that she had seen with René and her father. He moistened dry lips and his smile, obviously intended to put her at her ease, succeeded only in being quite ghastly.

'Fräulein.' He bowed and when he took her hand, his palm was damp.

'I've got a phone call to make,' Craig said. 'I'll be back in a minute.'

The door closed behind him. There was a long silence. Baum was sweating profusely now and took out a handkerchief to mop his brow.

'Major Osbourne tells me that you have some things for me that belonged to my sister.'

'Yes – that is so.' His smile was more ghastly than ever. 'And when he returns . . .' His voice trailed away and then he tried again. 'Can I get you anything? A glass of sherry, perhaps?' He was already at the cupboard in the corner, and turned with a bottle in one hand, a glass in the other. 'Not of the best, I'm afraid. Like so many other things these days.'

There was a photo on the mantelpiece in a black frame of a young girl of sixteen or seventeen, gently smiling. She had a kind of ethereal beauty.

Genevieve said instinctively, 'Your daughter?'

'Yes.'

'Still at school, I suppose?'

'No, Miss Trevaunce. She is dead.' The sad, quiet voice seemed to echo in her ears and the room really was cold now. 'It was the Gestapo – Vienna in 1939. You see, Miss Trevaunce,

I am an Austrian Jew. One of the luckier ones who got away.'

'And now?'

'I do what I can against her murderers.'

The voice was so gentle and yet the pain in those eyes was terrible to see. *We are all victims.* She'd read that somewhere and remembered the young Luftwaffe fighter pilot they'd carried into Casualty at Bart's one day, badly burned and shot to pieces. His face was unmarked, the hair very fair. He'd looked exactly like a sixth-former she'd fallen in love with when she was sixteen and still at school. Just a nice ordinary boy who kept smiling in spite of the pain and held her hand, still smiling as he died.

The door opened and Craig came in. 'Okay, that's taken care of. You'd better get started. I'll wait for you here.'

'I don't understand.' Baum looked extremely agitated. 'I thought you were going to handle this.'

There was a weary contempt on Craig's face. He put up a hand as if to cut off any further conversation. 'Okay, Baum, okay.'

He opened the door and stood to one side, waiting for her.

'Look, what game are you playing with me now?' she demanded.

'Something I think you should see.'

'What?'

'This way,' he said gravely. 'Just follow me.'

He went out and, in spite of herself, she went after him.

He opened a door at the end of the hall and they descended a dark stairway. There was a long corridor at the bottom, brick walls painted white, doors on either side. Where the corridor turned a corner, she could see a man sitting on a chair reading a book. He was perhaps fifty, heavily built with a broken nose and grey hair and wore a long white dust coat like the young man who'd admitted them earlier. A rhythmic banging started and as they reached the end of the corridor it increased to quite unbearable proportions. The man on the chair glanced up briefly, then returned to his book.

'He's quite deaf,' Craig said. 'He needs to be.'

He stopped at a metal door. The banging had ceased and it was very quiet. He moved a small panel, glanced in, then stood to one side. He didn't say a word and she moved forward as if hypnotised.

She had never smelled anything as foul as that room as she peered in through the bars. There was a ceiling light, but not a very good one. She could barely make out the outlines of a small bed with no blankets, an enamel slop bucket beside it and not much else. And then a movement, just out of sight, caught her eye.

There was someone in a rag of clothing crouched in the far corner. Impossible to tell whether it was male or female. It made a moaning sound and clawed at the wall. She could not have moved then if she had wanted to, caught by the horror of it. As if becoming aware that something was watching, it raised its face slowly and she gazed in terror upon her own face, twisted, broken, as if seen in one of those distorting mirrors in a penny arcade.

She couldn't even scream, fear cold inside her. They seemed to stare at each other for ever, that ruin of a face and Genevieve and then there were fingers reaching out through the bars, hooking into claws. She could not move to save herself, feet nailed to the floor. It was Craig who pulled her back, slamming the panel shut, cutting off the high-pitched animal scream.

She struck him then, back-handed with all her strength across the face. Once – twice, and then his hands were on her like iron, holding her still.

'It's all right,' he said calmly. 'We'll go now.'

The man in the chair looked up, smiled and nodded. The banging behind had reached the level of frenzy, and as they went along the corridor it was only Craig Osbourne's strong arm that kept her from falling.

They gave her brandy and she sat beside the electric fire, shaking like a leaf, hanging on to the glass for dear life while Baum lurked anxiously in the background.

'She left her car at the station as arranged,' Craig said. 'René went off to make contact with the local Resistance cell. Your sister changed her clothes, then started across country to the pick-up point on foot.'

'What happened?' Genevieve whispered.

'She was stopped by an SS patrol looking for partisans. Her papers, false, of course, seemed perfectly in order. To them she was just a good-looking village girl. They dragged her into the nearest barn.'

'How many?'

'Does it matter? René and a couple of his Resistance friends found what was left of her wandering the countryside afterwards. That's what the Lysander brought back two days ago.'

'You lied,' Genevieve said. 'All of you – even René.'

'To spare you, if we could, but you left us no choice, did you?'

'Can nothing be done? Does she really have to stay in that filthy place?'

It was Baum who answered. 'No – she is at the moment on a course of drugs which should gradually reduce her extreme violence, but it will be at least two weeks before these can take their full effect. Then, of course, we will make arrangements for her to be transferred to a suitable establishment.'

'Is there any hope?'

He mopped sweat from his brow again, then rubbed his hands on the damp handkerchief, his agitation clearly visible. 'Fräulein – please. What do you want me to say?'

She took a deep breath. 'My father must know nothing about this – you understand me? It would kill him.'

'Of course,' Craig nodded. 'He has his story. No need to change it now.'

She stared down into the glass. 'I never really had any choice from the beginning, did I, and you knew that.'

'Yes,' he said gravely.

'Right, then.' She swallowed the brandy which burned the back of her throat, placed the glass down carefully. 'What happens now?'

'Back to Munro, I'm afraid.'

'Then let's get on with it,' and she turned and led the way out.

Carter's face was grave as he led the way into the sitting room of the flat at Haston Place. Munro, still behind the desk, stood up and came round to her.

'So, now you know everything?'

'Yes.' She didn't bother to sit down.

'I'm sorry, my dear.'

'Save it, Brigadier.' She put up a hand. 'I don't like you and I don't like the way you operate. What happens now?'

'We keep the ground floor flat for guests. You can stay there overnight.' He nodded to Craig. 'You can stay with Jack in the basement.'

'And tomorrow?' Genevieve enquired.

'We'll fly you down to Cold Harbour from Croydon. It's in Cornwall. Only takes an hour by Lysander. We have a house there, Grancester Abbey. It's the sort of place used to prepare people in our line of work. Major Osbourne and I will accompany you.' He turned to Carter. 'You hold the fort, Jack.'

'What time, sir?' Carter asked.

'About eleven-thirty from Croydon, in deference to the Major's previous appointment.'

Craig said, 'What would that be then?'

'It seems someone recommended you for a Military Cross, dear boy, for that last little caper you pulled for SOE before you joined your own people. It's usual for His Majesty to pin these things on himself, so you're expected at the investiture at Buckingham Palace, ten o'clock sharp in the morning.'

'Oh, my God!' Craig groaned.

'I'll say goodnight then.' They turned to the door and Munro added, 'Just one thing, Craig.'

'Sir?'

'The uniform, dear boy. Do try to do something with it.'

They moved out on to the landing. Jack Carter said, 'The door's open and you'll find everything you need, Miss Trevaunce. I'll see you in the morning.'

He went down the stairs ahead of them and they followed to the ground floor. They paused outside the door to his flat.

Genevieve said, 'The basement for you. That sounds rough.'

'Very nice actually. I've stayed before.'

'Buckingham Palace. I'm impressed.'

'No big deal. I'll be one of many.' He turned away and paused. 'It's usual to take a couple of guests to these things. I won't have anyone. I was wondering . . . ?'

She smiled. 'I've never seen the King close up and I suppose it would be on the way to Croydon.'

'No point in just sitting in the car waiting,' he said.

She ran a finger down his tunic. 'Tell you what. You go and change, then let me have it. I'm sure I can put it in order with a sponge and iron.'

'Yes, ma'am.' He saluted and hurried down to the basement.

She went into the flat, closed the door and leaned against it, no longer smiling. She couldn't help liking Craig Osbourne, it was as simple as that, and where was the harm? A little warmth against the dark. Anything to blot out the memory of her sister's ravaged face.

*

It was raining heavily, St James's Park shrouded in mist as the limousine turned up Pall Mall towards Buckingham Palace. Dougal Munro and Genevieve sat in the rear seat. Having no hat, in deference to custom she'd found an old black velvet beret amongst the things in her case and wore that, a black belted raincoat and her last pair of decent stockings.

'I don't feel very dressed up,' she said nervously.

'Nonsense, you look marvellous,' Munro assured her.

Craig Osbourne sat on the jump seat opposite, his forage cap tilted at the regulation angle. She'd really done an excellent job on the olive drab battledress. His slacks were tucked into polished jump boots and instead of a tie, he wore a white scarf at his throat, an affectation of some OSS officers and men.

'He looks well, our boy, does he not?' Munro said cheerfully.

'I'm glad you think so. Personally, I feel terrible,' Craig said as they rounded the Victoria monument, paused at the main gate of the palace to be checked and were passed through to the courtyard.

There was quite a crowd pushing towards the main doors of the palace, uniforms from all the services, most of the civilians obviously being wives or relatives. Everyone was hurrying to get out of the rain.

It was anything but a solemn occasion. A sense of expectancy on most faces, an edge of excitement as they mounted the stairs to the picture gallery where rows of chairs waited for the party to be seated by court officials. The band at the other end playing light music was from the RAF.

That feeling of expectancy was heightened now, and then the band started to play 'God Save the King'. A moment later, King George and Queen Elizabeth entered and everyone rose. The royal couple seated themselves on the raised dais. Everyone sat down.

Decorations were called out in ascending order. Craig Osbourne was astonished at how nervous he was feeling. He listened to the names being called, one after the other, took a deep breath to steady himself and was aware of Genevieve's gloved hand sliding over his. He turned in surprise, she smiled encouragingly. On the other side of her, Munro smiled too and then the usher called his name.

'Major Craig Osbourne, Office of Strategic Services.'

And suddenly Craig found himself up there on the dais, the King smiling as he pinned the silver cross with the white purple ribbon to his uniform and the Queen was smiling too.

'We're very grateful, Major.'

'Thank you, Your Majesty.'

He turned and moved away as the next name was called.

At the bottom of the steps it was still raining. People were taking photos, smiling, happy. There was a general air of jollity.

Genevieve said to Craig as they walked to the car, 'What did he say?'

'He just said he was grateful.'

'You looked marvellous.' She put a hand up and adjusted his scarf in a slightly proprietorial way. 'Didn't you think so, Brigadier?'

'Oh, indeed I did. Very handsome,' Munro said sourly.

As they reached the car, Genevieve looked back at the crowd. 'They're all so happy. You'd never know there was a war on.'

'Well there is,' Munro said opening the door, 'so let's get moving.'

Six

Croydon was thick with mist and a heavy rain was falling. There was plenty of activity for it was used as a fighter station in the defence of London, but nothing seemed to be landing or taking off as Genevieve peered out of the window of the rather cheerless Nissen hut they'd been taken to on arrival. The Lysander, a squat, ugly high-wing monoplane was standing outside, a couple of RAF mechanics working on her.

René was sitting by the stove drinking tea and Munro moved across to Genevieve as rain spattered against the window. 'Damn weather.'

'Doesn't look good, does it?' she said.

'Mind you, those things can fly in anything.' He nodded out at the Lysander. 'Originally designed to carry a pilot and two passengers, but they can manage you four with a squeeze.'

René brought her tea in an enamel mug. She wrapped her hands around it for warmth as the door opened and Craig came in with their pilot. He was quite young with a fair moustache, dressed in RAF blue, flying jacket and boots. He had a map case in one hand which he dropped on the table.

'Flight Lieutenant Grant,' Craig said to Genevieve.

The young man smiled and took her hand. Munro said testily, 'Are we going to be delayed, Grant?'

'It's not the weather here that's the problem, Brigadier. We can take off in pea soup as long as it's clear up above. It's landing, and visibility is limited at the Cold Harbour end of things. They'll let us know as soon as there is a change.'

'Damn!' Munro said and he opened the door and went out.

'His liver must be acting up this morning,' Grant said and went to the stove and poured himself a mug of tea.

Craig said to Genevieve, 'It's Grant who'll be flying you across on Thursday night. You're in good hands He's done that kind of thing before.'

'Piece of cake really as long as one observes the formalities.' He stuck a cigarette in the corner of his mouth, but didn't bother lighting it. 'Flown before, have you?' he asked Genevieve.

'Yes, to Paris before the war.'

'Bit different, old girl, believe me.'

'Actually we could go over Thursday night's timetable,' Craig said. 'Fill in the time while we're waiting. You've already got a flight plan worked out, haven't you?' he said to Flight Lieutenant Grant.

'That's right,' Grant said. 'We take off at eleven-thirty from Cold Harbour. Estimated time of arrival, two o'clock our time. I'll explain how it goes.' He opened the map and they moved in as he traced a pencil across the Channel from Cornwall to Brittany.

'Major Osbourne will be coming with us for the ride. Not much room in these things, but they're good little kites. Never let you down.'

'What's your altitude on the Channel crossing?' Craig asked.

'Well, some people like to go in low – try and keep under their radar, but I favour going in around eight thousand all the way. That keeps us well below any bomber formations, which is what those Jerry nightfighters tend to be looking for.'

He was so calm, so terribly offhand about it all, and Genevieve realised that she was shaking a little.

'We'll be landing in a field about fifteen miles from St

Maurice. They'll have a flare path ready for us. Pretty crude. Cycle lamps, but good enough if the weather holds. Recognition code, Sugar Nan in morse. If we don't get that, we don't land, flare path or no flare path. Agreed?'

He had turned to Craig who nodded. 'You're the boss.'

'We've lost two Lysanders and a Liberator in the past six weeks because pilots landed and Jerry was waiting. Our experience is that as their aim is to get their hands on everybody intact, they don't start firing until a plane tries to take off again. Our latest instructions are to do the turnround as fast as possible. I'm not bringing anyone back, so the moment I land I'll taxi to the end of the field, you get Miss Trevaunce out fast and we'll get straight off again, just in case.' He folded the map. 'Sorry and all that, but one never really can be sure who's waiting out there in the dark.'

He went to the stove and poured himself a tea and Craig said to Genevieve, 'The chap who'll be waiting to take you in charge – Grand Pierre is his code name – is English. He's never actually met Anne-Marie. They've only spoken on the phone. He knows nothing about what happened, so to him you are who you appear to be.'

'And the station master at St Maurice?'

'Henri Dubois. The same goes for him, too. Only René and the two men with him when he found her know what happened, and they're a couple of mountain boys, way back in the hills by now. Grand Pierre will deliver you to Dubois before dawn. He's holding Anne-Marie's suitcases. You'll have plenty of time to change while René checks out the car. The night train from Paris arrives at seven-thirty. It will still be dark at this time of year. Three-minute stop, then it moves on. Nobody in the village will think it strange, even if they don't actually see you get off the train. It's a hotbed of the Resistance movement in that area.'

He had spoken without looking once at her directly, apparently very calm and yet a muscle twitched in his right cheek.

'Hey,' she said and put a hand on his arm. 'Don't tell me you're starting to worry about me?'

Before he could reply, the door was flung open and Munro roared in. 'I've seen the Station Commander,' he told Grant. 'He's given us permission to leave now. If we can't land when we get there we'll just have to come back. You have enough fuel, haven't you?'

'Of course, sir,' Grant told him.

'Then we're off.'

Everything seemed to be happening at once and Genevieve found herself running through the rain to the Lysander. Craig bundled her up into the rear of the cabin and he and René crowded in beside her. Munro followed, taking the observer's seat behind Grant. She was so busy strapping herself in that she was hardly aware of what happened after that, simply the deepening engine note and the sudden lurch as they lifted off.

It was a bad trip, noisy and confusing, the roar of the engine making it difficult to conduct any kind of conversation. Outside there was slate grey rain dashing against the Perspex hood. The whole aircraft seemed to shake constantly and every so often they dropped alarmingly in an air pocket.

After a while, she was humiliatingly sick, although they'd provided a bag for that kind of emergency. René followed her soon after which was some kind of comfort. She must have dozed off, for she became aware of a hand shaking her and realised that her legs were covered with a blanket.

Craig had a Thermos in one hand. 'Coffee? Good American coffee?'

She was very cold and her legs seemed to have lost all feeling. 'How long?'

'Fifteen minutes if everything goes all right.'

She took her time over the coffee. It was just what she needed, hot and strong and very sweet and, from the flavour, there was something stronger in it. When she was finished she returned the cup and Craig refilled it for René.

Grant had the radio speaker on. She heard a crackling and then a voice say: 'Lysander Sugar Nan Tare. Ceiling six hundred. Should give you no problem.'

Munro turned and said cheerfully, 'All right, my dear?'

'Fine.'

She was lying because suddenly she was shaking like a leaf as they were going down; and then there was a sudden roaring as the Lysander rocked violently in the slipstream of a great blackbird that came out of the cloud from nowhere, passing so close that she could see the swastika on its tailplane.

'Bang, bang, you're dead, old boy!' A voice crackled over the loudspeaker and the Junkers vanished as quickly as it had appeared.

Grant turned with a frown, 'Sorry about that. Joe Edge even more crazed than usual.'

'Stupid young idiot,' Munro said and then they broke through the mist and cloud at six hundred feet before Genevieve could ask what it was all about. Below, was the Cornish coast, the inlet of Cold Harbour, the cottages scattered alongside, the E-boat at the quay. The Ju88 was already skimming across the Abbey with its lake and dropping down on the grass runway with the windsock at one end.

'Right on target,' Grant called over his shoulder, dropped in over the line of pine trees and landed, taxi-ing towards the hangar. The Ju88 had already come to a halt where the mechanics waited with Martin Hare. Joe Edge got out of the cockpit to join them.

'My God, the uniform,' Genevieve said and clutched at Craig's sleeve.

'It's okay,' he told her. 'We haven't landed on the wrong side of the Channel. Let me explain.'

*

In the lounge bar of the Hanged Man, still a little bewildered by it all, she sat at one of the trestle tables in the window with the Brigadier, Craig and Martin Hare, eating bacon and eggs cooked by Julie Legrande in the back kitchen and served by Schmidt. The crew of the *Lili Marlene* lounged around the fire, talking in subdued voices, some of them playing cards.

Munro said, 'They're extraordinarily well behaved this morning.'

'Ah, well, sir, that would be the company.' Schmidt put fresh toast on the table. 'If you don't mind me saying so, Miss Trevaunce here's like a breath of spring, sir.'

'Bloody cheeky rascal,' Munro said. 'Go on, get out of it!'

Schmidt retired and Martin Hare poured Genevieve another cup of tea. 'All this must seem very weird to you.'

'You can say that again.' She had liked him at once on their first meeting up at the airfield, just as she had thoroughly disliked Edge. 'You must feel pretty strange yourself sometimes when you look in the mirror and see that uniform.'

'She's right, Martin,' Munro said. 'Do you ever wonder which side you're really on?'

'As a matter of fact I do sometimes.' Hare lit a cigarette. 'But only when I have to deal with Joe Edge. A disgrace to the uniform.'

'To any uniform,' Craig said. 'He's totally unbalanced in my opinion. Grant told me a pretty unsavoury story that just about sums him up. During the Battle of Britain a Ju88 lost one engine and surrendered to two Spitfire pilots who took up position on either side and started to shepherd it down to land at the nearest airfield. It would have been quite a coup.'

'What happened?' Genevieve asked.

'Apparently Edge came up on his rear, laughing like a maniac over the radio and blew him out of the sky.'

'That's terrible,' she said. 'Surely his commanding officer should have had him court-martialled?'

'He tried, but he was overruled. Edge was a Battle of Britain ace with two DFCs. It wouldn't have looked good in the papers.' Craig turned to Hare. 'Like I said, the war hero as psychopath.'

'I heard that story too,' Hare told him. 'The one bit you left out was that Edge's commanding officer was an American. Ex Eagle Squadron, so I understand. Edge never forgave him and he's hated Americans ever since.'

'Yes, well he's still the best damn pilot I ever saw,' Munro told them.

'If that's so, why isn't he doing the drop on Thursday instead of Grant?' Genevieve asked.

'Because he doesn't fly a Lysander, he pilots a German Fieseler Storch for that sort of flight and only on very special occasions,' Munro told her. 'The Thursday flight is comparatively routine.'

The door opened and Edge came in, the usual unlit cigarette dangling from the corner of his mouth. 'Everybody happy?' There was a sudden silence as he came across to the table. 'Grant got away okay, sir,' he told Munro. 'Back Thursday at noon.'

'Good show,' Munro said.

Edge leaned so close to Genevieve that she could feel his breath on her ear. 'Settling in all right, are we, sweetie? If you need any advice, Uncle Joe's always available.'

She pulled away, angry, and stood up. 'I'll see if Madame Legrande needs any help in the kitchen.'

Edge laughed as she walked away. Hare glanced at Craig with lifted brows. 'Not fit to be out, is he?'

Julie was washing dishes, elbow-deep in the sink when Genevieve entered. 'Madame Legrande, the breakfast was excellent.' She picked up a dishcloth, 'Here, let me help.'

'Julie, *chérie*,' the other woman said with a warm smile.

Genevieve suddenly remembered that Hortense had always called her that. Never Anne-Marie, only her. She liked Julie Legrande at once. She picked up a plate and smiled. 'Genevieve.'

'Everything all right?'

'I suppose so. I like Martin Hare. A remarkable man.'

'And Craig?'

Genevieve shrugged, 'Oh, he's all right, I suppose.'

'Which means you like him a lot?' Julie sighed. 'An easy thing to do, *chérie*, but he carries the pitcher to the well too often, that one, I think.'

'And Edge?' Genevieve said.

'From under a stone. Steer clear of him.'

Genevieve continued to dry plates. 'And where do you fit in to all this?'

'I run the house and this place. I'll take you up there later. Settle you in.'

The door opened and the Brigadier looked in. 'Craig and I are going up to the house now. Lots to do.'

Julie said, 'I'll bring Genevieve up later.'

'Fine.' He took a letter from his pocket and handed it to Genevieve. 'This is for you. I sent Carter round to Bart's first thing this morning to explain to the Matron that your leave would have to be extended because of family bereavement. She'd not forwarded that letter because she'd expected you back any day.'

It was open, slit neatly along the flap. 'You've read it?' Genevieve said.

'Of course.' He went out, closing the door behind him.

'Isn't he sweet?' Julie said sarcastically.

Genevieve put the letter down and carried on drying the dishes. 'Before. What were you doing before?'

'I was in France. My husband was Professor of Philosophy at the Sorbonne.'

'And now?'

'He is dead. They came for us one night, the Gestapo, and he held them off while I and the others made our escape.' She was lost for a moment, staring into space. 'But Craig went back for him. Saved his life. Helped us get out of England.' She sighed. 'He died of a heart attack last year, my husband.'

'And it was Craig Osbourne who saved him?'

'That's right.'

'Tell me about him,' Genevieve said. 'Everything you know.'

'Why not?' She shrugged. 'His father was an American diplomat, his mother French. As a child he lived for years in Berlin and Paris which explains his fluency in the languages He was working for *Life* magazine when the Germans took Paris in 1940.'

'Yes, that's when he knew my sister. Did you ever meet her?'

'No. He became involved with an underground ring engaged in smuggling Jews out through Spain and only got out by the skin of his teeth himself when the Germans discovered what he was up to. That's when he first came to England and joined their secret service. What they call SOE. Later, when the Americans joined in, they transferred him to OSS.' She shrugged. 'Names only. Everyone does the same thing. Fights the same war.'

'He went back to France?'

'Twice they dropped him in by parachute. On the third occasion, a Lysander was used. He operated a Maquis sabotage unit in the Loire valley for several months before they were betrayed.'

'Where did he go?'

'To Paris, a café in Montmartre, a staging post on the underground route out to Spain . . .' She paused.

'And?'

'The Gestapo were waiting. They took him to their

headquarters in Rue de Saussaies at the back of the Ministry of the Interior.'

'Go on!' Genevieve turned pale.

'He was photographed, fingerprinted – all the usual things, including an interrogation that lasted three days and involved considerable brutality. Notice his hands sometime. His finger-nails are misshapen because they were torn out at the time I describe.'

Genevieve felt slightly sick. 'But he escaped?'

'Yes, he was lucky. A car in which he was being transferred was involved in a collision with a truck. He got away in the confusion, hid in a church. The priest who found him got in touch with my husband who was leader of the underground movement in that part of Paris.'

'And who held the Gestapo off while you and Craig got away . . . ?'

'Let me explain, *chérie*,' she said patiently. 'Craig could hardly walk because they'd done things to his feet also.' She held Genevieve's right hand tightly for a moment. 'This was not some film made in Hollywood starring Errol Flynn that you go to see at your local cinema on a Saturday night. This was real. This is how it is over there. And things like this – they could also happen to you. This you must face now. After Thursday night it will be too late.'

Genevieve sat there staring at her. Julie carried on. 'We were taken to Amiens in a market truck. After three days they sent a Lysander.'

'What happened to Craig after that?'

'They made him a Commander of the Legion of Honour, his own people gave him the DSC and made him join OSS. The irony now is that he is back in Dougal Munro's clutches.'

'What's wrong with him?' Genevieve asked.

'He is, I think, a man who looks for death,' Julie said. 'Sometimes I think he would not know what to do with himself if he survived this war.'

'That's nonsense,' Genevieve told her, but shivered all the same.

'Perhaps,' Julie shrugged. 'But your letter – you haven't opened it.'

She was right, of course, and Genevieve did so. When she was finished reading, she crumpled it into a ball.

'Bad news?' Julie asked.

'Invitation to a party this weekend, so I couldn't have gone anyway. An RAF boy I met last year – a bomber pilot.'

'You fell in love?'

'Not really. I don't think I ever have, not in a lasting sort of way. It makes one feel like a lifelong wanderer.'

She laughed. 'At your age, *chérie*?'

'We went around together for a while. That's all there was to it. Mutual loneliness, I think, more than anything else.'

'And then?'

'He asked me to marry him, just before he was posted to the Middle East.'

'And you wouldn't?'

'He's just back. On leave at his parents' house in Surrey.'

'And still hoping?'

Genevieve nodded. 'And I can't explain. What a rotten way to leave it.'

'But you don't really care, I think?'

'Yesterday morning, perhaps yes, but now,' Genevieve shrugged. 'I find there are things in me I never knew existed. The possibilities are suddenly somehow limitless.'

'So, you are saved from what would have been a very bad mistake. You see, out of every unfortunate situation, something good always comes. And you will understand Craig a little better now, I think.'

The door opened before Genevieve could reply and Edge came in. 'Women at the kitchen sink. A lovely sight and so proper.'

'Why don't you go away and play with your toys, Joe. That's all you're good for,' Julie told him.

'Plenty to play with here, darling.' He moved in behind Genevieve and slipped his arms about her waist, holding her close. She could sense his excitement as he nuzzled her neck and ran his hands up to her breasts.

'Leave me alone!' she said.

'Look, she likes it,' he taunted.

'Like it? You make my flesh crawl,' Genevieve told him.

'Really? Oh, that's good, sweetie. I'd like to make your flesh crawl.'

She continued to struggle and then Edge gave a cry of pain and Martin Hare was there, had him by the arm, which he continued to twist even after Edge had released Genevieve. 'You really are a worm, Joe. Go on, get out of it.'

Schmidt appeared from nowhere, darted around him and got the back door open. Hare simply threw Edge through it and the pilot fell to one knee. He got to his feet and turned, his face contorted.

'I'll pay you back for this, Hare and you, you bitch.'

He hurried away. Schmidt closed the door. 'A real bad boy, if I may say so, sir.'

'Couldn't agree more. Get out to the boat and find Miss Trevaunce a pair of sea boots.'

'*Zu befehl, Herr Kapitän,*' Schmidt said cheerfully and went out.

Genevieve was still shaking with rage. 'Sea boots?' she demanded. 'What for?'

'We'll go for a walk.' He smiled. 'Salt air, the beach. Nothing like the beauties of nature to get things into perspective.'

And he was right, of course. They followed the narrow beach beyond the end of the quay where the inlet widened into the sea in a maelstrom of white water, spray lifting high into the air.

Genevieve said, 'God, this is wonderful. Every breath you take in London at the moment is tainted with smoke. The whole city stinks of war. Death and destruction everywhere.'

'The sea washes things clean. Ever since I was a boy vacationing at Cape Cod, I've sailed,' Hare told her. 'No matter how bad things are, you leave everything behind on the shore at your point of departure.'

'Your wife?' Genevieve said. 'Does she think the same way?'

'Used to,' Martin Hare said. 'She died of leukaemia in 1938.'

'I'm so sorry.' She turned, hands thrust into the pockets of the Kriegsmarine pea jacket Schmidt had given her. 'Have you any children?'

'Not possible. She was too frail. Struggled against that damned disease from the age of twenty-one.' He smiled. 'Left me some of the best water-colours I've ever seen. She was a fine artist.'

Instinctively, she took his arm. They had rounded the point now and the beach was much wider, following the cliffs. 'It's been a long war for you, I think.'

He shook his head. 'Not really. I take it day by day and that's all I expect – today.' He smiled, suddenly looking immensely charming. 'Night-by-night, I should say. That's when we operate most of the time.'

'And afterwards, when it's all over?'

'No such time. I've told you. Only today.'

'And Craig? Does he think in the same way?'

'You like him, don't you?' He squeezed her arm against him. 'Don't. There's no percentage in it. There's no future for people like me and Craig, so no future for you.'

'That's a terrible thing to say.' She turned to face him and he put his hands on her shoulders.

'Listen to me, Genevieve Trevaunce. War, played the way people like Craig and I play it, is like going to Monaco for a weekend's gambling. What you have to remember is that the odds are always against you. The house wins – you lose.'

She pulled away. 'I can't accept that.'

But he ignored her now, looking beyond her, a frown on his face. She turned and saw a man in a lifejacket a few yards away, bouncing around in the surf. Hare ran past her and she followed, pausing at the water's edge as he went in waist deep, secured a grip on the lifejacket and returned, towing the body behind him.

'Is he dead?' she called.

He nodded. 'Oh yes,' and pulled the corpse up on the beach.

It was that of a young man in black overalls with the German eagle on his right breast. His feet were bare. He had fair hair and a thin beard and the eyes were closed as if in sleep. He looked remarkably peaceful. Hare searched the body and found a wallet, sodden with water. He took from it an identity card, wet so that it was already falling apart.

He examined it and stood up. 'German seaman. Off a U-boat. Name of Altrogge. Twenty-three years of age.'

A seagull swooped overhead, cried harshly and flew out to sea. The surf washed in. Genevieve said, 'Even here, in a place like this, the war touches everything.'

'The house always wins, remember.' He put an arm around her. 'Come on – we'll go back and I'll arrange for some of my crew to bring him in.'

The room Julie Legrande had given her was very pleasant. There was a four-poster bed, Chinese carpets on the floor and an excellent view of the garden at the rear of the house from the bow window.

She stood there now, staring out, and Julie put an arm around her as Hare had done. 'You're sad, *chérie*?'

'That boy on the beach. I can't get him out of my mind.'

'I know.' Julie went and turned down the bed. 'It's gone on

too long, this war, but we have no choice. To you, he was just a boy, but to people like me . . .' She shrugged. 'If you could see what the Boche have done to my country. Believe me, the Nazis must be beaten. We have no choice.'

The door opened and Craig Osbourne came in. 'Ah, there you are.'

'You didn't bother to knock,' Genevieve said. 'Don't I get any privacy around here?'

'Not really,' he said calmly. 'In effect we've got two full days so I thought I'd let you know what to expect.' He sat on the window ledge and lit a cigarette. 'Number one, from now on we only speak French. Just to get you back into the habit. That includes me.'

He seemed different, a hard tough edge to him and she was annoyed. 'Are you sure you're up to it?'

'Whether I am or not doesn't really matter, but you sure as hell better be,' he told her.

Julie Legrande put a hand on her right shoulder and squeezed. Genevieve said in French, 'All right. Anything you say. What's next?'

'As Munro pointed out, we've no intention of trying to make a professional out of you, there isn't time. There are three main tasks and we have two days to cover them. Number one – to familiarise you with the present situation at the Château, the staff, both French and German, and so on. This will involve some lengthy sessions with René and we've also got a lot of photographic material to show you.'

'Then?'

'You'll need to fully understand the purpose of your mission and its background so that you know not only what to look for, but what's relevant and what isn't.'

'That sounds complicated.'

'It won't be. I'll take care of it and Munro will help.'

He started to get up. She said, 'You did say three main tasks, didn't you? You've only mentioned two.'

'Quite right. The third is of a more practical nature. No need to worry about radio and communication because René and his Resistance chums will take care of that, but there are one or two things which could be important from a survival point of view. Can you shoot?' She stared up at him. 'Hand guns,' he said patiently. 'Have you ever fired a pistol?'

'No.'

'Don't worry. It's easy when you know how. You just make sure you're standing close enough and pull the trigger, but we'll go into that later.' He glanced at his watch. 'I'd better get moving. We'll start in the library at eight.'

He went out. Julie made a face. 'It begins, *chérie*.'

'So it would appear,' Genevieve said, turned and looked out of the window.

Seven

Munro sat by the library fire in a wing-back chair working his way through a sheaf of papers on his knee. The table in the centre was covered with maps, photos and an array of documents. René sat on one side smoking one of his small cigars, saying nothing, waiting until he was required. Craig and Genevieve sat together opposite him.

Craig said, 'The most important thing to remember is that when you drive into that Château, you *are* Anne-Marie Trevaunce. On appearance alone everyone who knows you will accept that without hesitation. So much so that you should be able to get away with minor stupidities.'

'Well, that's a comfort,' she said. 'I would point out by the way that my German is totally non-existent.'

'That doesn't matter. All the staff officers speak French to a greater or lesser degree. Now, let's start with a few basic things that Anne-Marie would be familiar with. German uniforms, for instance.' He opened a book. 'The illustrations in here are quite good.'

She flipped through a few pages. 'Goodness, do I have to learn all these?'

'Just a few. The Kriegsmarine is simple and you've seen Joe Edge's Luftwaffe uniform which is quite different in style and colour from the Army. Blue-grey and yellow rank patches.'

She stopped at one page, an illustration of a combat soldier in three-quarter length camouflage smock. 'What's he? Doesn't even look like a German. The helmet's all wrong.'

'He's a Fallschirmjäger – a paratrooper. They wear a special rimless steel helmet, but you don't need to bother about that. Most of the Army uniforms are just as you've seen them in the movies. Here's an important one.'

He indicated a German soldier with a metal gorget suspended from his neck. 'Feldgendarmerie,' she said, reading the caption.

'Military police. The guy who stops your car on the road or stands guard at the Château gates. He might be Army, he could be SS, but that metal plate means police.'

'And I must always be nice to them?'

'Well, let's say a hint of stocking getting out of the car wouldn't come amiss.' Craig didn't even smile. 'The only other group of importance to you is the SS because there're plenty of those at the Château. Field grey uniforms like the Army and blue-green collars. The rank badges are worn on the collar. Up to Major, you'll notice the SS runes on one side of the collar. After that, it changes, but you needn't worry. Nobody would expect you to know the ranks. You'll always recognise anyone in the SS right up to Himmler himself by the silver skull and crossbones badge in his cap. All right?'

Genevieve nodded. 'Yes, I think so. The Luftwaffe look like Edge, then come the police with their gorgets, the Army and then the SS with the Death's Head badge.'

Craig said, 'All right, let's have a look at the Château now.'

They had a large-scale map of the surrounding countryside and then a plan of the house itself, Château de Voincourt in finest detail. As Genevieve looked more closely, it all came flooding back. Every stairway and passage, each nook and cranny that she had explored as a child. There was a sudden excitement at the thought of returning. She'd forgotten quite how much she'd loved the place.

'They have made no structural alterations except for

machine-gun posts.' René leaned over and indicated the positions with a black drawing pencil. 'The perimeter wall has been wired along its entire length to provide an electric warning system. The gate is guarded at all times and they have installed the usual swing barrier system. For the rest, their security depends upon a system of what they call prowler guards. These are all Waffen-SS and they are good, Mamselle. Make no mistake. They know their job. It is not necessary to like them to admit that.'

'What he's trying to tell you delicately without offending my finer American feelings is that they are the best soldiers in the world, man-for-man,' Craig Osbourne said. 'He's right. In this case, just to make it harder, most of them are accompanied by Alsatian or Dobermann guard dogs.'

She said, 'I always did like animals.'

'Good,' he said. 'Now let's get down to the really important details.' He glanced at his watch. 'We haven't got much time. The hairdresser's due soon.'

'The hairdresser?'

'Yes – the way you wear your hair might suit you, but not Anne-Marie. See for yourself. This photo was taken only a month ago.'

Genevieve wore her hair to her shoulders, Anne-Marie's was much shorter, sliced in a dark fringe very straight across her brow just above the eyes, Genevieve again, but a different Genevieve, with an arrogant smile on her mouth as if telling the whole damned world to go to hell. Unconsciously, Genevieve copied that expression and when she turned to look at Craig, Anne-Marie was smiling out at her from the mirror above the fireplace behind him, just as arrogant, just as hard.

He didn't like it. For the first time, she felt she had really got through to him in some strange way. There was something in his eyes as if for the moment he was afraid of what he saw. He snatched the photo from her roughly.

'Let's get on, shall we?' He placed another photo in front of her. 'You know this woman?'

'Yes, Chantal Chevalier, my aunt's personal maid.'

Dear Chantal of the rough tongue and the hard hand who had served Hortense through good times and bad for more than thirty years.

'She won't like me,' Genevieve said. 'Unless she's changed greatly. She never did.'

René nodded. 'It is as it always was. She never cared for Mamselle Anne-Marie. She was never a woman to hide her feelings.' He turned to Genevieve. 'But with you, Mamselle, it was different.'

But there was no point in going into that – not now. She said, 'Who else?'

'The chef, Maurice Hugo – you remember him?'

'Yes.'

'Everyone else is different, but as they're all servants at the lower end of the scale that a haughty bitch like you wouldn't tend to notice anyway, it doesn't matter. Your maid could be a problem. Here she is.'

She was small, dark-haired, with a petulant mouth, pretty enough in her own way. 'A *putain*,' René commented crisply. 'Maresa Ducray. She comes from a farm about ten miles away. Pretty clothes, men and money are the three most important things in her life and you can take them in any order. I've written a note on her family background for you.'

'You can read that later,' Craig said. 'Let's move on. This is the present Commandant at the Château, Major General Carl Ziemke.'

It was a blow-up from what had obviously been a group photo and there was a typed note on the back with his personal details right up to the present moment.

He was the wrong side of fifty, Army, not SS, silver in the hair and the clipped moustache. The face was a little too fleshy and so was his body. He had nice eyes with laughter lines around them, but no smile on his lips. He looked tired.

'A good man once,' Craig said, 'but now, they've put him out to grass. He and your aunt are lovers.'

'I can believe that.' Genevieve handed the photo back to him calmly. 'If you were trying to shock me, you're wasting your time. My aunt always did need to have a man around the house, and Ziemke looks rather nice.'

'He's a soldier,' René said grudgingly. 'I'll say that for him, and so is this bastard.'

He pushed a photo across to her. She had to lean on the table for a moment, so great was the shock of recognition. She had never seen this man before, and yet it was as if she had known him all her life. He was in uniform similar to Joe Edge's except for the SS collar tabs, an Iron Cross at his neck, black hair cut short, a strong, craggy face, eyes that seemed to look right through her and beyond. Not a handsome face and yet one you would turn to look at again, even in a crowd.

'Sturmbannführer Max Priem,' Craig Osbourne said. 'That means Major, to you. Knight's Cross holder, a first-rate soldier and a thoroughly dangerous man. He's in charge of security at the Château.'

'Why isn't a man like him at the Front fighting?'

'He took a bullet in the head in Russia last year serving with an SS parachute battalion. They had to put a silver plate in his skull, so he has to take care.'

'And how did he get on with Anne-Marie?' Genevieve asked René.

'They fought as equals, Mamselle. He did not approve of her and she did not like him. Her relationship with General Ziemke was excellent. She flirted with him outrageously and he treated her like a favourite niece.'

'Which all paid off very nicely with passes for those trips to Paris, freedom to come and go,' Craig said. 'But I must stress again how much the Germans value the de Voincourt connection. You and your aunt are collaborators, make no mistake about that. You continue to live in luxury and style while thousands of your countrymen toil in labour camps. And your friends, the French industrialists and their wives, who often help make up the parties at those weekend conferences, are amongst the most hated people in France.'

'You've made your point.'

'Only one more individual to be noted with particular care.' The photo wasn't nice. A young SS officer with very fair hair, narrow eyes, a generally vicious look to him that wasn't at all pleasant. 'Captain Hans Reichslinger. He's Priem's assistant.'

'Nasty,' Genevieve said.

'An animal.' René spat into the fire.

'Strange,' she said. 'He doesn't look Priem's sort.'

'And what sort would that be?' Craig demanded.

René said, 'Priem despises him and shows it.'

Craig picked up a large brown envelope and handed it to her. 'You'll find background information on every individual you're likely to run into in there. Study it as if your life depends on it, because it does.'

There was a knock at the door and Julie looked in. 'The hairdresser is here.'

'Good,' Craig said. 'We'll carry on later.' As Genevieve started to move away, he added, 'Before you go – just one more picture. Chief architect of the Atlantic Wall defence system. The man you'll be playing hostess to this weekend at Château de Voincourt.'

He placed, very carefully on the table in front of her, a photo of Field Marshal Erwin Rommel. She stood there, staring down at it in astonishment and Munro stood up and crossed to her, his papers in his left hand.

'So you see, my dear Genevieve, I wasn't exaggerating when I said that what you could accomplish for us this weekend might very well affect the course of the entire war.'

*

The hairdresser was a small, rather dapper, middle-aged man with black hair and white sideboards called Michael, and Julie obviously knew him quite well.

'Oh, yes,' he said. 'Remarkable – really quite remarkable,' when he first saw Genevieve.

He opened a scuffed brown suitcase that was filled with all sorts of things, make-up mostly, and took out a cardboard folder.

'I've studied the file, but this is even better than I'd hoped.' He removed his beige cord jacket, took out a comb and a cut-throat razor from the suitcase. 'Let's get started then.'

'You couldn't be in better hands,' Julie told her as she covered her shoulders with a towel. 'Michael was senior make-up man at Elstree Film Studios for years.'

'Quite right,' he said, stroking the comb through her hair. 'I was with Sir Alexander Korda and I worked on Mr Charles Laughton when he did Henry the Eighth. Now there was a job, I can tell you. Took hours, every morning. Of course, at my age you have to take life a little easier. I run a theatre i Falmouth now. Different show every week. We get plenty o sailors in, being a naval base, which is nice.'

As she watched in the mirror, she changed into Anne-Marie minute-by-minute. Not just the hair, that was easy, although he knew exactly what he was doing. There was the shade of lipstick, the rouge he carefully put on her cheeks, the mascara on the eyelashes and the perfume, Chanel No. 5, one that Genevieve never used herself.

The complete transformation took him about an hour and a half. When he had finished he nodded, obviously satisfied.

'Beautiful, though I do say it myself.' He took out a small make-up case in Moroccan leather. 'Everything you need in there, dear. Remember to put plenty on. That'll be your biggest problem. You'll skimp it because you're not the sort who uses much make-up, I can see that.' He snapped the case shut and patted Julie's cheek. 'Must fly. I've got a show tonight.'

The door closed behind him. Genevieve sat looking at herself. *Me and yet not me*, she thought.

Julie offered her a cigarette. 'Have a Gitane.' She began to refuse and Julie said, 'Anne-Marie would. You'll have to get used to the idea.'

Genevieve took the cigarette and the light which she was offering her and coughed as the smoke caught the back of her throat.

'Good,' Julie said. 'Now go and show yourself to Craig. He's in the basement, at the shooting range, waiting for you.'

The door to the cellar was next to the green baize one that led to the kitchen and when she opened it, she could hear the sound of shooting. The firing range had been made out of two cellars, part of one wall having been removed. The far end was brilliantly lit to reveal a row of cardboard figures resembling German soldiers against sandbags. Craig Osbourne was standing at a table loading a revolver, several other weapons laid out before him. He heard her approach, glanced over his shoulder casually, then froze.

'Good God!'

'Which obviously means I'll do.'

His face was quite pale. 'Yes, I think you could say that. It's quite astonishing. Still.' He snapped the revolver shut. 'You say you've never done any shooting before?'

'I fired an air rifle once at a funfair.'

He smiled. 'Nothing like starting from scratch. I'm not going to try and do more than explain the two handguns you're most likely to come across and how you should fire them.'

'From as close as possible, isn't that what you said?'

'You think it's easy, like in some cowboy film? Okay, let's see what you can do.' He gave her the revolver. 'Not too far, only fifteen yards. Aim for the middle target. All you do is squeeze the trigger.'

It was very heavy, which surprised her, but her hand fitted round the butt quite easily. And then there was the challenge, of course, to show him what she could do. She extended her arm, closed one eye, squinted along the barrel, pulled the trigger and missed completely.

'It's always a shock the first time,' he said. 'You don't think it's possible. I mean, how could you miss a man who is standing that close. Oh, and keep both eyes open.'

He turned, dropping into a crouch, the revolver extended, taking no apparent aim that she could see, firing very rapidly. As the echoes died away, she saw a neat pattern of four holes in the heart of the middle target. He stayed there for a moment, full of power and control, a kind of efficient deadly weapon. When he turned to look at her, she saw only the killer in the grey eyes.

'Now that would take some considerable practice.' He placed the revolver down and picked up two other guns. 'The Luger and the Walther are both automatic pistols and used a great deal by the German Army. I'll show you how to load them and how to shoot them. There isn't much more I can do in the time. I mean, this sort of thing isn't your cup of tea, is it?'

'No, I don't think so,' Genevieve said calmly.

He spent twenty minutes patiently showing her how to load a cartridge clip, how to ram it home and how to cock the gun for firing. Only when she had proved that she could do that did he take her forward to the other end of the range.

It was a Walther she was using now with a Carswell silencer on the end, specially developed by SOE for silent killing. When fired, it made only a strange coughing sound.

They stopped a yard from the targets. 'Close to your man,' he said, 'but not too close in case he tries to grab you, remember that.'

'All right.'

'Now hold it waist-high, shoulders square, and squeeze, don't pull.'

She closed her eyes when she fired, in spite of herself, and when she opened them again, saw that she'd shot the target in the stomach.

'Very good,' Craig Osbourne said. 'Didn't I tell you it was easy as long as you stand close enough? Now, do it again.'

She spent the late afternoon and early evening going over those background notes again and again until she really felt she knew her facts about all those people, then went to join René for another long session in the library.

Afterwards, there was dinner in the kitchen with Craig, Munro and René and Julie's cooking was superb. They had steak and kidney pudding, roast potatoes and cabbage and an apple pie to follow. There was also wine on the table, a very good red Burgundy, although even that didn't bring Craig out of himself. He seemed moody and preoccupied and the atmosphere was strained.

'A superbly traditional English meal.' Munro kissed Julie on the cheek. 'What a sacrifice for a French woman.' He turned to Craig. 'I think I'll take a walk down to the pub. Care to join me?'

'I don't think so,' Craig said.

'Suit yourself, dear boy. How about you, René? Fancy a drink?'

'Always, *mon Général*.' René laughed and they went out together.

Julie said, 'I'll bring coffee up to the Blue Room. Craig, show Genevieve the way.'

It was a pleasant sitting room next to the library with comfortable furniture and a fire burning and there was a rather nice grand piano.

Genevieve lifted the lid, fitting the rod under carefully.

There had been a time when this was what she had wanted to do more than anything else in the world, but then life rarely came out the way one expected it.

She started to play a Chopin prelude, deep, slow, crashing chords in the bass and the infinitely sweet crying of death at the top. Julie had come in with the tray and put it down by the fire and Craig came forward and leaned on the end of the piano, watching Genevieve.

His eyes were questioning as she started to play 'Claire de Lune', beautifully, achingly sad. She played well – better, she told herself, than she had done in a long time. When she finished and looked up, he had gone. She hesitated, put the lid down and went after him.

She could see him at the bottom of the steps on the terrace in the dark, smoking. She moved down and leaned against the parapet.

'You were good,' he said.

'As long as I stand close enough?' Genevieve asked.

'All right,' he said. 'So I've given you a hard time, but that's how it's got to be. You don't know what it's like over there.'

'What do you want, absolution?' she said. 'I've got to go, you said so yourself. There's no choice, because there is no one else. It's not your fault. You're just an instrument.'

He got to his feet and threw the cigarette end down. It rolled into the gravel and glowed red. 'We've a full day tomorrow,' he said. 'You've to see Munro again in the morning. Time for bed.'

'I'll be in soon.' She reached for his sleeve. 'And thanks for acting like a human being for once.'

His voice, when he replied, was strange. 'Don't be kind to me now, not now. We haven't finished with you yet.'

He turned and went inside quickly.

*

They came for her in the night. It was a rude awakening. A flashlight in her eyes, the bedclothes thrown back and then she was pulled upright.

'You are Anne-Marie Trevaunce?' a voice demanded harshly in French.

'Who the hell do you think you are?' She was thoroughly angry, tried to get up and received a slap across the face.

'You are Anne-Marie Trevaunce? Answer me.'

And then she realised that both of them, the shadowy figures just beyond the circle of light, were in German uniform and the reason for the whole nightmare struck her.

'Yes, I'm Anne-Marie Trevaunce,' she said in French. 'What do you want?'

'That's better – much better. Now, put your robe on and come with us.'

'You are Anne-Marie Trevaunce?'

It must have been the twentieth time they had put that question to her as she sat at the table in the library, blinded by the hard, white lights which they turned into her face.

'Yes,' she said wearily. 'How many times do I have to tell you?'

'And you live at Château de Voincourt with your aunt?'

'Yes.'

'Your maid, Maresa. Tell me about her family.'

She took a deep breath. 'Her mother is a widow and has a small farm about ten miles from the Château. She works it with one of her sons, Jean, who is a bit simple. Maresa has another brother called Pierre who is a corporal in a French tank regiment. He's working in a labour camp in Alderney in the Channel Islands.'

'And General Ziemke – tell me about him.'

'I've told you about him – all about him, at least four times.'

'Tell me again,' the voice said patiently.

Suddenly, it was over. Someone walked across to the door, and switched the main light on. There were two of them, as she had thought, and in German uniform. Craig Osbourne was standing by the fire lighting a cigarette.

'Not bad. Not bad at all.'

'Very funny,' she said.

'You can go to bed now.' She turned to the door and he called, 'Oh, Genevieve?'

She turned to face him again. 'Yes?' she said wearily.

There was a heavy silence, they looked at each other. She'd fallen for the oldest trick in the book.

'Try not to do that over there, won't you?' he said calmly.

Eight

In the morning, it seemed like a nightmare. Something which had never happened. One of the most frightening things about it had been the mingling of personalities that she had begun to feel. The constant insistence that she *was* Anne-Marie Trevaunce was something that she'd almost come to believe herself during the moments of most intense strain.

She sat at the window, smoking a Gitane, coughing a little less now and gradually it grew lighter and the first orange-yellow of the sun slipped up amongst the pale trees and glinted on the lake down there in the hollow.

What happened next was impulse. She found an old towelling robe hanging behind the bathroom door, put it on and went out. The hall was silent and deserted when she went down the main stairway, but there were kitchen noises somewhere at the rear of the house, Julie's voice raised in song, muffled and indistinct beyond the green baize door.

She tried another door and found herself in some sort of sitting room with French windows beyond, which opened on to a terrace. When she crossed it and stepped on to the grass, the cold morning dew sent a shiver through her entire body and she ran down the slope, her white robe flying out behind.

The small lake in the hollow was gold and silver in the early sun, what was left of a dying mist curling above the surface.

She took off her robe, pulled her nightdress above her head, waded out through the reeds and plunged into deep water.

It was so cold that she didn't even feel her body go numb, simply floated in a kind of limbo, watching the reeds sway in the breeze, the trees beyond. How still the water was, like black glass and she recalled, very clearly, a dream she'd had the night before of waters just as dark, Anne-Marie drifting up to meet her, hands in slow motion, reaching as if to pull her down to join her.

It was revulsion more than any panic that made Genevieve turn and swim back towards the reeds, wade through to dry land. She pulled on the robe and started to dry her hair with her nightdress as she walked up through the trees, back towards the house.

Craig was sitting on the balustrade of the terrace, smoking the inevitable cigarette, very still, so that she wasn't aware of his presence at all until she was half way across the sloping lawn.

'Did you enjoy your swim?'

'You were watching?'

'I saw you go out and I followed – yes.'

'Like any good intelligence officer? What did you think I might do – drown myself? That *would* have been inconvenient for you.'

'Highly.'

When she opened the door of her bedroom she found Julie arranging breakfast on a small table by the window. She wore a green velvet housecoat and looked very pretty.

'You're not pleased, *chérie*, I can tell. What's wrong?'

'That damn man,' Genevieve said.

'Craig?'

'Yes, I went for a swim in the lake. He followed me down. Watched me.'

She said soothingly, 'Drink your coffee and try the scrambled eggs. They're a speciality of mine.'

Genevieve did as she was told. 'We just seem to rub each other up the wrong way,' she said as she attacked her eggs.

Julie sat down opposite and sipped her coffee. 'Really? I should have thought it was the other way about.'

The door opened and once again Craig Osbourne looked in without knocking. 'There you are.'

'My God, it gets worse,' Genevieve said. 'Still no privacy.'

He ignored the remark. 'Munro would like to see you as soon as possible. Grant's flying in to take him back to London this morning. I'll be in the library.'

He went out, closing the door. Julie said, 'I wonder what Munro wants.'

'To wish me luck? Who knows.' Genevieve shrugged. 'He can wait. I'm going to have another cup of coffee,' and she reached for the pot.

What had happened to the men who had interrogated her the night before, she had no idea. The house was quiet, no sign of anyone else around as she went down the stairs. Craig was standing by the library fire reading a newspaper.

He glanced up casually. 'You'd better go straight in. The last door.'

She walked to the other end of the library, paused at the leather-covered door and knocked. There was no reply. She hesitated, opened it and went in. It had no windows and was furnished as a small office with another door in the far corner. Munro's Burberry was draped over a chair, and there was a briefcase on the desk holding down one end of a large-scale map. She could see what it was at once – a section of the French coast. The heading said Preliminary Targets, D-Day. As she stood looking down at it the door opened and Munro came in.

'So, there you are.' And then he frowned, crossed the room quickly and rolled up the map. She had a feeling he was going to say something, but changed his mind. Instead, he put the map in the briefcase and closed it. 'Amazing how different you look.'

'Isn't it?'

'Have they been giving you a hard time?' He smiled. 'No, don't answer that. I know how Craig operates.' He stood at the desk with his hands behind his back, suddenly serious. 'I know this hasn't been easy for you, any of it, but I can't impress the importance of it too much. When the big day comes, when we invade Europe, the battle is going to be won on the beaches. Once we get a foothold, the final victory is only a matter of time. We know that and so do the Germans.'

It sounded as if he was making a speech to a group of new young officers.

'That's why they put Rommel in charge of co-ordinating their Atlantic Wall defences. You see now why any information you can get us from that conference this weekend could be vitally important.'

'Of course,' she said. 'I can win the war for you at one fell swoop.'

He managed to smile. 'That's what I like about you, Genevieve. Your sense of humour.' He reached for his Burberry. 'Well, I've got to go.'

'Haven't we all,' she said. 'Tell me, Brigadier, do you enjoy your work? Does it give you job satisfaction?'

He picked up his briefcase and when he looked at her his eyes were bleak. 'Goodbye, Miss Trevaunce,' he said formally. 'I look forward to hearing from you.' And he walked out.

When Craig returned, she was standing by the library fire. 'Has he gone?'

'Yes. He wasn't too pleased. What did you do to him?'

'Lifted a corner of his personal stone.'

He stood with his hands in his pockets, looking at her gravely. 'Hardly calculated to please.' He moved to the table. 'I've got something for you.'

He passed her a cigarette case made of silver and onyx. It was really very beautiful. She opened it and found it was neatly packed with Gitanes.

'A going-away present?' she asked.

'Rather a special one.' He took the case from her. 'See the engraving, here in the back?' He pushed his thumb nail in and a wafer-like flap of silver fell down to show the tiniest of lenses and a camera mechanism. 'The genius who put this together for us insists it will take good, sharp pictures even when the light is poor. So, if you see any documents or maps, you know what to do. Twenty exposures and it's loaded and ready to go. All you have to do is point it and pull this thing here.'

'Always remembering to stand close enough?'

Somehow she'd hurt him now, she could see that and took no pleasure in it. She could have bitten her tongue, but it was too late.

He gave her the cigarette case back and moved to the table, all business again. 'The rest of the day I suggest you go over your notes again and the photo and case histories until you're word perfect.'

'And tomorrow?'

'I'll go over everything again with you until you know it backwards. Tomorrow night we take off a little after eleven.'

'We?'

'Yes, I'll be going with you as far as your drop-off point.'

'I see.'

'If everything goes according to plan, you and René will be picked up by the local Resistance people, who will transport you to St Maurice by road. You'll wait there in the station-master's house until the night train from Paris has passed through. Then René will go and collect your car as if you've just got off the train, and drive you home to the Château.'

'Where I'll be on my own?'

'You've got René,' he said. 'Any information you have, you pass straight to him. He has a radio. He can contact us here through the coastal booster station.'

'Here?' she said. 'But I haven't seen anyone else in the place except for those friends of yours last night.'

'They just keep out of the way, that's all. We have a very efficient radio room, I can assure you and then there's the costume department. Julie runs that. Not much she can't supply in the way of uniforms or clothing or documents.'

They stood there, a silence between them. Finally, he said, strangely gentle, 'Is there anything I can do for you?'

'Anne-Marie. I'm worried about her. If anything happens to me . . .'

'I'll take care of it. I give you my word.' He lifted her chin with a finger. 'And nothing is going to happen to you. You've got luck. I can tell.'

She was almost in tears, suddenly vulnerable. 'And how in the hell can you know a thing like that?'

'I'm a Yale man,' he said simply.

She worked on the papers all morning. Julie had told her she would be going down to the pub at lunchtime so just after noon Genevieve stopped work, borrowed a sheepskin jacket she found hanging in the hall cupboard and walked down to the village.

She stopped on the quay to look down at the *Lili Marlene* where a couple of members of the crew swabbed the decks. Hare leaned out of the wheelhouse window.

'Come aboard, why don't you?'

'Thank you. I will.'

She descended the narrow gangplank gingerly and one of the men gave her a hand.

'Up here,' Hare called.

She went up the steel ladder and followed him into the wheelhouse. 'This is nice,' she said.

'You like boats?'

'Yes – very much.'

'The Germans call this a fast boat, *Schnellboot*, because that's what they are. Hardly a pleasure craft, but about the most efficient thing of its kind afloat.'

'How fast?'

'Three Daimler-Benz diesels, plus a few improvements the Brits have added, give us about forty-five knots.'

She ran her hands over the controls. 'I'd love to go to sea in her.'

'Come on, I'll show you around.'

He took her down to the engine room, the tiny galley, the wardroom, his own minute cabin. She inspected the two torpedo tubes, sat behind the 20mm ack-ack gun in the fore-deck well and inspected the Bofors gun which had been fitted in the afterdeck.

When they were finished, she said, 'It's awe-inspiring. So much packed into such little space.'

'I know,' he said. 'Very thorough, the Germans, very efficient. I should know. My mother was one.'

'Are you ashamed of that?' she asked.

'Of Hitler, Goebbels and Himmler? Yes. But thank God for Goethe, Schiller, Beethoven and a few more I could mention.'

She reached up and kissed his cheek. 'I like you, Martin Hare.'

He smiled warmly, 'Oh, keep it up – please. I've almost a quarter of a century on you, girl, but you could be in trouble.'

'Promises,' she said. 'That's all I get.'

'No you don't. You get lunch,' and he took her hand and led her up the gangplank.

Everyone seemed to be at The Hanged Man. The entire crew of the *Lili Marlene*, Craig, even Joe Edge at the end of the bar attempting to play hail fellow well met with everyone. Julie was passing hot Cornish pasties from the kitchen which Schmidt was dispensing to the others with his usual good humour.

He brought three across to Genevieve, Hare and Craig at the table by the window. 'Nothing kosher about these, but they smell bloody marvellous,' he said.

Craig seemed more cheerful. He and Hare exchanged jokes and drank beer with their pasties while Genevieve tried another Gitane. She didn't like to admit it, but she was actually beginning to enjoy them.

Craig said, 'Excuse me for a moment, I need to see Julie about something.'

He went behind the bar into the kitchen. Hare was obviously enjoying the pasty. Genevieve was aware of Edge at the end of the bar, watching her, eyes glittering. She began to feel uncomfortable.

Hare said, 'God, that pasty was marvellous. I think I'll have another.'

He stood up and Genevieve said, 'Actually, I could do with some air. I think I'll go for a walk.'

She went out, aware of Edge following her with his eyes. She was angry then for it was as if he'd driven her out and she started to walk fast, head down, following the path up through the trees to the headland. A moment later, Edge emerged from the pub and hurried after her, cutting to one side after a while, following another track and starting to run.

Martin Hare, in the window seat, took the pasty Schmidt passed to him and turned at the same moment to see Genevieve disappear into the trees, Edge running after her. He put the pasty down and stood up.

'I think I'll leave this till later.'

'I think it might be an idea, sir,' Schmidt said.

Hare went out quickly and started to hurry along the track.

Craig leaned against the sink, smoking, and watched Julie roll more pastry.

'You want something special, is that it?' she asked.

'Dinner,' he said. 'You, me, Martin, René, Genevieve. I mean, it's her last full night. I think it would be nice.'

'Why not?' she said. 'Just for you. I've got some lamb, just a bit mind, but it'll do. Oh, and there are three bottles of champagne still in the cellar. Moët, I think.'

'What could be better.'

'And be nice to her, Craig.' She put a hand on his sleeve, touching him with flour. 'She likes you, that girl.'

The door opened and Schmidt came in. 'Excuse me, guvnor.'

'What is it?' Craig demanded.

'A little potential drama, I think. Miss Trevaunce went off for a walk up the track to the wood. Then we see Flight Lieutenant Edge running after her. Well, sir, the Commander didn't think too much of that. He went after them.'

'So?' Craig said.

'For Christ's sake, sir, if you'll pardon the expression,' Schmidt said, 'he's only got one good lung. I mean, if it gets physical,' but Craig was already on his way out of the door, moving very fast indeed.

It started to rain a little as Genevieve moved on through the trees. She came into a clearing and found a half ruined building, relic of the tin mining explorations of the previous century.

She hesitated in the entrance then moved inside. It was very dark and mysterious in there, no roof above her head, only the inside of a kind of beehive tower.

Edge said, 'Whither away, oh maiden, so palely loitering?' She turned, saw him leaning in the doorway and moved to pass him. He put up an arm to bar her way. 'What does it take to make you just a little more friendly?'

'Nothing you have to offer.'

He grabbed her by the hair, pulling her close, his free hand groping between her legs. She cried out and beat at his face with a clenched fist. He slapped her back-handed and she staggered back, catching her foot on a stone, and fell down. In a second, he had dropped on his knees, straddling her.

'Now then,' he said. 'Let's teach you your manners.'

Martin Hare had run the last hundred yards, something he had been advised very earnestly not to do by his doctors. His heart was pounding and he was gasping for breath as he ran in through the entrance. He had just enough energy to grab Edge by the hair and pull him off.

Edge, on his feet, turned with a cry of rage and punched him high on the right cheek. Hare tried to raise his arms, but suddenly found it almost impossible to breathe. He keeled over and Edge raised a knee in his face. Genevieve grabbed him by the jacket from the rear and Edge cursed and struck out at her as Hare fell to his knees.

Edge turned and had Genevieve by the throat as Craig Osbourne arrived on the run. Craig delivered a thoroughly dirty blow to Edge's kidneys, knuckles extended. Edge screamed and Craig punched him again in exactly the same way, grabbed him by the neck and ran him out through the doorway.

As he turned, Genevieve was helping Hare to his feet. The Commander smiled ruefully. 'A fat lot of use I turned out to be.'

'You'll always be a hero to me,' Genevieve told him.

'See,' Craig said. 'It's the thought that counts. Come on, I'll buy you a drink. And you,' he turned to Edge, 'try anything like that again and I'll personally see you court-martialled.'

They went out, totally leaving Edge on his hands and knees, gasping for breath, and walked back towards Cold Harbour.

It was not possible to dress as Anne-Marie just yet. Her suitcases were with the Rolls-Royce hidden by René at St Maurice. However, Julie found her a blue silk dress of pre-war vintage and when Genevieve went downstairs and paused at the foot of the stairs, her reflection in the great cheval-mirror was disturbingly satisfactory.

Julie had laid the table in the library and had decked it with the best the Abbey could provide. Silverware, tablecloths of finest linen, exquisite plates of bone china. It was a wonderful atmosphere, the only illumination coming from the flickering candelabra and the log fire.

Julie, very attractive in the typically French little black dress, her hair tied back with a velvet bow, wore a white apron and insisted on handling everything in the kitchen herself, helped only by René who acted as a waiter.

'This is a French evening,' she said. 'No one else must do a thing. And the cooking, *mes amis*, will very definitely be French now that the Brigadier, God bless him, is no longer with us.'

It was exquisite. A liver pâté with toast, the leg of lamb with herbs, some Cornish early new potatoes, a green salad, and afterwards a concoction of fruit and whipped cream that melted in the mouth.

'I thought there was supposed to be a war on,' Craig observed as he went round the table refilling the glasses, handsome in uniform.

Martin Hare sat opposite Genevieve, still playing the officer of the Kriegsmarine, wearing a collar and tie in deference to the occasion, a medal at his throat.

Genevieve reached across to touch it. 'What is that decoration?' she asked.

'The Knight's Cross.'

'What's it for?'

'It's similar to our Congressional Medal of Honor or your Victoria Cross. It usually means the wearer should really be dead.'

Genevieve turned to Craig. 'Didn't you say Max Priem has one of those?'

'With Oak Leaves and Swords,' Craig said. 'That means three awards. He really is on borrowed time, that boy.'

'A brave man, though,' she said.

'I'll grant you that.' Craig raised his glass. 'Let's drink to brave men everywhere with this excellent champagne.'

Julie bustled in with coffee on a tray. 'Wait for me,' she called, put the tray on the table and picked up her glass.

The fire flared up as in a sudden draught, Genevieve shivered, the champagne ice-cold as she swallowed and her skin crawled as if touched by a cool breeze. She could see the french window reflected in the great mirror above the fire, curtains drawn, and then they billowed outwards, came apart, and three men stepped through and stood there, just inside the room.

They were straight out of the book of German uniforms Craig had shown her, paratroops in the rimless steel helmets and the peculiarly long camouflage jackets. Two of them held machine pistols at the ready, hard, dangerous looking men. The one in the middle had a similar weapon suspended from his neck across his chest and held a Walther in his right hand with a silencer on the end similar to the one Craig had shown her.

'Finish your drinks, ladies and gentlemen, by all means.' He crossed to the table, took the champagne bottle from the bucket and examined the label. 'Nineteen thirty-one. Not bad.' He poured himself a glass. 'Your health. My name is Sturm, Hauptman, Special Duty Squadron, 9th Parachute Regiment.' His English was quite reasonable.

'And what can we do for you?' Craig Osbourne asked.

'Why, exactly as you are told, Major. The special duty tonight is to convey you, the young lady here and the Fregattenkapitän to territory occupied by the forces of the Reich as fast as possible.'

'Really? I don't think you'll find that so easy.'

'I don't see why not.' Sturm savoured the champagne. 'The parachute drop was the difficult part, hitting the beach with the tide just right. Much simpler to slip out to sea in the E-boat so thoughtfully provided by your Kriegsmarine friend here.'

Genevieve saw it all then and barely stopped herself from laughing out loud. But she forced herself to react as Anne-Marie would and turned towards Osbourne, a cynical smile on her face.

Only Craig wasn't smiling and René, his face contorted with rage, thrust a hand inside his coat and pulled out a pistol. 'Sale Boche!' he cried.

Sturm's hand swung up, the Walther coughed once, René fell back into his chair, dropping the pistol, a hand to his chest. He looked at the blood on it in a kind of wonder, turned to Genevieve in mute appeal then slid to the floor.

Julie cried out in fear, her hands to her face, turned and started to run along the length of the library towards the door at the far end. Sturm's arm swung up.

'No!' Genevieve called.

His Walther coughed again, Julie seemed to trip, lurched to one side and fell on her face. Genevieve started towards her, but Sturm caught her arm.

'You will stay where you are, Fräulein.'

His two men covered them with the machine pistols and

Sturm walked the length of the room and dropped to one knee beside Julie. He stood up and came back.

'Dead, I'm afraid. A pity.'

'You butcher!' Genevieve said.

'I suppose that depends on whose side you are on.' Sturm turned to Hare. 'Is your crew on board the E-boat at the present time?' Hare made no reply and Sturm said, 'Come now, Commander. We'll find out soon enough when we get down there. You might as well tell me.'

'All right,' Hare said. 'I believe the engineer is doing some work below and Obersteuermann Langsdorff is keeping watch.'

'And the rest will be at this inn they use as a mess? They can stay there. I'm sure that you can put to sea with no difficulty, aided by this engineer and the Obersteuermann.' He turned to Craig. 'I understand you have a reputation for action, Major Osbourne. I would most earnestly advise against it on this occasion.' He took Genevieve by the arm and touched the silencer to her cheek. 'The consequences for Fräulein Trevaunce, caught in the crossfire, could be severe. Do I make myself plain?'

'Perfectly,' Craig told him.

'Good. Then we go now, I think. We'll leave your jeep in the courtyard, gentlemen, and proceed on foot by way of the garden. No need to advertise our presence.'

He took Genevieve by the hand like a lover and led the way out through the french windows, holding the Walther against his thigh in the other hand. Craig and Hare followed, menaced by the machine pistols of the other two paratroopers.

It was cold and Genevieve shivered as they passed through the garden into the wood and reached the first cottages at the edge of the village.

'Are you all right, Fräulein?' Sturm enquired. 'You're trembling.'

'So would you be if you were only wearing a silk frock. It's bloody cold.'

'Never mind. You'll be on board soon.'

And then what? she thought. What waited on the other side? And what could have gone so disastrously wrong? They were passing The Hanged Man now, curtains drawn at the windows, only a chink of light showing. There was laughter and singing, all curiously remote.

There was only a dim light up in the wheelhouse and the deck of the *Lili Marlene* was shrouded in darkness. They went down the gangplank, one by one.

Sturm said, 'Now Commander, we have words with the Obersteuermann while one of my men goes below to reason with your engineer.'

The door to the companionway was flung open, light flooded out and Schmidt appeared. He was laughing as if he'd just been talking to someone, but now, the laugh faded.

'Here, what the bleeding hell is going on?' he demanded in English.

Again Sturm's Walther swung up and the German shot him at close quarters, sending Schmidt back down the companionway.

Sturm gestured to one of his men. 'Get below and watch the engineer. The rest of you – on the bridge.'

He went up the ladder first followed by Genevieve then Hare and Craig, covered from behind by the other paratrooper. Langsdorff was seated at the chart table and he looked up, then stood in amazement.

'Get this thing moving,' Sturm said.

Langsdorff glanced at Hare who nodded. 'Do as he tells you.'

There was a slight pause. Langsdorff called down to the engine room. A moment later and the engines rumbled into life.

'We need to cast off,' Hare said.

Sturm turned to Craig. 'Get on with it and come back.'

Craig did as he was told. The lines splashed softly into the water. A minute later and the *Lili Marlene* moved away from the quay and drifted out into the harbour.

'See how simple life can be?' Sturm said. 'Only one thing and it's been annoying me. Brave men have died for that medal, Commander. I object to your use of it. It's not for play actors.'

He tore the Knight's Cross from Hare's neck and Hare, in the same moment, grabbed his wrist, forcing the Walther to one side. There was a dull thud as it discharged. Genevieve ran her nails down the side of Sturm's face and kicked him on the shins.

'Get her out of it, Craig! Now!' Hare cried as he and Sturm swayed together.

Craig wrenched open the door, reaching for Genevieve's hand, pulling her after him. She lost a shoe, stumbled, and below on the afterdeck the other paratrooper fired his machine pistol from the shelter of the two rubber dinghies stored there. Craig pushed her to the rail to one side of the ladder.

'Jump, for God's sake! Now!'

She got one foot on the second rail, he lifted her up, a hand to her back and then she was falling, hit the water and went under and Craig vaulted over to land beside her as she surfaced. The E-boat was already slipping away into the darkness. There were sudden stabbing fingers of flame as the machine pistol fired again ineffectually and then silence. They floated there alone.

'You all right?' he asked her, coughing.

'Yes, I think so. But Martin, Craig?'

'Never mind that now. This way. Follow me.'

They started to swim through the darkness. It was bitterly cold and then she heard the dull rumble of the E-boat's engines again.

'It's coming back,' she said in a panic.

'Never mind. Keep swimming.'

The engines were quite close now. She thrashed forward

and then suddenly a searchlight picked them out of the water and then another light was turned up on the quay. There was a ragged cheer. She floated, looking up. The crew of the *Lili Marlene* were up there and Dougal Munro in a heavy overcoat, hands in pockets.

'Well done, Genevieve,' he called.

The *Lili Marlene* coasted in beyond them. Lines were thrown to the quay. In the light, she could see Martin Hare standing beside Sturm and Schmidt at the rail.

She turned to Craig, laughing, in spite of herself. 'Oh, you bastard.'

Willing hands reached down to help them up the ladder to the top of the quay. Someone gave her a blanket and Munro came forward, Sturm and Hare behind him.

'Excellent, Genevieve. Good as a film. Allow me to introduce Captain Robert Shane, Special Air Service.'

Shane grinned and said, 'Pleasure to do business with you.' He put a hand to his scratched face. 'Some of the time.'

Julie came through the crowd, René behind her. 'I thought we were all pretty damn good. Now let's get inside before you catch pneumonia. Scotch all round, I think.'

They turned and walked towards The Hanged Man. Craig put an arm around her shoulders. 'Just a taster,' he told her, 'of how rough things might get. You did well.'

'Don't tell me you're proud of me,' she said, teeth chattering.

'Something like that,' and he opened the door of the pub and ushered her inside.

Nine

It was just after seven on the following morning when Heinrich Himmler got out of his car and entered Gestapo Headquarters at Prinz Albrechtstrasse in Berlin. He had a bad habit of turning up at unreasonable hours which meant that in a way, his appearance was not unexpected. Guards sprang to attention as he entered, clerks hurriedly busied themselves over meaningless pieces of paper. He wore full black dress uniform as Reichsführer-SS and the face behind the silver pince-nez was a blank as usual.

He went up the marble stairs, turned along the corridor and entered his office suite. In the ante-room, his secretary, a middle-aged woman in the field grey uniform of an SS Auxiliary, stood up behind her desk. Himmler had his office personnel working shifts twenty-four hours a day.

'Is Hauptsturmführer Rossman in the building?' Himmler asked.

'I saw him having breakfast in the canteen a little while ago, Reichsführer.'

'Send for him at once.'

Himmler went into his office, placed his briefcase and cap on his desk and went to the window where he stood, hands behind his back. After a while, there was a knock at the door. The young captain who entered was in black uniform and the silver cuff title on his sleeve carried the legend, RFSS.

Reichsführer der SS. The cuff title of Himmler's personal staff. He clicked heels.

'At your order, Reichsführer.'

'Ah, Rossman.' Himmler sat behind his desk. 'You've had the night shift? You're due to go home?'

'Yes, Reichsführer.'

'I'd appreciate it if you'd stay.'

'No problem, Reichsführer. My pleasure to serve.'

'Good.' Himmler nodded. 'I was with the Führer last night. He raised the matter of this conference which is to take place at Château de Voincourt in Brittany this weekend. Do we have a file?'

'I believe so, Reichsführer.'

'Bring it to me.'

Rossman went out. Himmler opened his briefcase, took out some papers and looked at them. A moment later, Rossman came in again with the file. He passed it across and Himmler took out the contents and worked his way through them. Finally, he sat back.

'Atlantic Wall conference?' He laughed coldly. 'The Führer was concerned about this affair last night and rightly so, Rossman. There is devilry afoot.' He looked up. 'I have always been able to count on your loyalty?'

'To the death, Reichsführer.' Rossman sprang to attention.

'Good, then I will tell you now of things I've had to keep very personal, very private. There have been numerous attempts on the Führer's life, but then you know that.'

'Of course, Reichsführer.'

'By the mercy of God they have always been foiled, but there is evil behind all this.' Himmler nodded. 'Generals of our own High Command, men who have taken a holy oath to serve the Führer are engaged in a conspiracy to assassinate him.'

'My God!' Rossman said.

'Amongst others I'm having watched are Generals such as

Wagner, Stieff, von Hase.' He took a sheet of papers from his briefcase. 'And others on this list, some of whom may surprise you.'

Rossman ran his eye over the list and looked up in astonishment. 'Rommel?'

'Yes, the good Field Marshal himself. The people's hero.'

'Unbelievable,' Rossman said.

'So,' Himmler told him. 'As the Führer so rightly said, we would be failing in our duty not to suspect that this conference at Château de Voincourt was not simply a cover for something more. Atlantic Wall conference. What nonsense!' Himmler laughed entirely without mirth. 'A cover, Rossman. Rommel himself will be present. Why does he go all the way to Brittany for such an affair?'

Rossman, who had always found it politic to agree, nodded eagerly. 'I'm sure you are right.'

'This General Ziemke, for example, who's in charge of the place. I'm sure he is involved.'

Rossman, looking for some way of involving himself to his own advantage, said, 'There is one thing in our favour about the de Voincourt set-up, Reichsführer.'

'And what is that?'

'That security there is in the hands of the Waffen-SS.'

'Really?' Himmler looked up, immediately alert. 'You're sure of this?'

'Oh, yes, Reichsführer.' Rossman sifted through the file. 'See, the officer responsible for all matters of security and intelligence. Sturmbannführer Max Priem.'

Himmler examined Priem's record. 'Quite a hero, this Priem.'

'Knight's Cross with Oak Leaves and Swords, Reichsführer. The only reason he is not at the Front would seem to be the severe nature of wounds received in Russia.'

'I can see that.' Himmler tapped his fingers on the desk while Rossman waited nervously. 'Yes,' Himmler said. 'I think this Major Priem will serve our purpose very well. Get him on the phone, Rossman. I'll speak to him personally.'

At that precise moment, Max Priem was running through the wood on the other side of the lake from Château de Voincourt. He was an inch under six feet, the short black hair tousled, sweat on his face. He wore an old track suit, a scarf around his neck and one of the security guard's Alsatians ran with him.

'Remember in future,' the surgeon had told him on the day of his release from hospital. 'For a man with a silver plate in your head, you've done very well, but walk from now on. Walk, don't run. That must be your new motto.'

'Well, to hell with that,' Priem told himself, rounded the lake and went across the lawn to the main entrance in a final burst of speed, with the Alsatian, Karl, hard on his heels.

He went up the steps past the sentries, who saluted, and into the great entrance hall. He went along the corridor to the right, stopping at the cloakroom to get a towel with which to mop his face. The first office was that of his aide, Hauptsturm-führer Reichslinger. Priem passed on, aware of the phone ringing in his own office. He opened the door, still mopping his face and found Reichslinger, who had come through from his own office, answering the phone.

'Yes, this is Sturmbannführer Priem's office. No, but he's just come in.' He paused, then turned and held out the phone to Priem, his narrow eyes widening. 'My God, it's Reichsführer Himmler himself.'

Priem held out his hand for the phone, his face giving nothing away. He pointed to the other office. Reichslinger went through, closed the door, then hurried to his desk and picked up his phone gently.

He heard Himmler say, 'Priem?'

'Yes, Reichsführer.'

'You are a loyal member of the SS brotherhood? I may rely on your help and discretion?'

'Of course, Reichsführer.'

'You have a remarkable record. We're all very proud of you.'

'What's the bastard got up his sleeve now?' Priem wondered.

'Listen to me attentively,' Himmler said. 'The life of your Führer could be in your hands.'

Priem fondled the Alsatian's ruff as it sat beside him. 'So, what would you wish me to do, Reichsführer,' he asked when Himmler was finished.

'Surveillance of this conference at the weekend which I'm convinced is spurious. This General Ziemke seems heavily suspect to me and as for Rommel – the man is beyond the pale. A disgrace to the officer corps.'

In spite of having Germany's greatest war hero dismissed in such a fashion, Priem stayed calm. 'We are not talking arrests here, I take it, Reichsführer?'

'Of course not. Total surveillance, a log of everyone who is present and naturally, a record of all telephone calls the Field Marshal and any other general officer make. This is a direct order, Priem.'

'*Zu befehl, Reichsführer,*' Priem said automatically.

'Good. I look forward to your report.'

The phone went dead, but Priem still had the receiver to his ear. There was the faintest of sounds. He glanced at the adjoining door, smiled slightly, put his phone down gently and crossed the room, followed by the Alsatian. When he opened the door, Reichslinger was just replacing the receiver He turned, guilt written all over his face.

Priem said, 'Listen, you miserable little toad. If I ever catch you doing that again, I'll give Karl here permission to feed off your balls.'

The Alsatian stared fixedly at Reichslinger, its tongue hanging out. Reichslinger, face ashen, said, 'I meant no harm.'

'You are, however, now privy to a state secret of the utmost gravity.' Priem suddenly barked, 'Heels together, Reichslinger.'

'*Zu befehl, Sturmbannführer.*'

'You took an oath to protect your Führer, a holy oath, repeat it now.'

Reichslinger gabbled, 'I will render unconditional obedience to the Führer of the German Reich and People, Adolf Hitler, Supreme Commander of the Armed Forces, and will be ready, as a brave soldier, to stake my life at any time on this oath.'

'Excellent, so keep your mouth shut or I'll have you shot and remember – failure is a sign of weakness.'

As he opened the door to his office, Reichslinger called, 'I would remind the Major of one thing.'

'And what would that be?'

'You also took the oath.'

Max Priem had been born in Hamburg in 1910, the son of a schoolteacher who had been killed on the Western Front as an infantry corporal in 1917. His mother had died in 1924, leaving him a small legacy, enough to enable him eventually to enter the University of Heidelberg where he had studied law.

By 1933 he was well qualified, but without employment. The SS, with the rest of the Nazi party, were looking for bright young men. Priem, like so many others, joined more for employment than anything else. His language ability had caused him to be recruited by the SD, SS intelligence, but on the advent of war, he had managed to secure an appointment to an active service unit of the Waffen-SS. When the 21st SS Paratroop Battalion was formed, he was one of the first to apply, serving in Crete, North Africa and Russia. Stalingrad had finished him. The bullet in the head from a Russian sniper. So now he sat here behind a desk, miles from the war, living in a fairy tale château in the midst of beautiful Breton countryside.

He went upstairs to his room, showered and changed, inspecting himself in the mirror when he was ready. Except for the silver death's head in his cap and his SS rank badge, his uniform was all paratrooper. Not the Luftwaffe blue-grey, but the field grey of the Army. Flying blouse, baggy jump trousers tucked into jump boots. A gold wound badge, Iron Cross First Class and gold and silver paratrooper's qualification badge studded his left breast, the Knight's Cross with Oak Leaves and Swords hung from his neck.

'Very pretty,' he said softly. 'Nothing like keeping up appearances.'

He went out on the landing as Maresa, Anne-Marie's maid, passed with a stack of towels. 'Is General Ziemke with the Countess, do you know?' he asked in excellent French.

She curtseyed. 'I saw him go into her suite five minutes ago. They ordered coffee.'

'Good. Your mistress returns tomorrow?'

'Yes, Major.'

He nodded. 'Go ahead, get on with your work.'

She walked away and Priem took a deep breath, then walked across the landing above the great hall and went up the steps leading to the Countess de Voincourt's bedroom.

At Cold Harbour, it was raining steadily, mist draped across the trees, shrouding the Abbey in mystery as Genevieve and Julie, wearing yellow storm coats and sou'westers, walked down to the village.

'So much for the weather forecast,' Julie said. 'They always get it wrong, those people.'

'But what will happen?' Genevieve said.

'God knows. They'll come up with something.'

They came to where the *Lili Marlene* was tied up to the

quay. Hare came out of the wheelhouse and up the gangplank. 'Going to the pub?' he asked.

'That's right,' Julie said. 'I've got to get lunch ready.'

Hare smiled at Genevieve. 'Are you over last night?'

'Just about.'

'Good. I'll join you. Craig and Munro went in a little while ago with Grant. I think they're having a council of war.'

Inside The Hanged Man, they found the three men sitting at the table by the window. Munro looked up. 'Ah, there you are. We're just having words. Join us.'

Craig said, 'As you may have noticed, the weather isn't too good. Tell them, Grant.'

The young pilot said, 'We were supposed to have a moon tonight and dry weather. Ideal conditions, but this stinks. You see, it isn't just the visibility. We land in ordinary fields. If they get waterlogged by heavy rain, it would be impossible to take off again.'

'So what happens?' Genevieve asked.

Craig said, 'There's an outside chance, according to the Met. people, that it might clear by seven or eight this evening.'

'And if not?'

'You have to go, my dear, we can't delay,' Munro told her. 'So, if there's no plane it will have to be a fast boat and a passage by night, courtesy of the Kriegsmarine here.'

'Our pleasure,' Martin Hare said.

'Good, we'll leave it till seven this evening, then make the decision.'

Julie stood up. 'Coffee, everyone?'

Munro sighed. 'How many times do I have to remind you, Julie, I'm a tea person.'

'But Brigadier,' she told him sweetly, 'I'm always reminded of what you are every time I look at you,' and she went into the kitchen.

*

Priem knocked on the door, opened it and went into the ante-room. Chantal was sitting in a chair by the bedroom door. She was, as always, thoroughly unfriendly.

'Yes, Major.'

'See if the Countess will receive me.'

She opened the door, went in and closed it. After a while, she returned. 'You may go in now.'

Hortense de Voincourt was propped up against pillows. She wore a silk gown and a kind of cap covered the red-gold hair. She had a tray in front of her and was eating a buttered roll.

'Good morning, Major. Did I ever tell you that you look like the Devil himself coming through the door in that preposterous uniform?'

Priem liked her immensely. Always had. He clicked heels and gave her a military salute. 'You are as radiant as the morning, Countess.'

She sipped champagne and orange juice from a tall crystal glass. 'What piffle! If you want Carl, he's reading the paper on the terrace. I will not allow a German paper to be read in this house.'

Priem smiled, saluted again and went out through the french windows. Ziemke was seated at a small table on the terrace, a glass of champagne in front of him. He was reading a two-day-old copy of a Berlin newspaper. He looked up and smiled.

'I see from the front page that we are winning the war.' Priem stood there, looking at him, and Ziemke stopped smiling. 'What is it, Max?'

'I've had a phone call from Reichsführer Himmler.'

'Really?'

'Yes.' Priem lit a cigarette and leaned on the parapet. 'It seems that Château de Voincourt is a hotbed of conspiracy. Not only yourself, but most other Generals who stay here including Rommel himself, are suspected of designs on the Führer's life.'

'Dear God!' Ziemke folded his paper. 'My thanks for telling me, Max.' He got up and put a hand on Priem's shoulder. 'My poor Max. A hero of the SS and yet you're not even a Nazi. It must make life terribly difficult.'

'Oh, I manage,' Priem told him.

There was a murmur of voices inside and Chantal appeared a moment later. 'An orderly left this, General.'

Ziemke read the signal, then laughed out loud. 'The cunning bastard. Still the chicken farmer at heart. He's buying your services in advance, Max. Listen to this. *"From Reichsführer SS to Max Priem. In recognition of services to the Reich above the call of duty, by special order of the Führer, you are promoted to the rank of Standartenführer from this date. Heil Hitler."'*

Priem took it from him, bemused, and Ziemke pushed him into the bedroom. 'What do you think, darling?' he said to the Countess. 'Max here has been promoted twice at the same time. He's now a full Colonel.'

'And what does he have to do for that?' she demanded.

Priem smiled ruefully. 'I look forward to your niece's return. Tomorrow, I think.'

'Yes, we're going to need her to entertain Rommel at the weekend,' Ziemke said. 'I thought we should have something special this time. A ball more than a dance.'

'An excellent idea,' Priem said.

'Yes, Anne-Marie has been staying at the Ritz,' Hortense de Voincourt said to Priem.

'I know,' he told her. 'I've rung three times, but she's always out.'

'What do you expect? Shopping in Paris is still shopping in Paris in spite of this dreadful war.'

'Yes, well I must be about my duties.' Priem saluted and went out.

Hortense looked up at Ziemke. 'Trouble?'

He took her hand. 'Nothing I can't handle and not from Max. He's caught in the middle.'

'A terrible shame.' She shook her head. 'You know something, Carl? I really like that boy.'

'So do I, *liebling*,' and he took the champagne from the bucket and refilled her glass.

Towards evening it was already getting dark at Cold Harbour, rain drumming relentlessly against the window of the kitchen. Julie and Genevieve sat opposite each other at the kitchen table and the French woman was shuffling a pack of Tarot cards. The gramophone was playing a man's voice, very appealing, backed by a swing band. The song was 'A Foggy Day in London Town.'

'Very appropriate considering the weather,' Julie said. 'Al Bowlly. The best ever for me. He used to sing in all the great London nightclubs.'

'I saw him once,' Genevieve told her. 'I had a date with an RAF pilot. It was back in 1940. He took me to the Monseigneur restaurant. That was in Piccadilly. Bowlly was singing there with the Roy Fox band.'

'I'd have given anything to see him in the flesh,' Julie said. 'He was killed in the Blitz, you know.'

'Yes, I know.'

Julie held up the Tarot cards. 'They tell me I have a gift for these things. Shuffle them and give them back with your left hand.'

'You mean you can foretell my future? I'm not sure I want to know.' But Genevieve did as she was told and handed back the cards.

Julie closed her eyes for a moment, then spread the cards face down on the kitchen table. She looked across. 'Three cards, that is all you need. Select one and turn it over.'

Genevieve did as she was told. The cards were very old. The painting was dark and sombre, the title in French. There was a pool guarded by a wolf and a dog. Beyond it, two towers and in the sky above, the moon.

'This is good, *chérie*, for it is in the upright position. It tokens a crisis in your life. Reason and intellect have no part – only your own instincts will bring you through. You must, at all times, flow with the feeling. Your own feeling. This alone will save you.'

'You've got to be kidding,' Genevieve told her and laughed uncertainly.

'No, this is what the card says to me,' Julie told her earnestly and reached to put a hand on hers. 'It also tells me you will come back from this thing. Choose another.'

The card was the Hanged Man, a replica of the sign which hung outside the inn on the quay.

'It does not mean what you think. Destruction and change, but leading to regeneration. A major burden is removed. You go forward as your own person for the first time, owing nothing to others.'

There was a pause. Genevieve took a third card. It was reversed, a knight on horseback, a baton in his hand.

Julie said, 'This is a man close to you. There is conflict for its own sake.'

'Would that be a soldier?' Genevieve asked.

'Yes.' Julie nodded. 'Probably.'

'A crisis that only my own instincts will carry me through. Change, a major burden removed. A man, possibly a soldier, interested in conflict for its own sake.' Genevieve shrugged. 'I mean, what does it all add up to?'

'The fourth card will tell. The card you did not know you must draw.'

Genevieve hesitated, finger poised, then pulled out the card. Julie flipped it over. Death stared up at them, a skeleton with a scythe mowing not corn, but corpses.

Genevieve tried to laugh, but her throat was dry. 'Not too good, I presume?'

Before Julie could reply, the door opened and Craig came in. 'Munro wants us in the library now. It's decision time.' He paused, smiling. 'God, have you been messing around with those things again, Julie? You'll be getting yourself a tent next at the spring fair at Falmouth.'

Julie smiled and scooped the cards together. 'An interesting idea.'

She got up as Genevieve did, came round the table and squeezed her hand as they followed him.

Munro and Hare were in the library bending over the table examining a large-scale Admiralty chart of the Channel between Lizard Point and Finisterre in Brittany. René sat by the fire smoking one of his little cigars, simply awaiting orders.

Munro looked up. 'Ah, there you are. The weather as you can see hasn't improved and the weather boys still can't actually guarantee that it will if we follow your original schedule which you'll recall was take-off at eleven.'

The door opened and Joe Edge came in. Munro said, 'Any further word?'

'I'm afraid not, Brigadier,' Edge told him. 'I've just spoken to Group Captain Smith in London who's running the weather department for SHAEF at the moment. He confirms what we already know. Things could get better, but there's a better than fifty per cent chance that they won't.'

Genevieve glanced at him curiously. He'd been keeping out of the way since the incident in the woods, had even kept out of The Hanged Man. His face was blank, no expression at all, but the eyes said it all, only hatred there.

Munro said, 'That does it. Can't leave it any longer because you'll need to leave earlier if it's to be a sea passage.' He turned to Hare. 'You're sailing now, Commander.'

'Fine, sir.' Hare nodded. 'We leave at eight. I know that won't give you much time, Genevieve, but there it is. The fog is rather lighter at sea level, variable in patches. The forecast after three to four miles was with rain squalls. Should be perfect for a nice invisible run.'

'To where?' Genevieve asked.

Hare turned to Osbourne. 'Craig?'

The American said, 'We've already spoken to Grand Pierre on the radio just in case.' He traced a pencil along the chart. 'Here's Leon and Grosnez light, the bay where the *Lili Marlene* picked me up. Grand Pierre tells us that the Germans closed the light down two days ago.'

'Why?' Genevieve asked.

'They've been closing lights down progressively for some time now,' Hare put in. 'Invasion fever.'

'The point is,' Craig told her, 'that directly below the Grosnez light there's a quarry in the cliffs. Hasn't been worked since the 1920s, but there's a deep water pier there that the boats used in the old days when they went in for the granite.'

'Perfect for our purposes,' Hare said.

Craig carried on. 'We'll call Grand Pierre to confirm the new arrangement. He'll be waiting with suitable transport. You'll still be at St Maurice on schedule.'

'Using that pier at Grosnez we can go straight in and straight out,' Hare told her. 'No problem.'

'And if anyone did happen to be in the vicinity, what would they see?' Munro demanded. 'The pride of the Kriegsmarine going about its business.'

Genevieve looked down at the chart, feeling strangely calm. 'That's it, then,' she said softly.

Ten

Genevieve and Craig and René stayed below at Hare's request as the *Lili Marlene* left harbour. Sitting at the table in the tiny ward room Genevieve found herself reaching for a Gitane almost as a reflex action. Craig gave her a light.

'You're really enjoying those things now, aren't you?'

'A bad habit.' She nodded. 'I've had the horrible idea that it might haunt me for the rest of my life.'

She leaned back and thought of the leave-taking in the rain on the quay. Munro, strangely serious in his old cavalry coat as he shook hands, Edge in the background, watching her malevolently all the time. And then Julie's quick, affectionate embrace, the final whisper.

'Remember what I told you.'

The movement of the E-boat was quite pronounced and a door opened as Schmidt came in from the galley balancing himself, three mugs on a tray. 'Tea,' he said. 'Hot and sweet. Lots of lovely condensed milk.' Genevieve made a face. 'No, you drink it down, sweetheart. Good for the stomach on this kind of trip. Stops you being sick.'

She doubted that, but took him at his word and somehow managed to get some of the sickly brew down. After a while, he glanced in again. 'The guvnor says you can come up top if you want to.'

'Fine,' Genevieve turned to Craig. 'Coming?'

He looked up from the newspaper he was reading. 'Later. You go.'

Which she did, leaving him with René, going up the companionway. When she opened the door the wind dashed rain into her face. The *Lili* seemed vibrant, full of life, the deck heaving beneath her feet as she held on to the lifeline and struggled towards the ladder going up to the bridge. She felt totally exhilarated, rain on her face, pulled herself up and got the wheelhouse door open.

Langsdorff was at the helm, Hare at the chart table. He swung to face her in the swivel chair and stood up. 'Sit here. You'll be more comfortable.'

She did as she was told and looked around her. 'This is nice. Exciting.'

'It has its points.' He said to Langsdorff in German, 'I'll take over for a while. Take a coffee break.'

'*Zu befehl, Herr Kapitän,*' the Obersteuermann said formally and went out.

Hare increased speed, racing the heavy weather which threatened from the east. The fog was patchy so that at times they travelled in a private, dark world and at others, burst out into open water, for the moon was clear on occasion in spite of rain squalls.

'The weather doesn't seem to know what to do,' she said.

'It never does in this part of the world. That's what makes it so exciting.'

'Different from the Solomon Islands.' It was a statement, not a question.

'You can say that again.'

It was rougher now, the *Lili Marlene* rolling occasionally, barrelling forward, the floor of the wheelhouse tilting so that Genevieve had to brace her feet firmly to stay in the chair. Visibility was poor again and as the waves broke, there was a touch of phosphorescence on the water.

The door opened and Schmidt lurched in, the oilskin over

his pea jacket streaming. He had a Thermos jug in one hand, a tin biscuit box in the other. 'Coffee in the jug, love, and sandwiches in the box,' he told her cheerfully. 'You'll find mugs in the cupboard under the chart table. Enjoy.'

He retreated, banging the door and Genevieve got the mugs out. 'He's quite a character, that one. Always a quip for every situation, just like a comedian.'

'True,' Hare agreed as she handed him a mug, 'But have you ever noticed that he doesn't smile all that much? Sometimes humour is simply a cover for pain. Jews know more about that syndrome than any other race on earth.'

'I see,' she said.

'Schmidt, for example, had a cousin he adored. A nice Jewish girl from Hamburg who lived with his family in London for a few years. She went back on a visit just before the war because her widowed mother had died unexpectedly. They tried to persuade her not to go. She was still a German citizen, you see. She was too late for the funeral anyway, but there were family affairs to see to and then nobody in England really believed the stories they were hearing.'

'What happened?'

'Schmidt insisted on going with her. They were both picked up by the Gestapo. The British Consul in Hamburg saved him, of course, as a British citizen. He was given a two-day deportation order.'

'And his cousin?'

'He made enquiries. She was a pretty blonde girl. Seems she was allocated to the programme servicing troops' brothels in spite of the fact that sexual relations with Jews are illegal. The last word he got, she'd been put on a train going east to the border just before the Polish invasion.'

'How horrible,' she said, deeply shocked.

'That's what it's like over there, Genevieve. Let me tell you how the Gestapo operate.'

'I know,' she told him. 'I've seen Craig's fingernails.'

'You know how they break women agents down? No hot irons, no whips, no pincers. Multiple rape. They take turns, one after another, then they take turns again. Revolting, yes, but appallingly effective.'

Remembering Anne-Marie, Genevieve said, 'Oh, yes, I can imagine only too well.'

'Damn my big mouth!' Hare glanced at her, genuine concern on his face. 'I was forgetting your sister.'

'You know about that?'

'Oh, yes, Munro explained. He felt it best I should know the full background.'

She found a Gitane. 'I'll just have to soldier on, I suppose.'

'Not quite the right phrase for a flight officer.'

'A what?' Genevieve asked, the lighter flaring in her hand.

'All women agents going into the field are sent as officers of one sort or another. Frenchwomen are usually commissioned into the Corps Auxiliaire Feminin. A lot of the English girls officially join the Nursing Yeomanry.'

'The FANY?'

'That's right, but Munro likes to keep a tighter hold than that. As I understand it, you were commissioned as a flight officer in the WAAF yesterday. Actually, RAF blue will suit your colouring if you ever get a chance to put the uniform on.'

'He didn't say a word to me about this.'

'Munro?' Hare shrugged. 'A devious old dog, but there's method in his madness. In the first place, being a commissioned officer is supposed to help you if you fall into enemy hands.'

'And in the second?'

'It gives him personal control over you. Disobey an order in wartime and you could be shot.'

'I sometimes think there was never any other time,' she said.

'I know the feeling well.'

The door opened and Craig came in. 'How's it going?'

'Fine,' Hare said. 'We're on time.' He turned to Genevieve. 'I'd go below if I were you. Try and catch a little sleep. Use my cabin.'

'All right, I think I will.'

She left them there, negotiated the heaving deck and went down to his tiny cabin. The bunk was so small that she could hardly stretch out on it and she lay there, knees up, staring at the ceiling. So much had happened and it was all whirling around in her head and yet, in spite of that, she drifted into sleep after a few minutes.

Off the coast of Finisterre it was still foggy in patches, the moon breaking out from behind a cloud occasionally. The *Lili Marlene* eased in towards the shore, her silencers on. The crew were at battle stations, manning the guns fore and aft and Hare had a pistol in its holster ready on his hip.

Langsdorff had the helm and Hare and Craig surveyed the shore with nightglasses. Genevieve waited behind, René at her shoulder. There was a sudden pinpoint of light dead ahead.

'There they are,' Hare said. 'Perfect.' He put a hand on Langsdorff's shoulder. 'Nice and easy now. Dead slow.'

The pier at Grosnez loomed out of the darkness about them, a tall, skeletal structure, waves booming hollowly underneath, splashing around the great rusting iron pilings. They bumped against the lower jetty and some of the crew were instantly over the side with lines. She noticed Schmidt down there on the deck, a Schmeisser machine pistol at the ready.

There was a light at the top of the pier and a voice called in French, 'Is that you?'

'Grand Pierre,' Craig said. 'Let's move it.'

She and René went ahead, Craig followed with Hare. On the jetty, she turned to look back to the deck. Schmidt smiled up at her. 'Don't let the bastards grind you down, lovely one.'

Craig moved close. 'Present for you.' He gave her a Walther and a spare clip. 'Stick those in your pocket. No girl should be without one.'

'Not in these parts,' Hare said and put an arm about her. 'You take care now.'

Craig turned to René. 'Bring her back in one piece or I'll have your balls.'

René shrugged. 'If anything happens to Mamselle Genevieve, it happens to me also, Major.'

Craig said calmly. 'Okay, angel, up you go. The greatest performance of your career. As they say in show business, break a leg.'

She turned quickly, almost in tears, and went up the steps to the upper level, René following. There was a truck at the end of the pier, shapes moving in the darkness and then a man stepped out to confront them. She had never seen a more villainous looking individual in her life. He wore a cloth cap, dirty old moleskin jacket and leggings and a collarless shirt. The three-day stubble on his chin didn't help, nor the scar on his right cheek.

'Grand Pierre?' René called.

Genevieve put a hand in her right-hand pocket to find the Walther. 'This can't be our man,' she whispered urgently to René, so thrown that she spoke in English.

Scarface paused a yard or so away and smiled. 'Terribly sorry to disappoint you, old girl,' he said in the most stunningly beautiful Oxford accent, 'but if it's Grand Pierre you're looking for, then I'm your man.'

Behind him, a dozen or so more moved out of the darkness carrying rifles and Sten guns. They stood there, staring at her, not saying a word.

She whispered to Grand Pierre, 'I don't know what they do to the Germans, but they certainly frighten me.'

'Yes, they are rather splendid, aren't they?' He clapped his hands. 'Come on, you rat-pack,' he called in very fluent

French. 'Let's get moving and watch your language. We have a lady with us remember.'

The truck was what was known as a gazogene, operated by gas generated by a charcoal-burning stove in the rear. Grand Pierre's men had left a mile back along the road and he was driving quite fast, whistling tunelessly between his teeth.

She said, 'What if we run into a German patrol?'

'A German what?' He really did smell awful at such close quarters.

'Patrol,' she said.

'Not round here. They only move about when they have to. That means during the day and in strength. Anyone out tonight within fifteen miles of here and I'd know it, believe me.'

She could have laughed out loud because the whole thing was so beautifully macabre. 'You've really got it organised then?'

'You always sounded rather delectable on the phone. Nice to be able to put a face to you,' he said. 'Ever get up to Oxford at all?'

'No.'

'Norfolk?'

'I'm afraid not.'

They came over the brow of a hill and at the same moment, the clouds parted to reveal the moon again. In its light she could see the line of the railway track in the valley below, the cluster of houses that was St Maurice.

'Pity,' he said. 'I used to shoot a lot up there. Near Sandringham where the King has his country estate. Lovely place.'

'Do you miss it?'

'Not really. Pretend I do, just to keep me going. I mean, what would I do without all this lot? Smell me. Beautiful, isn't it? Talk about back to nature.'

'What did you do before?'

'The war, you mean? Taught English Literature at a rather second-rate public school.'

'You enjoy doing this sort of thing?'

'Oh, yes, scouting for boys and all that. The worst sores in life are caused by crumpled rose leaves, not thorns, Miss Trevaunce, wouldn't you agree?'

'I'm not even sure I understand.'

'That's exactly what my pupils used to say.' They were entering the village now and he started to slow. 'Goods yard coming up.'

They turned in between massive gate posts, rattled across a cobbled yard to the house in the corner. The truck braked to a halt. A door opened, someone peered out. René scrambled down. Genevieve followed.

'Thanks very much,' she said.

'We aim to please.' Grand Pierre smiled down at her. 'Crumpled rose leaves. You think about it.'

He drove away and she turned and followed René inside.

She sat in front of the mirror in the small bedroom, Anne-Marie's suitcases on the bed, handbag open, her papers on the bed beside it. There was her French identity card, the German *Ausweis*, ration cards, a driving licence. She carefully applied mascara and the door opened as Madame Dubois entered. She was a small, dark-complexioned woman with a careworn face and wore a shabby grey dress. There were holes in her stockings and her shoes looked ready to fall to pieces.

She didn't approve, Genevieve could see that, and her lips set in a thin line as she took in the finery displayed on the bed. The navy blue suit from Paris with the pleated skirt, the silk stockings, the oyster satin blouse.

Remembering who she was supposed to be, Genevieve said sharply, 'Another time, knock first. What do you want?'

Madame Dubois shrugged defensively. 'The train, Mamselle. It has just come in. My husband sent me to tell you.'

'Good. Tell René to fetch the car. I'll be down soon.'

She withdrew. Genevieve applied a little lipstick, hesitated, then put on some more, remembering what Michael, the hairdresser, had said at Cold Harbour. She dressed quickly – underwear, stockings, slip, blouse, skirt – all Anne-Marie's. As she put on each item, it was as if she removed another layer of herself.

She wasn't afraid as she pulled on her jacket and checked herself in the mirror, simply coldly excited. The truth was that she really did look rather good and she knew it. She snapped the suitcase shut, draped the caped greatcoat of blue worsted over her shoulders and went out.

She found Henri Dubois in the kitchen with his wife. He was a small, sallow-faced man, very ordinary looking, the last person one would have imagined to want to involve himself in such a business.

'René is bringing the car now, Mamselle.'

She took the silver and onyx lighter from her handbag and selected a Gitane. 'Bring down my bags.'

'Oui, Mamselle.'

He went out. She lit the cigarette and walked to the window, aware of the woman's eyes on her, hostile, disapproving, but that didn't matter. Nothing mattered now except the job in hand.

The Rolls-Royce emerged from one of the goods sheds and drove up to the door to meet her. René got out and she opened the door. He stood at the bottom of the steps, looking up at her impassively, wearing chauffeur's uniform now. He opened the car door for her without a word and she got into the rear seat.

Dubois appeared with the suitcases. He placed them in the boot, then came round to the window as René got behind the wheel. 'You will convey my respects to the Countess, Mamselle?'

Genevieve didn't reply, simply wound up the window and tapped René on the shoulder. As they drove out of the yard, she was aware of his eyes in the driving mirror, watching her, a touch of fear in them again.

'And now it really does begin,' she thought, leaned back filled with restless excitement, and took out another Gitane.

As they drove on, the countryside became increasingly familiar, green fields and forest, the mountains on her left capped with snow, the river gleaming in the early morning sun in the valley below. A shepherd in sheepskin jacket moved his flock across the hillside above.

'The hills of childhood, René. Nothing changes.'

'Or everything, Mamselle.'

He was right, of course. She held her coat around her for it was rather cold. They moved down towards a small village, a place she remembered well called Pougeot.

She leaned forward. 'When we were children, you used to stop the car here at a café in the square so that we could have ice cream. Old Danton and his daughter ran the place. Is he still there?'

'He was shot last year for what the Boche called terrorist activities. His daughter is in prison in Amiens. The property was confiscated then sold. Comboult bought it.'

'Papa Comboult? But I don't understand.'

'It's quite simple. Like so many, he works with them, trades with them and in the process makes his fortune. They feed on the flesh of France, people like him. As I said, Mamselle, everything changes.'

There were women working in the fields and as they went through the village itself, she found the streets strangely deserted. 'Not many people about.'

'Most able-bodied men have been shipped off to labour camps in Germany. The women run the farms. They'd have even taken an old dog like me, one eye and all, if it had not been for the Countess.'

'And she could not do anything for the others?'

'What she can, she does, Mamselle, but in France these days, most things are difficult. This you will find out for yourself very soon now.'

They came round a bend in the road and became immediately aware of a black Mercedes on the grass verge. The bonnet was raised and a German soldier worked on the engine. An officer stood beside him smoking a cigarette.

'God in heaven, it's Reichslinger,' René said as the officer turned and raised a hand. 'What shall I do?'

'Stop, of course,' Genevieve said calmly.

'She has nothing but contempt for this one, Mamselle, and shows it.'

'And he tries all the harder?'

'Exactly.'

'Good. Let's see how we get on then, shall we?'

She opened her handbag, took out the Walther Craig had given her and slipped it into her right-hand pocket. The car slid to a halt and she wound down the window as Reichslinger approached.

He was exactly like his photo. Fair hair, narrow eyes beneath the peaked cap, a generally vicious look to him, and the uniform, with the SS runes on the collar, did nothing for him at all.

He smiled, contriving to look even more unpleasant than ever. 'Mademoiselle Trevaunce. My luck is good,' he said in French.

'Is it?' Genevieve enquired coldly.

He gestured towards the car. 'The fuel pump is giving trouble and this fool of a driver is apparently unable to do anything about it.'

'So?' she enquired.

'Under the circumstances I must beg a lift from you.'

She let it hang there for a moment, made him wait, his sallow cheeks flushing slowly, then said, 'The master race being masterful? What can I say except yes.'

She leaned back and wound up the window. He hurried round to the other side, scrambled in beside her and René drove away.

She took out another cigarette and he hastily produced a lighter. 'I trust you had a pleasant stay in Paris?' His French was good enough in its way, but his accent was terrible.

She said, 'Not really. Service is abominable now and one is constantly stopped and searched which is very inconvenient. Still, you soldiers do have to play at something, I suppose.'

'Mamselle, I can assure you it is all very necessary. My comrades of the SS in Paris have had considerable success in tracking down terrorists.'

'Really? I'm surprised all those soldiers haven't succeeded in putting down the Resistance movement entirely.'

'You don't understand the difficulties.'

'To tell you the truth, I don't want to. Not very interesting.'

He was angry then, but she gave him one of the beautiful smiles for which her sister was famous and had the satisfaction of seeing him swallow hard.

'How is the General?' she asked. 'In good health, I trust?'

'As far as I am aware.'

'And Major Priem?'

'Standartenführer since yesterday.'

'Colonel? That's nice.' She laughed. 'He does take himself rather seriously, but he really is most efficient, you must admit that.'

Reichslinger scowled. 'With others to do the work for him.' He was unable to hold back.

'Yes, it must get very boring for you. Why don't you apply for a posting? Russia would suit you very nicely, I should imagine. Lots of honour and glory there.'

She was actually enjoying herself now because it was working, because he had totally accepted her as Anne-Marie Trevaunce. In a sense, she saw now that running into him had been the luckiest thing imaginable.

'I am pleased to go where the Führer sends me,' he said stiffly.

At that moment they came round a corner and René had to swerve violently to avoid an old woman leading a cow along the road on a halter. Genevieve was thrown into the corner, Reichslinger with her and she became aware that his hand was on her knee.

'Are you all right, Mamselle?'

His voice was hoarse, the grip on her knee tightened.

She said icily, 'Please remove your hand, Reichslinger, otherwise I'll have to ask you to get out of the car.'

They were coming up towards the village of Dauvigne and René, scenting trouble, started to pull in at the side of the road. Reichslinger, who had gone too far to draw back, moved his hand a little higher.

'What's wrong?' he demanded. 'Aren't I good enough, is that it? I'll show you I'm as good a man as Priem on any day of the week.'

'Not really,' she said, 'Because the Colonel is a gentleman which you are very definitely not. To be perfectly honest, I find you just a little beneath me, Reichslinger.'

'You arrogant bitch, I'll show you . . .'

'Nothing.' Her hand came out of her pocket holding the Walther. She slid off the safety catch in one smooth movement as Craig Osbourne had taught her and pushed the muzzle into his side. 'Get out of this car!'

They came to a halt as René braked. Reichslinger pulled away from her, eyes wild. He got the car door open and stumbled out. She closed it behind him and René drove away instantly. She looked back and saw Reichslinger standing at the side of the road looking strangely helpless.

'Did I do well?' she asked René.

'Your sister would have been proud of you, Mamselle.'

'Good.'

She leaned back in the seat and lit another Gitane.

They came over the hill and she saw it half-a-mile away, nestling at the foot of the mountains amongst the trees. Château de Voincourt, grey and still in the morning sun. House of nobility, survivor of religious wars, of revolution, of one bad time after another. As always since childhood, whenever she had returned to this place, there was the same feeling of calm. Of total happiness just at the sight of it.

It vanished for a few moments, as they followed the narrow road, pine trees crowding in and then there it was again, a couple of hundred feet above as they climbed the slope, like a fortress behind those grey walls, waiting for her as it had always done.

The gates stood open, but the way was blocked by a swing bar. There was a wooden guardhouse just inside and a sentry holding a machine pistol. He was only a boy in spite of being SS and he leaned down and said uncertainly in bad French, 'Papers?'

'But I live here,' she said and he looked totally bewildered. 'Don't you know me?'

'I am sorry, Mamselle, my orders are firm. I must see your papers.'

'All right,' she said. 'I'll give myself up. I'm a British agent and I've come to blow up the Château.'

A quiet voice cut in, speaking in German. She didn't understand a word, but the sentry did, running to lift the barrier at once. She turned to the man who had emerged from the guardhouse, the SS Colonel in the paratrooper's flying blouse of field grey, Knight's Cross at his throat, the Death's Head in his cap gleaming in the morning sun. One thing was certain. She didn't need René to tell her who this man was.

'Max, how nice.'

Max Priem opened the door and got in. 'Drive on,' he told René. 'The boy, by the way, has only been here for three days.' He kissed her hand. 'I'll never understand the pleasure you get from baiting my soldiers. It's bad for morale. Reichslinger gets very upset about it.'

'Not at the moment,' she commented. 'He has other things on his mind.'

The vivid blue eyes were suddenly very alert. 'Explain.'

'His car broke down near Pougeot. I gave him a lift.'

'Really? I don't see him.'

'I put him out again on the other side of Dauvigne. I don't know where he did his training, but it certainly didn't include how to behave in the company of a lady.'

His mouth was smiling, but his eyes were not. 'And he went quietly? Reichslinger? Is this what you are telling me?'

'With a gentle prod from my friend here.'

She produced the Walther and he took it from her. 'This is German Army issue. Where did you get it?'

'A friendly barman in Paris. Such things are readily available on the black market and a girl needs all the protection she can get these days.'

'Paris, you say?'

'Now don't expect me to tell you the name of the bar.'

He weighed the pistol in his hand for a moment, then returned it to her and she slipped it into her handbag.

'So, you enjoyed your trip?' he said.

'Not really. Paris isn't what it was.'

'And the train journey?'

'Abominable.'

'Is that so?'

There was, for some reason, a certain irony to his voice and she glanced at him quickly from under her lashes, out of her depth a little and not understanding why. They stopped at the foot of the steps leading to the front door. He handed her out and René went round to the boot and got her suitcases.

'I'll take those,' Priem said.

'You really are mortifying the flesh today,' she told him. 'An SS Colonel with a bag in each hand like a hotel porter? I should have a camera. They'll never believe it in Paris. Congratulations on your promotion, by the way.'

'One of our several mottos,' he said, 'is that to the men of SS, nothing is impossible.'

He started up the steps. René said loudly, 'Will there be anything else, Mamselle?' and whispered, 'The Rose Room is your bedroom, remember. The Countess next door.'

It was an unnecessary point to make for they had discussed the layout of the Château thoroughly enough at Cold Harbour. He was a little afraid now, she could see that. There was sweat on his brow.

She said, 'Nothing, thank you, René,' turned and went up the steps after Priem.

There was a sentry on each side of the door, but the hall was exactly as she remembered, right down to the ornaments, the pictures on the walls. They ascended the wide marble staircase together.

She said, 'How is the General?'

'His bad leg is a little stiff. All the rain we've been having. I saw him earlier, walking in the sunken garden.'

They reached the top corridor. She paused outside the Rose Room and waited. He sighed, put down one suitcase and opened the door for her.

As a child, she had slept in this room often. It was light and airy, tall french windows opening on to a balcony. There were red velvet curtains and the furniture was completely unchanged. Polished mahogany. Bed, dressing table, wardrobe. Everything.

Priem pushed the door shut, came across and put the suitcases on the bed, then turned. There was a slight, grave smile on his mouth, a strange air of expectancy as if he was waiting for something.

'Well?' she said.

'Well yourself.' He smiled. 'Poor Anne-Marie. Was Paris really that bad?'

'I'm afraid so.'

'Then we'll have to try and make it up to you.' He clicked his heels formally. 'But duty calls. I'll catch up with you later.'

She was aware of an overwhelming surge of relief as the door closed behind him. She tossed her coat on the bed, opened the french windows and went out on the balcony. It overlooked part of the garden only. The main entrance was to the right, her aunt's balcony around the corner.

There was an old rocking chair in hand-carved beech that she remembered well. She sat down in it, gently rocking, the sun warm on her face. How often had Anne-Marie done this?

Priem walked along the landing and paused at the top of the marble staircase, aware of the boots of the SS sentries slamming in salute outside. A moment later, Reichslinger entered.

'Reichslinger!' Priem called.

'Colonel?' Reichslinger looked up.

'My office. Now.'

Reichslinger looked hunted, walked across the hall and disappeared into the corridor. Priem went down the steps slowly, paused at the bottom to light a cigarette, then crossed the hall. When he entered his office the young Hauptsturm-führer was standing at his desk. Priem closed the door.

'I hear you've been playing naughty boys again?'

Reichslinger looked sullen. 'I don't know what you mean.'

'Mademoiselle Trevaunce. I get the impression you didn't try hard enough to be the gentleman.'

'She had a pistol, Standartenführer, a Walther.'

'Which you provoked her into using?'

'The penalty for a civilian found in possession of a weapon is death, as the Standartenführer well knows.'

'Reichslinger,' Priem said patiently. 'There are wheels within wheels here. Things you know nothing about. In other words, mind your own business.'

And Reichslinger, unable to hold his anger, said viciously, 'That the Trevaunce girl is your business, I understand only too well, Standartenführer.'

Priem seemed to go very still, his face calm and yet suddenly, Reichslinger was afraid. The Colonel moved close and, very gently, fastened a button which was undone in the other man's tunic.

'Careless, Reichslinger. Won't do. I can't have one of my officers setting such a bad example to the men.' He went round his desk and took a document from his in-tray. 'A signal from Berlin. Rather depressing. SS battalions in Russia are desperately short of officers. They enquire if we can spare anyone.'

Reichslinger's throat went dry. 'Standartenführer?' he whispered.

'An indifferent posting, especially as the Army is in total retreat there.'

Reichslinger said, 'I'm sorry, sir, I didn't mean . . .'

'I know exactly what you meant.' Suddenly, Priem looked like the Devil himself. 'If you ever speak to me like that again, if you step out of line just once.' He held up the signal.

Reichslinger's face was ashen. 'Yes, sir.'

'Now get out.' The young man hurried to the door and got it open. Priem added, 'And Reichslinger.'

'Standartenführer?'

'Interfere with Mademoiselle Trevaunce again in such a way and I will most certainly have you shot.'

Sitting in the rocking chair on the balcony of the Rose Room, Genevieve, for no accountable reason, remembered an incident when she was fourteen, crouched on the landing in the dark, watching the guests at one of Hortense's balls when she and her sister should have been in bed. Anne-Marie had discovered that the best-looking young man there was also one of the richest in France.

'I shall marry him if I find I haven't enough money when I'm older. We'd make a perfect couple. He's so fair and I'm so dark.'

Genevieve had believed her totally. The voice echoed down the years and then she realised suddenly that Anne-Marie *must* have changed to some degree because everything in life did. The girl she remembered from childhood who, excepting Hampstead, she had last seen four years ago, must be different. Had to be. In a way, the whole thing needed rethinking.

She'd always had a fear of being swallowed up by Anne-Marie, just as she always had the feeling that in some strange way she should never have been born. Sitting there, thinking about it all, she saw that there had always been some kind of bond between them. A kind of mutual resentment of the fact of each other's existence.

Strange how this quiet place could cause such thoughts and then she became aware of movement in the room. She stood up and went in. Black dress, white apron, dark stockings and shoes, the perfect lady's maid. Maresa was leaning over her suitcases.

'Leave them!' Genevieve ordered.

Her voice was angry, for inside, she was a little scared. Here was another to convince, someone else who knew her intimately.

'I want to sleep,' she said. 'The train was awful. You can unpack later.'

For a moment, she thought she saw hatred in the dark eyes and wondered what Anne-Marie could have done to earn that.

Maresa said, 'Perhaps I could run Mamselle a hot bath?'

'Later, girl.'

She closed the door behind Maresa and leaned against it, hands shaking. Another hurdle passed. She glanced at her watch and saw that it was just after noon. Time she braved the lioness in her den. She smoothed her skirt, opened the door and went out.

Eleven

When Genevieve went into her aunt's sitting room, it was like entering another world. One wall was entirely covered by a mural some famous Chinese artist had done for her. It was exquisite, beautiful, intricate details as finely painted as the green trees and the strange, unfamiliar figures and temples. Heavy blue silk curtains hung from ceiling to floor and she knelt on the faded *chaise-longue* by the window and looked down into the garden.

When she had last been here it had been lush and beautiful in the warmth of early summer, roses climbing over the statue of Venus. No flowers now, but the important things were still there like the large stone fountain with a boy on a dolphin in the middle of the lawn.

General Ziemke was sitting on the bench by the high wall over to her right. His hair was silver, more silver than in the photos, his face more arresting at a distance, giving him the air of a man still in his prime. A greatcoat with an enormous fur collar was draped over his shoulders and he smoked a cigarette in a long holder. He appeared to be deep in thought, but every so often rubbed that bad leg of his as if he would restore feeling to it.

'What do you want?'

Genevieve turned and there she was, totally unchanged since the last time she had seen her. 'Chantal – you gave me a shock.'

Her grim ugly face didn't relax in the slightest. 'What do you want?' she repeated.

'To see my aunt, of course. Any objections?'

'She's resting. I won't let you disturb her.'

Hatchet-face, they used to call her, grim and unrelenting and no one had ever been able to do anything with her.

Genevieve said patiently, 'Do as you're told for once, Chantal. Ask Hortense nicely if she'll see me. If you won't, then I'll go in anyway.'

'Over my dead body.'

'I'm sure that can be arranged.' Suddenly she was impatient, Anne-Marie taking over completely. 'Don't be so irritating for God's sake.'

Chantal's eyes darkened at the blasphemy for she was very religious. 'You know where you'll go, don't you?'

'Just as long as you're in the other place.'

The door behind her was slightly ajar. As Genevieve turned to it, she heard the voice, so familiar in spite of the years and her mouth went dry, the heart beat a little faster.

'If she's so anxious to see me, she must want something badly. Let her in.'

As Chantal pushed the door open, Genevieve could see Hortense beyond her sitting up in bed against the pillows, reading a newspaper. She smiled sweetly as she went past. 'Thank you, dear Chantal.'

But once inside the room, she found herself totally at a loss. 'What do I say?' she thought. 'What would Anne-Marie say?' She took a deep breath and went forward. 'Why do you put up with her?' she asked, flinging herself down in a chair by the fireplace and looking towards the bed.

She was conscious of a feeling of the most intense excitement, wanted only to go to her aunt. To tell her that it was she, Genevieve, come back after all these years.

'Since when have you cared?' She was a disembodied voice behind the newspaper. Now, she lowered it, and Genevieve had one of the greatest shocks of her life. She was still Hortense, but infinitely older than when she had last seen her.

'Give me a cigarette,' she snapped.

Genevieve opened her handbag, took out her lighter and the silver and onyx case and threw them on to the bed. 'This is new,' Hortense said as she opened the case. 'Very pretty.'

She lit a Gitane. Genevieve picked up the silver case, put it back in her handbag and put out her hand for the lighter, the wide silk sleeve of her blouse sliding up her arm. Hortense hesitated, her eyes blank, then gave it to her.

'Paris was a bore,' Genevieve told her.

'I dare say.' She inhaled deeply. 'Chantal thinks I shouldn't smoke. If I ask for a packet of cigarettes, she conveniently forgets.'

'Get rid of her.'

Hortense ignored her for a moment, giving her a chance to adjust. When Genevieve had last seen her, she hadn't looked a day over forty, but that had always been so. The truth was not that she was old, only that she had got older by more than the four years since Genevieve had last seen her.

'You want something?' Hortense said.

'Do I?'

'Usually.' She took another puff at her cigarette and handed it to Genevieve. 'You finish it, just to satisfy Chantal.'

'She won't believe you. The original bloodhound, that one.'

'A game we play.' Hortense shrugged. 'There's little else to do.'

'What about General Ziemke?'

'Carl's all right in his way. A gentleman at least, which is more than you can say for the others downstairs. Scum like Reichslinger, for example. They think breeding is something to do with horses.'

'And Priem? What about him?'

'I understand he carried your bags up from the car. Is he in love with you?'

'You tell me. You are, after all, an authority on the subject.'

She sat back against the cushions, staring at Genevieve, eyes narrowed: 'I know one thing. He's a man, that one. Just himself.'

'Indeed.'

'Not one to play games with. I'd give him a wide berth if I were you.'

'Is that a suggestion or an order?'

'You never were very good at doing as you were told,' she said, 'but I never took you for a fool. You know I'm usually right in this sort of thing.'

Genevieve was in a real difficulty now, for Hortense was the one person who could tell her everything that went on in this house and yet she dared not involve her; certainly never tell her about herself. For her own sake, it was better that she remain totally uninvolved.

'What if I told you why I'm here?'

'You'd probably be lying.'

'A Swiss banker, desperately in love with me?'

'True love at last? You, Anne-Marie?'

'You don't believe a word I say, do you?'

'Isn't that always safer? Now, tell me what you're up to and give me another of those cigarettes.'

She reached for Genevieve's handbag, had it open before she could stop her and rummaged inside. There was a pause, she went quite still, then took out the Walther.

'Be careful,' Genevieve said and reached for it, her sleeve sliding back up her arm again.

Hortense dropped the pistol and grabbed her right wrist, a grip of incredible strength so that she was pulled forward on to her knees beside the bed.

'Once, when you were a little girl of eight, you waded into the fountain in the lower garden – the boy with a trumpet. You told me later that you wanted to climb up to drink the water as it spouted from his mouth.' Genevieve shook her head dumbly. The grip tightened. 'One of his bronze fingers was broken. When you slipped, you caught your arm. Later, here in this very room, you sat on my knee, holding me tight as Doctor Marais repaired the damage. How many stitches was it – five?'

'No!' Genevieve struggled wildly. 'You're mistaken. That was Genevieve.'

'Precisely,' Hortense traced a finger along the thin white scar clearly visible on the inside of the right forearm. 'I saw you arrive, *chérie*,' she said. 'From my window.' Her grip slackened, a hand stroked Genevieve's hair. 'From the moment you stepped out of the car – from that moment. Did you think I would not to able to tell?'

There were tears in Genevieve's eyes. She threw her arms about her. Hortense kissed her gently on the forehead, held her close for a moment, then said softly, 'And now, *chérie*, the truth.'

When she had finished, she still knelt by the bed. There was a long pause, then Hortense patted her hand. 'I think I would very much like a glass of cognac. Over there – the Chinese lacquer cabinet in the corner.'

'But is that wise?' Genevieve said. 'Your health . . .'

'What on earth are you talking about?' Hortense was frowning now.

'They told me you'd had trouble with your heart. Brigadier Munro said you were in poor health.'

'What nonsense. Do I look ill to you?'

She was almost angry. Genevieve said, 'No, you look marvellous, if you really want to know. I'll get your brandy.'

She went to the cabinet and opened it. So, another piece of dishonesty on Munro's part, just to push her a little harder in the direction he'd wished her to follow and Craig Osbourne had gone along with it. Her hand shook a little as she poured

Courvoisier into a crystal glass and carried it to her aunt.

Hortense took it down in one quick swallow and looked into the empty glass pensively. 'Poor Carl.'

'Why do you say that?'

'You think I could bear to have his hands on me now, knowing what those animals did to Anne-Marie?' She placed the glass down on the bedside cabinet. 'We lived in a state of armed conflict, Anne-Marie and I. She was selfish, totally ruthless where her own desires were concerned, but she was my niece, my blood, my flesh. A de Voincourt.'

'And acted like one these past few months.'

'Yes, you are right and we must see that what she did is not wasted.'

'Which is why I am here.'

Hortense snapped her fingers. 'Give me another cigarette and tell Chantal to run my bath. I'll soak for an hour and think about things. See what can be done to pay a little back on account to those gentlemen below. You take a walk, *chérie*. Come back in an hour.'

At Cold Harbour it was raining when Craig went into the kitchen in search Julie. She took in the fact of his uniform, the trenchcoat.

'You're leaving?'

'For the moment. The weather's lifted at Croydon. I'm flying up there with Munro in the Lysander.' He put an arm about her. 'Are you okay? You don't seem yourself.'

She smiled wanly. 'I know I amuse you with my Tarot cards, Craig, but I do have the gift. I get feelings. I just know when something isn't as it should be.'

'Explain,' he said.

'Genevieve – her sister. There's more to this than meets the eye. Much more. I don't think Munro is telling anything remotely like the truth.'

And he believed her, his stomach contracting into a knot. 'Genevieve,' he said softly and his hands tightened on Julie's shoulders.

'I know, Craig. I'm afraid.'

'Don't be. I'll sort it.' He smiled. 'You've got Martin to lean on. Talk it over with him. Tell him I intend to do some digging when I get to London.' He kissed her on the cheek. 'Trust me. You know what a wild man I am when I get angry.'

He sat beside Munro when they took off. The Brigadier produced papers from his briefcase and studied them. No point in a frontal attack at that stage, Craig knew.

He said, 'She'll be well into things by now.'

'Who will?' Munro glanced up. 'What are you talking about.'

'Genevieve. She should be there by now. Château de Voincourt.'

'Oh, that.' Munro nodded. 'We'll have to see how it goes. She is an amateur, of course, one must remember that.'

'That fact didn't bother you before,' Craig told him.

'Yes, well I hardly wanted to depress her, dear boy, did I? I suppose what I'm trying to say is that one mustn't expect too much. Two-thirds of all women agents we've put in the field have come to a bad end.'

He returned to his documents, unperturbed and Craig sat there thinking. Julie was right. There *is* more. He tried to analyse it step-by-step, the factors involved, the way everything had happened. Central to it all was Anne-Marie, of course. If what had happened to her hadn't happened, if it hadn't been so essential for Munro to see her face-to-face. Craig thought of her as he'd last seen her and shuddered. The wretched girl, down there in that cellar at Hampstead and Baum, in whose care she was entrusted, and yet who couldn't bear to go near her himself.

He straightened in his seat. Strange, that. Very strange. A doctor actually afraid to go near his own patient. There had to be an answer to that one.

The rest of the flight was uneventful. As they were walking across to the limousine waiting at Croydon, he said to Munro, 'Will you need me tonight, sir?'

'No, dear boy. Enjoy yourself, why don't you.'

'I will, sir. Might try the Savoy,' Craig said and opened the car door for him.

'The conferences are always held in the library,' Hortense said. 'The rest of the time, Priem uses it as his main office. He even sleeps there on a camp bed. He has a smaller office next to Reichslinger, but that's for routine business.'

'How very dedicated of him,' Genevieve said. 'The camp bed, I mean.'

'Any important papers are always kept in the library safe.'

'Behind the portrait of Elizabeth, the eleventh Countess?'

'Ah, you remember?'

'How can you be sure about all this?'

'Sooner or later, *chérie*, any man in my life discloses all, a habit I have always encouraged. Carl is no different, I assure you. You see, he is not a Nazi, God help him. He doesn't approve, which means that when he gets angry, he talks. A kind of release.'

'You know that Rommel will be here the day after tomorrow?'

'Yes. To discuss their coastal defence system.'

'The Atlantic Wall?'

'And that's what you are here for?'

'Any information I can get on it.'

'Which means getting into the safe because that's where anything worth looking at will be.'

'Who has the key – the General?'

'No, Priem. Carl has great difficulty in getting into it himself. He's always complaining. When they first came, I was compelled to hand over the key.'

'Didn't you always keep a spare?' Genevieve asked.

Hortense nodded. 'They asked for that, too. They're very thorough, the Germans. On the other hand.' She opened the drawer of her bedside cabinet, took out a trinket box and lifted the lid. She rummaged amongst some assorted jewellery and produced a key. 'I didn't give them this. The spare to the spare, you might say.'

Genevieve said, 'That's marvellous.'

'Only a beginning. Such papers, if removed, would soon be missed.'

'I have a camera.' Genevieve took out the silver and onyx case, fiddled at the back until the flap dropped. 'See?'

'Ingenious.' Hortense nodded. 'So, the conference is to be held during the afternoon. In the evening, there will be a reception and ball, after which Rommel will return to Paris overnight. This means that if you are to see the contents of the safe, it will have to be during the ball itself.'

'But how?'

'I'll think of a way, *chérie*. Depend on it.' Hortense patted her cheek. 'Now, leave me for a little while. I need to rest.'

'Of course.' Genevieve kissed her and crossed to the door.

As she reached for the handle, Hortense said, 'And one more thing.'

Genevieve turned. 'What's that?'

'Welcome home, my darling. Welcome home.'

When she got back to her room, she found that she was really tired. Her head was throbbing, hurting almost to the point of nausea. She drew the curtains and lay down fully clothed on the bed. So, Munro had been less than honest with her. In a sense, she could accept his actions, but Craig Osbourne . . .

On the other hand, it had brought her back to Hortense. For that, at least, she was grateful.

She woke to find Maresa shaking her gently by the shoulder. 'I thought Mamselle would wish a bath before dinner.'

'Yes, thank you,' she said.

Maresa was obviously slightly bewildered by the gentleness of her tone and Genevieve realised at once that she wasn't playing her part.

'Well, go on, girl!' she said sharply.

'Yes, Mamselle.' Maresa disappeared into the bathroom and Genevieve heard the sound of running water. When the maid came back she said, 'You can unpack and tidy up here while I'm having my bath.'

She moved into the bathroom, dropping her clothes on the floor in an untidy heap as her sister had done since the age of five, and got into the bath. She wasn't sure about Maresa at all and wondered whether she kept a watching brief on Anne-Marie Trevaunce for anyone. She was beautiful in a heavy, passive kind of way and not stupid. Apparently quiet and correct, and yet there had been that look of hate in her eyes when Genevieve had first arrived.

She luxuriated in the hot water and after a while, there was a discreet knock. 'It's half-past six, Mamselle. Dinner is at seven tonight.'

'If I'm late, I'm late. They'll wait.'

For a while, she'd thought of snatching a further breathing space by staying in her room and pleading tiredness, but there was the General to consider. The sooner they met, the better.

She abandoned the bath reluctantly, reached for the silk dressing gown behind the door and went back into the bedroom. She sat down in front of the dressing table and Maresa immediately started to brush her hair, something Genevieve had always found intensely irritating, but she forced herself to sit there as Anne-Marie would have done.

166

'And what will Mamselle wear tonight?'

'God knows. I'd better have a look.'

Which was the only sensible solution for the wardrobes were crammed with dresses of every description. Her sister had style, there was no doubt about that, and expensive tastes to go with it. In the end, she slipped into something in chiffon, subdued blues and greys, floating and elegant. The shoes were a little tight, but she'd have to get used to that. She glanced at the clock. It was five-past seven.

'Time to go, I think.'

Maresa opened the door. As Genevieve went past, she could have sworn the girl was smiling to herself.

Chantal appeared from the stairway carrying a covered tray.

'What's this?' Genevieve demanded.

'The Countess has decided to eat in her room tonight.' She was angry as usual. 'He's in there.'

Genevieve opened the door for her. Hortense was sitting in one of the wing-back chairs by the sitting room fire, wearing a spectacular Chinese housecoat in black and gold. General Ziemke leaned against the back of the chair, resplendent in full uniform. He really did look rather handsome. When he turned and saw Genevieve, his face broke into a smile of welcome that was very real.

'At last,' Hortense said. 'Now perhaps I can get a little peace. There are times when I seem to be surrounded only by fools.'

Ziemke kissed Genevieve's hand. 'We've missed you.'

'Oh, get out of here,' Hortense said impatiently. She beckoned to Chantal to bring the tray forward. 'What have you got there?'

Ziemke smiled. 'An essential quality for any good general is to know when it pays to retreat. I suspect this is one of those moments.'

He opened the door for Genevieve, inclined his head and she went out.

There were about twenty people at the dining table, mostly men. A couple of women who looked like secretaries and wore evening gowns and two rather pretty girls in uniform with a lightning flash on their left arms. Female signal personnel from the radio room. René had warned her about them. Much in demand amongst the officers, he had said. Looking at them, Genevieve could well believe it.

Max Priem sat opposite her and she noticed Reichslinger at the far end of the table with some other SS officers. When he glanced towards her, his eyes glittered with hate, reminding her strangely of Joe Edge. She'd made an enemy there, for certain.

A couple of orderlies in dress uniform and white gloves came round with wine and she remembered that Anne-Marie couldn't stand red, but was capable from an early age of putting away far larger amounts of white than Genevieve ever could. She also noted, wryly, that the wine was a Sancerre, the pride of her aunt's wine cellars which must have been pretty ravaged by now.

Reichslinger laughed loudly above the buzz of general conversation. From the expressions on the faces of his companions, he wasn't exactly popular.

Ziemke leaned close. 'I trust the Countess will feel in better spirits tomorrow?'

'You know her moods as well as I do.'

'The day after, Field Marshal Rommel himself visits us. We are naturally giving a reception and ball for him afterwards and if the Countess were to have one of her headaches . . .' He shrugged. 'It would be most unfortunate.'

'I understand you perfectly, General.' Genevieve patted his hand. 'I'll do my best.'

'I would be loath to order her to be there. In fact,' he added frankly, 'I'd be afraid to. You weren't here at the time, but the day Priem and I arrived here . . . My God, how she ran rings around us. Isn't that so, Priem?'

'I fell in love with her instantly,' the Colonel said.

'People have a habit of doing that,' Genevieve told him.

She found his smile so disquieting that she had to look away from the penetrating blue eyes, her heart beating quickly. She had the strangest feeling that he could see right through her.

The General was speaking again. 'The day we came, you were in the village as I recall. Your aunt barred the door to us for quite some time. When we finally gained admittance, there were several conspicuous spaces on the walls.'

'Have you tried the cellars?'

He laughed delightedly and for the rest of the meal was in the highest of spirits. As for Genevieve, the strain of playing her role was beginning to tell and she found that she was becoming increasingly tense.

'Coffee in the drawing room, I think,' Ziemke finally announced.

There was a momentary confusion as everyone rose and she was aware of Priem at her shoulder. 'May I have a word?'

But he was definitely someone to avoid, at least for the moment. 'Perhaps some other time,' she said and moved towards the General.

'My dear,' he said, 'I must introduce you to a countryman of yours, now serving with the Charlemagne Brigade of the SS, here for tonight only with dispatches.'

The officer bowed to her. She noticed his cuff title, the tricolour on his left sleeve as he smiled and carried her hands to his lips as only the French can. He was blond, blue-eyed, handsome, more like a German than anyone there, an incredible contrast to Max Priem standing a few feet away.

'Enchanted,' he said and she noticed how well the uniform suited him and wondered what would happen if the Maquis ever got him up a back alley, this Frenchman in the SS.

Ziemke steered her across the room and out through the french windows to the terrace. 'That's better,' he said. 'Fresh air. Cigarette?'

As she took it, she said, 'You're worried about this conference. Is it so important?'

'Rommel himself, my dear. What would you expect?'

'No, it's more than that,' Genevieve said. 'You don't agree with them – not any more. Isn't that it?'

'You make it too complicated,' he said. 'We'll be talking about defences and I know what most of the others think.'

This, of course, was exactly the kind of conversation she'd come to hear. 'And you disagree?'

'I do.'

'But surely this is only a preliminary?'

'Yes, but the conclusions, in the main, will hold. Unless the Führer makes a sudden decision to change it all.'

'He's got you this far,' she said lightly.

'We will lose the war.'

She reached for his hand. 'I wouldn't say that too loudly if I were you.'

He held her hand and stared out into the dark grounds, seemingly lost in thought. She didn't mind, that was the strange thing. He was kind and he was unhappy and she liked him and that hadn't been part of the scheme at all. There were footsteps and she pulled away.

'Sorry to disturb you, Herr General,' Max Priem said, 'but there's a call from Paris.'

The General nodded heavily. 'I'll come.' He kissed her hand. 'Goodnight, my dear,' and went back into the drawing room.

Max Priem stood to one side. 'Fräulein,' he said formally. She caught the mocking in his eyes and, strangely, something else too. Anger.

Twelve

She slept well and didn't dream and woke so suddenly that she knew something must have caused it and lay there, trying to work out what it was. Then the shots came and she was out of bed very fast, reaching for her dressing gown and running to the balcony.

Someone shouted in German, an object spun up very fast and was shot to pieces. She looked down. Just below, Priem was reloading a shotgun, snapping the barrels back into position. Behind him, an orderly crouched on the ground beside a box. They were clay pigeon shooting.

Priem shouted, the soldier released the spring and another disc spun into the blue sky. The barrels of the gun were up and following, he squeezed the trigger. She watched the disc explode, shading her eyes against the bright sky.

'Good morning,' she called.

He paused in the act of reloading and looked up. 'Did I wake you?'

'You could say that.'

He handed the shotgun to his orderly. 'Breakfast in the dining room in ten minutes. Are you joining us?'

'No, I think I'll have a tray in my room this morning.'

'As you wish.' He smiled. She turned, slightly breathless and went inside.

*

Hortense sent Chantal for her just after she'd finished breakfast. She was in her bath when Genevieve went in.

'I've decided to go to Mass this morning. You can come with me,' her aunt said.

'But I've already eaten.'

'How inconsiderate of you. You will come anyway. It is necessary.'

'For the salvation of my immortal soul?'

'No, to give that little slut, Maresa, a chance to search your room. Chantal overheard Reichslinger giving her her instructions late last night.'

Genevieve said, 'He suspects me then?'

'Why should he? You made a bad enemy there, that's all. This is probably just the start of his campaign to get back at you any way he can. An RAF propaganda leaflet would be enough for that one to denounce you as an enemy of the Reich. We must see if we can't make his little plan backfire.'

'What do I do?'

'When you return you will make the unpleasant discovery that your diamond earrings are missing, which they will be because by then, Chantal will have transferred them to some suitably stupid hiding place in Maresa's bedroom. You will naturally raise the Devil. Go straight to Priem who is, after all, in charge of security.'

'And then what happens?'

'Oh, he is a very astute man. He will find the earrings in Maresa's bedroom very quickly. She will protest her innocence, but the facts will speak for themselves. It is at that point that the silly girl will begin to cry . . .'

'. . . and will confess that she was acting under Reichslinger's instructions?'

'Exactly.'

'You could beat the Devil himself at cards, I suppose you know that?'

'Of course.'

'But will Priem believe her?' Genevieve said.

'I think we may rely on it. No public announcements – no fuss. He'll deal with Reichslinger in private perhaps, but he'll deal with him. He is, I think, a hard man, this Colonel of yours, when he has to be.'

'Mine? Why do you say that?'

'Poor Genny.' Nobody had called her that for years. 'Since you were old enough to climb on my knee, I have been able to read you like an open book. He fills you with unease, this man, am I not right? Your stomach turns hollow with excitement just to be near him.'

Genevieve took a deep breath to steady herself and stood up.

'I'll do my best to resist the temptation, I think you can rely on that. Have you told Chantal?'

'Only that Anne-Marie is up to her neck in subversive activities. I think you will find that she will smile on you more warmly now. Her brother, Georges, is in a labour camp in Poland.'

'All right,' Genevieve said. 'Now, as to a plan of campaign.'

'All sorted out. We'll discuss it later. Be a good girl and tell Maresa to inform René that I'll need the Rolls.'

Genevieve was a child again to do her bidding. She did exactly as she was told, of course. Nothing changed.

Their first shock came when they went out of the front door and down the steps. There was no sign of René or the Rolls, only Max Priem and a black Mercedes.

He saluted gravely. 'Your car, it would appear, is out of order this morning, Countess. I've told our own mechanics to do what they can. In the meantime, I am wholly at your service. You wish to go to church, I believe?'

Hortense hesitated, then shrugged, got inside and Genevieve followed her.

He drove them himself and Genevieve had to sit there, looking at the back of his neck, acutely uncomfortable. Hortense ignored him and glanced at her watch. 'We're late. Never mind, the *curé* will wait for me. He's seventy, if he's a day, you know. The first man I ever fell in love with. Dark and handsome and with so much belief. Faith is an attraction in a man. I never went to so many services.'

'And now?' Genevieve asked.

'His hair is white and when he smiles, his skin crinkles so much that his eyes are hidden.'

Genevieve became uncomfortably aware that Priem was watching her in the driving mirror, his eyes full of laughter, and so did Hortense.

She said coldly, 'I understand the SS do not believe in God, Colonel?'

'I have it on the most reliable authority that Reichsführer Himmler does, however.' Priem turned the car in beside the church gate, got out and opened the rear door. 'If you please, ladies.'

Hortense sat there for a moment, then took his hand and got out. 'You know, I like you, Priem. 'It's a great pity . . .'

'That I'm a German, Countess? My grandmother, on my mother's side, came from Nice. Will that help?'

'Considerably.' She turned to Genevieve. 'No need for you to come in. Pay your respects to your mother. I shan't be long.'

She pulled down her veil and went up the path between the gravestones to the porch of the ancient church.

Priem said, 'A remarkable woman.'

'I think so.' There was a slight pause as he stood there,

hands clasped behind him, a kind of fantasy figure in that magnificent uniform, the cross at his throat. She said, 'If you'll excuse me, I'd like to visit my mother.'

'But of course.'

She entered the churchyard. It was an ideal setting in the far corner, shaded by a cypress tree. The headstone was beautifully simple as Hortense had intended it to be and there were fresh flowers in the stone vase.

'Hélène Claire de Voincourt Trevaunce,' Max Priem said, moving to the other side and then he did a strange thing. He saluted briefly, a perfect military salute, nothing Nazi about it. 'Well, Hélène Claire,' he said softly, 'you have a very beautiful daughter. You would be proud of her, I think.'

Genevieve said, 'What about your family?'

'My father died in the last war, my mother a few years later. I was raised by an aunt in Frankfurt, a schoolmistress. She was killed in a bombing raid last year.'

'So, we have something in common?'

'Oh, come now,' he said, 'what about this English father of yours, the doctor in Cornwall? The sister of whom you so seldom speak? Genevieve, isn't it?'

She was frightened then at the fact that he knew so much, was aware of a desperate feeling of being balanced on some dangerous edge. She was saved because of a sudden shower. As it burst upon them, he seized her hand.

'Come, we must run.'

They reached the shelter of the church porch and she noticed that he appeared to be having some difficulty with his breathing. He slumped down on the stone bench.

She said, 'Are you all right?'

'It's nothing, believe me.' He managed a smile and produced a silver case. 'Cigarette?'

'You were wounded in Russia?' she said.

'Yes.'

'It was bad there in the Winter War, they tell me.'

'I think you may say it was an unforgettable experience.'

She said, 'Reichslinger and the others – you inhabit different worlds. You're . . .'

'A German whose country is at war,' he said. 'It's really very simple. Very unfortunate perhaps, but very simple.'

'I suppose so.'

He sighed, his face softening a little. 'Always since I was a boy I have loved the rain.'

'Me, too,' she said.

He smiled gravely. 'Good, then we do have something in common after all.'

They sat there waiting for Hortense as the rain increased and her aunt had been right as usual for she had never felt so excited in her life before.

In London, Craig Osbourne rang the bell at Munro's flat in Haston Place. When the door opened, he went upstairs and found Jack Carter waiting to greet him on the landing.

'Is he in, Jack?'

'I'm afraid not. He was called to the War Office. A good job you're here. I was about to send the bloodhounds out after you. Your people have been trying to get hold of you.'

'OSS? What for?'

'Well, the way things worked out, you were never debriefed over the Dietrich affair. They're annoyed at Munro using Ike's authority to steal you but rather pleased at the way you handled things. I think another medal might be in the offing.'

'I've got a medal,' Craig said.

'Yes, well be a good lad and get over to Cadogan Place, just to keep them happy. What did you want anyway?'

'I promised Genevieve I'd keep an eye out for her sister. Thought I'd drop in at the nursing home, but the guards refused me admittance.'

'Yes, well security has been tightened there for various reasons.' Carter smiled. 'I'll give Baum a call. Tell him to expect you.'

'Fine,' Craig said. 'I'll go and take care of things at OSS Headquarters then,' and he turned and hurried down the stairs.

In a spy film Genevieve had seen, the hero had placed a hair from his head across a door so that he could tell later whether his room had been entered. She had employed the same ruse with two of the drawers in her dressing table. It was the first thing she checked when she got back from church. They'd both been opened.

Maresa was not around because she'd told her before going out that she wouldn't need her again until after lunch, so she lit a cigarette, just to fill in a little time, then went in search of Priem. She found him at his desk in the library, Reichslinger at his side, going over some list or other together.

They both looked up. She said, 'It really is too much, Colonel. That your security people should search our rooms from time to time is something that one must regrettably take for granted. What I am not prepared to overlook is one pair of very valuable diamond earrings, pearls set in silver, a family heirloom. I really would be infinitely obliged to you if you would see they are returned.'

'Your room has been searched?' Priem said calmly. 'How can you be sure?'

'A dozen different ways – things not as I left them – and the earrings, of course.'

'Perhaps your maid was simply tidying up. Have you spoken to her?'

'Not possible,' Genevieve said impatiently. 'I gave her the morning off before leaving for church.'

He said to Reichslinger, 'Do you know anything about this?'

Reichslinger's face was pale. 'No, Standartenführer.'

Priem nodded. 'After all, there would be no question of you undertaking such a search without my authority.'

Reichslinger stayed silent. Genevieve said, 'Well?'

'I'll deal with it,' Priem told her, 'and come back to you.'

'Thank you, Colonel.' She turned and walked out quickly.

Priem lit a cigarette and looked up at Reichslinger. 'So.'

'Standartenführer?' Reichslinger's face was already damp with sweat.

'The truth, man. Five seconds is all you've got. I warned you.'

'Standartenführer, you must listen. I was only doing my duty. The Walther – it worried me. I thought there might be other things.'

'So you force Mademoiselle Trevaunce's maid to search her mistress's room and in the process, the stupid little bitch gets sticky fingers? Very helpful, Reichslinger. I'm sure you'll agree.'

'Standartenführer, what can I say?'

'Nothing,' Priem said wearily. 'Just find Maresa and bring her to me.'

Genevieve waited in her room a little nervously, sitting by the open window to the balcony, trying to read. But Hortense, after all, had been right. In a little more than an hour after her visit to the library, there was a knock at her door and Priem entered.

'You have a moment?' He crossed the room, held up the earrings and dropped them into her lap.

'Who?' she asked.

'Your maid. You see, I was right.'

'The ungrateful little slut. You're certain?'

'I'm afraid so,' he said calmly and she wondered what had passed between him and Reichslinger.

'Right – it's back to the farm for her.'

'An impulse of the moment, I would say, more than anything else. A stupid girl who persisted in her innocence of the charge in spite of the fact that I had discovered the earrings in her room. In any case, she could hardly have hoped to get away with such a thing.'

'Are you suggesting that I give her another chance?'

'That would require a little charity, a commodity in short supply in these hard times.' Priem looked out across the balcony. 'It really is a most pleasant view from here. I hadn't realised.'

'Yes,' Genevieve said.

He smiled gravely. 'So. There is much to do if we are to be ready for the Field Marshal's visit tomorrow. You will excuse me now?'

'Of course.'

The door closed behind him. She waited for a couple of minutes, then left herself, quickly.

'Maresa is having an affair with one of the soldiers,' Hortense said, 'or so Chantal informs me.' She glanced up at her grim old maid. 'You may bring her to me now.'

'This means something?' Genevieve asked.

Hortense allowed herself a tiny smile. 'Maresa's soldier is on extra guard duty on the terrace outside the library tonight and tomorrow and she's not pleased. I believe she thinks you are to blame.'

Genevieve stared blankly at her. 'I don't understand.'

'The soldier at the gate when you arrived,' her aunt explained. 'You wouldn't show him your papers. By the time the story reached Reichslinger, the boy had become rude and ill-behaved. His captain felt this reflected on himself and took appropriate action. Maresa was very angry with you, according to Chantal.'

179

'You intend that we use her in some way? That's what all this has been about, isn't it?'

'Naturally. If you are to get into the library, it must be during the ball. You will have to make an excuse to slip away for a while. The catch on that third french window is still broken after thirty years. If you push hard enough, it will open. How long will it take you to open the safe and use this camera of yours. Five minutes? Ten?'

'But the guard outside,' Genevieve said. 'On the terrace.'

'Ah, yes, Maresa's young man. Eric, I believe the name is. I think we can rely on her to take him off into the bushes for a reasonable length of time. After all, everyone else will be enjoying themselves.'

'My God,' Genevieve whispered. 'Are you sure there isn't any Borgia blood in the family?'

Maresa arrived a couple of minutes later, shepherded by Chantal, her face swollen, ugly with weeping.

'Please, Mamselle,' she pleaded. 'I didn't take your earrings, I swear it.'

'But you searched my room on Reichslinger's orders, didn't you?'

Her mouth gaped in shock and she was obviously too shaken even to attempt to deny it.

'You see, we know everything, you stupid girl, just like Colonel Priem,' Hortense said. 'He made you tell him the truth, didn't he and then told you to shut up about it?'

'Yes, Countess.' Maresa dropped to her knees. 'Reichslinger's a terrible man. He said he'd have me sent off to a labour camp if I didn't do as he told me.'

'Get up, girl, for goodness sake.' She did as she was told and Hortense continued, 'You want me to send you back to the farm? Disgrace your mother, eh?'

'No, Countess – please. I'll do anything to make it up to you.'

Hortense reached for a cigarette and smiled up at Genevieve coldly. 'You see?' she said.

Craig Osbourne had found himself trapped for most of the day at OSS Headquarters. It was evening before he got away, seven o'clock when he arrived at the nursing home in Hampstead. The guard didn't open the gate, simply spoke through the bars.

'What can I do for you, sir?'

'Major Osbourne. I think you'll find Dr Baum is expecting me.'

'I believe he's out, sir, but I'll check.' The guard went into his office, returned a moment later. 'I was right, sir. He went out an hour ago, just before I came on.'

'Damn!' Craig said and started to turn away.

'Would it be urgent, sir?' the guard asked.

'Actually, it is.'

'I think you'll find him in the snug at the Grenadier, sir. That's a pub in Charles Street. Just down the road. You can't miss it. He's there most nights.'

'Why, thank you,' Craig told him and he turned and hurried away.

The officers were holding a small party at the Château that evening as a preparation for the great event and Ziemke had asked Genevieve to be there, especially as Hortense had again indicated her intention of dining in her room.

'I've promised to perform for Rommel,' she told the General, 'and that will have to suffice.'

Genevieve was dressed and ready to go down just before seven, had dismissed Maresa, when there came the lightest of taps on the door. She opened it and found René Dissard standing there, holding a tray.

'The coffee Mamselle ordered,' he said gravely.

Her hesitation was only fractional. 'Thank you, René,' she said and stood back.

She closed the door, he put down the tray and turned quickly. 'A moment only, Mamselle. I've received word to go and visit one of our most important contacts in the Resistance.'

'What about?'

'A message from London perhaps.'

'Can you get away from the Château all right?'

'Don't worry about me. I know what I'm doing.' He smiled. 'It goes well?'

'Perfect so far.'

'I'll contact you some time tomorrow, but I must go now, Mamselle. Goodnight.'

He opened the door and went out. For the first time, she was conscious of a feeling of real unease. Stupid, of course. She poured some of the coffee he'd brought and went and sat by the window to drink it.

They were using the old music room for dancing. There was a grand piano in the corner on a slightly raised section, in shadows now. She remembered the last time she'd played for Craig Osbourne and hoped that no one would ask her to repeat the performance.

Anne-Marie had always been more accomplished, had worked harder at it. She could have been a professional, but she was careful not to become quite that good. It wasn't, she maintained, what people wanted her to be. She was probably right – as usual.

Genevieve played the aristocrat to the hilt, a way of keeping at a distance people she was probably supposed to know. Someone opened the window to the terrace and coolness rushed in. There was quite a crowd. That afternoon an SS Brigadier General named Seilheimer had arrived with his wife and two daughters and an Army Colonel with one arm in a sling, who seemed to be held in high esteem by the younger officers. Some kind of war hero from the way they hung around him. Ziemke's presence and that of the Brigadier put rather a strain on things. Perhaps they noticed, because they left early to talk and the music became a little more lively.

Two young officers spent the first hour seeing to the gramophone between them, but soon relinquished the task to one of the orderlies and tried their luck with the Brigadier's daughters who both looked no more than seventeen and were flushed with excitement at all the attention they were receiving.

They were looking forward to the ball, of course, and the chance to meet the great Erwin Rommel. The youngest, with an irritating giggle, said she had never met so many handsome young men in one room before and what did Genevieve think of the dark Colonel in the Waffen-SS? She spoke in French which most of the Germans made a determined effort to do.

This last was said just a little too loudly. Max Priem, a glass of cognac in one hand, kept his face very straight as he talked to the Army Colonel, but there was wry amusement in those blue eyes when he glanced at Genevieve briefly.

She watched him for a while, this man who was nothing like what she had expected. All Germans were Nazi brutes like Reichslinger. She had believed that because that was what she was supposed to believe.

But Priem was different from anyone she had ever known. When she looked at him, she knew what they meant by the phrase 'a born soldier'. And yet there was the fact of what he and people like him had done. She had already seen something of that for herself in the past couple of days and there were other, darker things. The camps, for instance. She shivered slightly. Such thoughts were stupid. She was here for a purpose and must hold on to that fact.

The music was a curious mixture and not always German. There was French and even a little American Boogie. Tomorrow would be nothing like this. The lights would be bright and strong and the music dignified, an orchestra. They would drink punch from the de Voincourts' silver bowls and lots of champagne, and soldiers would wait upon them in white gloves, dress uniforms.

A young lieutenant approached and asked her to dance so diffidently that she flashed him Anne-Marie's most brilliant smile and said she'd be delighted. He was a beautiful dancer, probably the best in the room and blushed when she complimented him.

While the record was being changed, she stood in the centre of the room, chatting and a voice said, 'My turn now.'

Reichslinger pushed between the boy and Genevieve so that the young lieutenant had to step back.

'I like to choose my company,' she said.

'So do I.'

As the music began, Reichslinger took a firm grip of her waist and hand. He was smiling all the time, enjoying his temporary mastery, knowing there was little she could do about it until the record ended.

'The last time we met,' he was saying, 'you told me I was no gentleman. I must learn to mend my manners, then.'

He laughed as if he'd said something exceptionally witty and she realised he was more than a little drunk. As the record ended, they stopped by the open french windows and he pushed her out on the terrace.

'I think that's enough,' she said.

'Oh, no, not yet.' He grabbed both arms and held her back against the wall. They struggled while he laughed, enjoying himself, using only half his strength and then she brought her heel down hard on his instep.

'You bitch!' he said.

His arm swung up to strike and then there was a hand on

his shoulder, pulling him away. 'Didn't anyone ever tell you that isn't good manners?' Max Priem told him.

Reichslinger stood there, glaring and Priem faced him, hands on hips, looking strangely menacing. 'You are on duty at ten, is this not so?'

'Yes,' Reichslinger said thickly.

'Then I suggest you go about your business.' Reichslinger glanced at Genevieve wildly. Priem said, 'An order, not a suggestion.'

The iron discipline of the SS was in control now. Reichslinger's heels clicked together. '*Zu befehl, Standartenführer.*' He gave a perfect Nazi salute and marched away.

'Thank you,' Genevieve said, rather inadequately.

'You weren't doing too badly. Is that what they taught you at finishing school?'

'The syllabus was extremely varied.'

Another record started and she recognised the voice with something of a shock. Al Bowlly, Julie's favourite.

'I, too, like to choose my company,' Priem said. 'May I have this dance?'

They went through the french windows and moved on to the floor. He was an excellent dancer and suddenly, it was all rather pleasant. And yet, she was a spy, surrounded by the enemy. If they found out, what would they do to her? Those Gestapo cellars in Paris where Craig Osbourne had suffered? It was hard to reconcile such facts with the laughter, the gay conversation.

'Of what are you thinking?' he murmured.

'Nothing very special.'

It was rather marvellous drifting there, the light swimming in a haze of smoke. The music throbbed and then she realised what Bowlly was singing – 'Little Lady Make-Believe'.

A curious choice. Last time she had heard the song was during the London Blitz. A probationer nurse with a few hours off duty and too tired to sleep. She had gone to one of the clubs with an American pilot from the Eagle Squadron. Al Bowlly had just been killed by a Nazi bomb and the American had laughed when she said it was eerie and she had tried to make herself be in love with him, just because everyone else seemed to be in love. And then he'd shattered her eighteen-year-old romantic dream by asking her to sleep with him.

Priem said, 'You may have noticed the music has stopped.'

'Which shows how tired I am. I think I'll go to bed. I've had what you might call an interesting evening. Say goodnight to the General for me.'

An orderly appeared with a message for him. He took the piece of paper and read it and curiosity made her stay just to see if it was important. Not a muscle moved in his face. He slipped the paper into a pocket.

'Goodnight, then,' he said.

'Good night, Colonel.'

She felt dismissed and had a strange feeling about that paper as if it meant something she ought to know. How ironic if Rommel wasn't coming. If everything was cancelled. No, it wouldn't be ironic, it would be bloody marvellous. She'd stay on at the Château. They'd drift along until the war was won and hopefully, she'd be able to go home to her father. It was a while, she thought uneasily, since she'd considered him.

She moved up the stairs and along the corridor to her room. When she went in, she could feel Anne-Marie there for the first time, a dark presence, and had to get out, at least to the balcony, where there was no wind, only a cool stillness.

She sat in the rocking chair in the shadows, remembering Anne-Marie and what had happened to her. And they had been men of the Waffen-SS, her executioners, which was what it came down to, just like Max Priem. But that was nonsense. He was different.

There were quiet footsteps below and she looked down to see a figure silhouetted by the light from the room he'd just left. He stood quite still and she found that she had stopped rocking, was scarcely breathing.

She was not sure how long she watched, safe in the shadows, but he didn't move at all. It created a still harmony between them, all the more magnetic because he was unaware of it. He turned, the light from one of the windows on his face, and looked up at the balcony.

'Hello, there,' she said from the shadows.

It was a moment or so before he replied and she let the silence ride, peaceful. 'Aren't you cold?' he asked.

Somewhere by the boundary wall, a guard dog howled, splitting the silence, and others joined. Priem strode to the parapet and leaned on it, his body rigid and tense. The eeriness of that first cry was gone now. The dogs were very real. There was lots of noise down in the lower garden, voices raised, the flicker of torchlight.

A searchlight was turned on and its beam travelled like a yellow snake along the ground until it caught the tail-end of the pack, five or six Alsatians, and then the quarry, a man, leaping just ahead of them. They caught him by the lower fountain. He went down and then the dogs were all over him. A moment later the guards arrived to beat them off.

Genevieve was cold with horror, watching as the wretched man was lifted to his feet, covered with blood. Priem called out in German and a young sergeant turned and ran across the lawn to report. After a few moments, the sergeant returned to the group by the fountain and the snarling dogs, the prisoner, were led away.

'A local poacher after pheasant,' Priem called softly. 'He made a bad mistake.'

She hated him then, there at that moment, for what he stood for. The brutality of war, the violence that could so easily touch the lives of ordinary people, but she was a de Voincourt after all. A family who, in an earlier century, would have had that poacher's right hand in exchange for the pheasant.

She took a deep breath to steady her voice. 'I think I'll go to bed now. Good night to you, Colonel Priem.'

She backed into the shadows. He stayed where he was, the light on his face, looking up. It was quite some time before he turned and walked away.

Thirteen

The Grenadier in Charles Street was on the corner of a cobbled mews. When Craig went in he found himself in a typical London pub, marble-topped tables, a coal fire burning in a small grate, a mahogany bar, bottles ranged against an enormous mirror behind. It wasn't too busy. A couple of air raid wardens in uniform played dominoes by the fire. Four men in working overalls sat in a corner enjoying the beer. A motherly looking middle-aged blonde in a tight satin blouse looked up from the magazine she was reading behind the bar. Her eyes brightened at the sight of his uniform.

'What can I get you, love?'

'Scotch and water,' he told her.

'I don't know, you Yanks expect the earth. Haven't you heard of rationing?' She smiled. 'Still, I suppose there could be a drop for you.'

'I was hoping I might find a friend of mine here. A Dr Baum.'

'The little foreign doctor from that nursing home up the road?'

'That's right.' She was filling a glass out of sight of the other customers behind the bar. 'He's in the snug through that glass door, love. In there most nights. Likes to be on his own.'

'Thanks.' Craig paid her and took his drink.

She said, 'He ain't half putting it away these days – the booze I mean. See if you can get him to slow down.'

'He's one of your regulars then?'

'I should say so. Ever since he's been running the clinic and that's got to be three years now.'

There was information to be gained here, he knew it. He took out his cigarettes and offered her one. 'He hasn't been drinking hard all that time, has he?'

'Good lord, no. Used to come in every night, same time, sit on the stool at the end of the bar, read *The Times*, drink one glass of port then go.'

'So what happened?'

'Well his daughter died, didn't she?'

'But that was some time ago. Before the war.'

'Oh, no, love, you're wrong there. It was about six months ago. I remember it well. Dreadfully upset he was. Went in the snug and leaned on the bar with his head in his hands. Crying he was. I gave him a large Scotch and asked him what was wrong. He said he'd just had bad news. He'd heard his daughter had died.'

Craig managed to stay calm. 'I obviously got it wrong. Never mind. I'll have a word with him now.' He emptied his glass. 'Bring us another of those and whatever Baum's drinking.'

He opened the Victorian frosted glass door and found himself in the long snug. The main bar extended into it. In other days it had been intended for ladies only. Leather benches fringed the wall and there was another small coal fire in a grate, Baum sitting beside it, a glass in his hand. He looked seedy and neglected, clothes hanging on him. The eyes were bloodshot and there was a stubble on his chin.

Craig said, 'Hello, Doctor.'

Baum looked up in surprise. His speech was slightly slurred. Obviously the drink had already taken effect. 'Major Osbourne. How are you?'

'I'm fine.' Craig leaned against the bar and the blonde lady came round the partition with the drinks.

'Ah, Lily, for me? How nice,' Baum said.

'You take it steady, Doctor,' she said and went back in the main bar.

'Jack Carter said he'd give you a ring. Arrange for me to call at the nursing home,' Craig told him. 'I promised Genevieve Trevaunce I'd check on her sister.'

Baum ran a hand across his face, frowned and then nodded. 'Yes, Captain Carter did phone me.'

'How is the sister?'

'Not too good, Major.' He shook his head and sighed. 'Poor Anne-Marie.' He reached for the fresh glass of port. 'And Miss Genevieve – have you heard from her yet?'

'Heard from her?' Craig asked.

'From over there. The other side.'

'You know about that then?'

Baum assumed an expression of cunning and put a finger to his nose. 'Not much I don't know. Fast boat, passage by night. She must be a wonderful actress that girl.'

Craig just let it flow, nice and easy. 'Lily was telling me your daughter died six months ago.'

Baum nodded, maudlin now, his eyes filling with tears. 'My lovely Rachel. A terrible thing.'

'But if she was in Austria, how could you find out?' Craig said gently. 'The Red Cross?'

'No,' Baum answered automatically. 'It was my own people. The Jewish underground. You know the one? Friends of Israel?'

'Of course,' Craig said.

And then Baum suddenly looked worried. 'Why do you ask?'

'It's just that I always understood your daughter died before the war when you fled to this country.'

'Well, you're wrong.' Baum seemed to have sobered up and got to his feet. 'I must go. I have work to do.'

'What about Anne-Marie? I'd like to see her.'

'Some other time perhaps. Goodnight, Major.'

Baum went into the bar, Craig followed. Lily said, 'He went off like a rocket.'

'Yes, he did, didn't he?'

'Another one, love?'

'No thanks. What I need is a nice long walk to clear my head. Maybe I'll see you later.'

He smiled with total charm and went out. One of the air raid wardens come over. 'Two pints, Lily. Gawd, did you see that Yank's medals?'

'He certainly had a chestful.'

'Load of bull,' he said. 'Give them away for anything, that lot.'

It was half-nine when Craig went up the steps to the door of the Haston Place flat and rang the bell of the basement flat. 'It's Craig, Jack,' he said into the voice box.

When the door opened, he went in and walked along the corridor to the basement stairs. Carter was standing at the bottom.

'How did you get on with OSS?'

'They kept me most of the day.'

'Come on.' Carter turned and went into the flat and Craig followed him.

'Drink?' Carter asked.

'No, thanks. I'll just have a smoke if you don't mind.' He lit a cigarette. 'Thanks for phoning Baum for me.'

'You saw him then?' Carter poured himself a Scotch.

'Yes, in a manner of speaking. Not at the nursing home. I found him at the local pub. He's really pouring the stuff down these days.'

Carter said, 'I didn't know that.'

'It apparently started six months ago when he got word from Friends of Israel that his daughter had died in German hands.'

'Yes, well I think that would be enough to start me drinking.' Carter spoke without thinking.

'Only one thing wrong with all this, of course,' Craig said. 'As I understood it, Baum got out of Austria by the skin of his teeth just before the war after the Nazis had killed his daughter. Munro told me that himself one night over a drink at Cold Harbour. I was interested in what went on at the Rosedene Nursing Home having been a patient there myself and then there was Anne-Marie.'

'So?' Carter said calmly.

'Munro told me Baum offered his services to Intelligence. He wanted revenge. They gave him a thorough vetting and decided he wasn't suitable to use in the field.'

'Yes, I believe that's true,' Carter said.

'What's true – what's false, Jack? Did his daughter die in '39 or six months ago.'

'Look, Craig, there's a lot you don't know about this business.'

'Try me,' Craig said. 'No, let me try you. How about this as a possibility. The Nazis hold Baum's daughter and suggest that if he wants her to continue to exist, he flees to British Intelligence, continuing to work for them or else.'

'You've been reading too many spy stories,' Carter told him.

'And then something goes wrong. The girl dies in the camps. Baum's masters don't tell him, but the Jewish underground does. Baum, a decent man in the first place, only did what he did for his daughter's sake and now he really wants revenge.'

'And how would he achieve that?'

'By going to Dougal Munro and confessing all. No question of punishment. He's too valuable as a double agent.' Carter said nothing and Craig shook his head.

'But there's more. Anne-Marie and Genevieve. There's more to it than meets the eye. What is it, Jack?'

Carter sighed, went and opened the door. 'My dear Craig, you're overwrought. You've been through too much. Take the ground floor flat. Get yourself a decent night's sleep. You'll feel better in the morning.'

'You're a good man, Jack, a decent man. Just like Baum.' Craig shook his head. 'But that one upstairs worries me. He really does believe the end justifies the means.'

'Don't you?' Carter asked.

'No way, because if it does, it makes us just as bad as the people we're fighting. Night, Jack.'

He went upstairs and Carter immediately picked up the house phone by the door and rang Munro in his flat. 'Brigadier, I'd better see you. Craig Osbourne is on to something. The Baum business. Right, I'll come up.'

The door was slightly ajar. In the darkness of the passage above Craig had heard everything. Now, as Carter ascended the stairs, the American tiptoed to the front door and let himself out quietly.

It was raining hard and just after ten when Craig arrived back at the nursing home in Hampstead. He lurked at the other end of the street for a while under the shelter of sycamore trees, watching the gate. No point in trying that way. It made sense that Baum, frightened, would leave orders that he was not to be admitted.

He tried a lane at one side leading into a small mews of terraced cottages. There was a two-storeyed building at the end that looked like a workshop, an iron staircase going up one side. He went up quietly and stood on the platform at the top. The wall of the nursing home was no more than three feet away. It was ridiculously easy to climb over the rail, step across and drop down into the garden.

He moved cautiously towards the home, avoiding the front door. There were a couple of faint lights upstairs, but the ground floor was in darkness and then, when he moved round to the rear, light showed through a chink in the curtains of a room looking out over the terrace.

He went up the steps to the terrace and peered through the gap in the curtains. Inside was a book-lined study. Baum sat at a table, head in hands, a bottle of Scotch and a glass in front of him. Very gently, Craig tried the handle of the french window, but the catch was down. He thought about it for a moment and then knocked on the window smartly. Baum looked up in surprise.

Trying to sound as English as possible Craig called, 'Dr Baum. It's the gate guard.'

He stepped back and waited. A moment later the french window opened and Baum peered out. 'Johnson. Is that you?'

Craig moved in fast, had a hand round his throat in an instant and pushed him back into the room. Baum's eyes were starting from his head as Craig ran him across to the chair.

'What is it?' he demanded hoarsely when Craig released him. 'Are you crazy?'

'No.' Craig sat on the edge of the table and selected a cigarette. 'But I think a few crazy things have been happening around here so it's question and answer time for you and me.'

'I've nothing to say.' Baum quavered. 'You're mad. When the Brigadier hears about this it will mean your commission.'

'Fine,' Craig said. 'It'll leave me free to take up a more honest line of work.' He held up his left hand. 'See how crooked they are? The Gestapo did that in Paris. They broke each finger in turn and pulled out the nails with pinchers. They also tried the water torture where they dump you in a bath until you actually drown then they bring you back to life and start again. They booted me in the crotch so much I ended up with a nine-inch rupture.

'My God!' Baum whispered.

'Unfortunately He must have been busy elsewhere at the time. I'm an expert, Baum. I've been there. I stopped caring a long time ago.' Craig grabbed Baum by the chin and squeezed painfully. 'Genevieve Trevaunce is infinitely more important than you are, it's as simple as that. I'm willing to do whatever is necessary to make you talk, so why not go easy on yourself and just answer the questions like a good boy.'

Baum was utterly terrified now. 'Yes,' he gabbled. 'Anything.'

'You didn't escape from the Nazis. They held your daughter hostage and told you to claim political asylum, pretend she was dead and offer your services to British Intelligence.'

'Yes,' Baum moaned. 'It's true.'

'How did you communicate?'

'I had a contact at the Spanish Embassy. He sent out messages in the diplomatic pouch. Bomb damage, troop movements. That sort of thing. For emergencies there was another agent, a woman who lives in a village in Romney Marsh. She has a radio.'

'And it worked? You got away with it until the Jewish underground told you six months ago that your daughter really was dead?'

'That's right.' Baum mopped sweat from his face.

'So you went to Munro of your own accord and spilled the beans?'

'Yes.' Baum nodded. 'He ordered me to carry on as if nothing had happened. They even left the woman in Romney Marsh in place.'

'Her name?'

'Fitzgerald. Ruth Fitzgerald. She's a widow. Married to an Irish doctor, but originally a South African. Hates the English.'

Craig stood up and walked to the other side of the table. 'And Anne-Marie Trevaunce? What's the truth there?' Baum looked wildly from side to side and Craig picked up an old-fashioned mahogany ruler from the desk and turned. 'The fingers of your right hand for starters, Baum. One at a time. Very inconvenient.'

'For God's sake, it wasn't my fault,' Baum said. 'I just gave her the injection. I was doing what Munro told me.'

Craig went very still. 'And what injection would that be?'

'A kind of truth drug. A new idea they decided to try on every agent who came in from the field, just in case. You understand. Excellent when it works.'

'And for her it didn't?' Craig said grimly.

Baum's voice was almost a whisper. 'An unfortunate side effect. The damage to the brain is irreversible. The only good thing is that she could die at any time.'

'Is there more?'

'Yes,' Baum said wildly. 'I was ordered to blow the Trevaunce girls' cover.'

Craig stared at him. 'Munro told you to do that?'

'Yes, I passed a message to the Fitzgerald woman at Romney Marsh three nights ago to transmit on the radio, letting them know about Genevieve.' Behind Craig the door opened quietly, but Baum didn't see. 'He wants her caught, Major. I don't know why, but he wants them to take her.'

'Oh, dear me, what a loose tongue we have,' Dougal Munro said.

Craig turned and found the Brigadier standing there, hands in the pockets of his old cavalry coat. Jack Carter stood beside him, leaning on his stick, a Browning in the other hand.

'You bastard,' Craig said.

'A sacrificial lamb is required occasionally, dear boy. A bad fortune of war that on this occasion it has to be Genevieve Trevaunce.'

'But why?' Craig said. 'The Atlantic Wall conference. Rommel. Was it all lies?'

'Not at all, but you don't really think an amateur like our Genevieve would stand an earthly of getting hold of that information. No, Craig, Overlord is coming soon. D-Day and deception is the name of the game. It is essential that the Germans think we're invading where we're not. Patton is head of a non-existent army in East Anglia whose apparent task will be to invade the Pas de Calais area. Various other little projects will reinforce the suggestion.'

'So?' Craig said.

'And then I had a rather bright thought which was the real reason I sent for Anne-Marie. When Genevieve had to take over, we kept to the same plan. I allowed her to see, by accident, a plan on my desk at Cold Harbour. It was of the Pas de Calais area and it was headed Preliminary Targets – D-Day. The brilliance of that little stroke is that she doesn't appreciate the importance of that information. It will make it seem all the more genuine when they sweat it out of her which they will. She'll be all right for the time being, of course. This chap Priem will do nothing yet. Just to see what she gets up to. That's what I'd do. After all, she's nowhere to run.'

Craig said, 'You intended the same thing with Anne-Marie? You'd have sold her out too?'

Craig's face was terrible to see. He took a step towards him and Carter raised the Browning. 'Stay where you are, Craig.'

Craig said to Munro, 'You'd do anything, wouldn't you? You and the Gestapo have a lot in common.'

'We've a war on. Sacrifices are sometimes necessary. You assassinated General Dietrich the other week. You knew before you did it that it would cost innocent lives yet you went ahead. What was the body count? Twenty hostages shot?'

'To save even more lives,' Craig said.

'Exactly, dear boy, so why are we arguing.' Craig stood there, fists clenched and Munro sighed. 'Put him in the cellar, Jack. Lock him up tight and tell Arthur to take extra care. We'll have words in the morning.'

He turned and went out. Craig said, 'How do you like working for him now, Jack?'

Carter's face was troubled. 'Come on, old son, don't give me any fuss.'

Craig walked ahead of him and down the back stairs to the

basement. It was very quiet, no sound from Anne-Marie, but deaf Arthur in his white coat sat on his chair reading a book as if nothing had happened in between.

Carter stayed well away from Craig as they paused at another cell door. 'Inside, there's a good chap.' Craig did as he was told as Arthur stood up and came forward. Carter spoke full into the man's face so that he could lip-read. 'Keep an eye on the Major for me, Arthur. The Brigadier and I will be back in the morning. And take care, he's a dangerous man.'

Arthur, who was built like a brick wall, flexed his muscles. When he spoke his voice was strangely metallic. 'Aren't we all?' he said and turned the key in the door.

The grille was not one which closed and Craig looked out through the bars. 'Sleep well, if you can, Jack.'

'I'll do my best, old son.'

He started to turn away and Craig called, 'Jack, just one thing.'

'Yes.'

'René Dissard? Where did he fit in?'

'We told him Anne-Marie'd had a mental breakdown. The rape story was necessary to give Genevieve the right motivation. The Brigadier persuaded Dissard it was of vital importance that he go along with that story.'

'So even her old friend René let her down.'

'Goodnight, Craig.'

Carter's footsteps faded and Craig turned to inspect his quarters. There was an iron camp bed with a mattress and nothing else. No window, not even a bucket for the usual purposes and no blankets. The door's construction was of the strongest. No way out there.

He went and sat on the bed which sagged alarmingly. He pulled the mattress back and saw that the heavy coiled springs had rusted with age. It gave him an idea. He took a small penknife from the pocket of his tunic and started to work.

*

It was almost six o'clock in the morning when Anne-Marie started to scream. Craig, lying on the bed waiting for the hoped-for check-up from Arthur which had never come, got to his feet and went to the door, the heavy coil of bed spring swinging from his hand. When he peered through, he could just see Arthur's seat. It was empty. The terrible moaning continued. Five minutes passed and then he heard the sound of approaching footsteps. He glanced the other way and saw Arthur coming, an enamel mug in one hand.

Craig stuck a hand out. The man turned and looked at him. 'I need the lavatory,' Craig said. 'I haven't been all night.'

Arthur didn't reply, simply walked away. Craig's heart sank and then a few moments later, the man re-appeared, the key in one hand, an old Webley service revolver in the other.

'All right. Out you come and watch it,' he said in that strange voice. 'One wrong move and I'll break your right arm.'

'I wouldn't be such a fool,' Craig told him as they moved into the corridor then swung on one foot, the coil spring lashing across the hand holding the revolver. Arthur cried out, dropping the weapon and the coil spring arced, catching him across the side of the head. Craig grabbed for the man's right wrist, hoisted the arm up behind him in an unarmed combat hold and ran him head first into the cell. He slammed the door shut and turned the key. As he went along the corridor, Arthur started to shout and beyond him in the other cell Anne-Marie's voice rose to a crescendo, drowning him out. Craig closed the padded door at the end of the corridor, cutting off the sound and went upstairs.

But what to do now, that was the problem. The house was very quiet. He stood listening in the hall then slipped into Baum's study and closed the door gently. He sat behind the desk, picked up the phone and asked the operator to get him the Grancester Abbey number. It rang for quite some time at the other end before it was picked up and Julie answered, her voice full of sleep.

'It's Craig. Sorry if I got you out of bed, but it's urgent.'

'What is it?' she asked, suddenly alert.

'You are right about something being wrong only you couldn't imagine how wrong in your wildest dreams. Listen carefully . . .'

When he was finished she said, 'What are we going to do?'

'You spell it out to Martin Hare. Tell him I need a fast passage to France. I don't think he'll say no when he knows the facts. I'll be there as soon as I can.'

'How do you intend to come. Fly?'

'You know something, that's quite an idea. See you soon.'

He replaced the receiver, took out his wallet and found his SOE security card. He smiled softly. It always did pay to go in hard. Nothing to lose, anyway. He let himself out by the french window, slipped through the shrubbery to the wall, pulled himself on top and stepped across to the iron landing. A moment later, he was hurrying through the mews and turning into the main road. His luck was good. As he reached the next corner, a taxi driver, on the way to start his shift, spotted him and pulled in.

'Where to guvnor?' He grinned. 'I bet you've had a good night. Gawd, you Yanks.'

'Baker Street,' Craig told him and got in.

He was taking a chance now, gambling on the fact that his dispute with Munro was still private. He dismissed the cab, went up the steps to the entrance to SOE Headquarters in Baker Street, produced his pass and was checked through by security. The place was already busy, but then, like the Windmill Theatre, they never closed. He went up the back stairs two at a time and entered the Transport Office. His luck was still good. The night duty officer, still on till eight, was a retired infantry Major named Wallace, brought back for the war. Craig had known him since his early days with SOE.

'Hello, Osbourne,' Wallace said in surprise. 'What brings you out so bright and early?'

'Big flap on. Munro wants to go down to Cold Harbour. I'm meeting him at Croydon. Give me the usual authorisation for the RAF then phone through to Croydon to tell them to expect us. We'll need the Lysander.'

'We're trying to win the war in a hurry again, are we?' Wallace opened a file, took out the appropriate document and filled it in.

'Frankly, I think he might be more interested in the fishing.' Craig sat on the edge of the desk calmly and smoked a cigarette. 'Oh, you'd better give me a chit for the motor pool.'

'Anything to oblige.'

Wallace handed him the documents. Craig said, 'Marvellous. I'd better get moving then and you'll phone Croydon?'

'Of course,' Wallace said patiently and reached for the phone as Craig went out.

It was raining steadily at Croydon, but visibility was good as Craig, in the passenger seat of the jeep, was passed through the main gate. They drove straight to the usual departure point where the Lysander already waited, a couple of mechanics standing beside it. Craig dismissed his driver and went into the Nissen hut where he found Grant in his flying clothes having a cup of tea with the orderly officer.

Grant said, 'Hello, old son, thought I was getting the day off. Where's the Brigadier?'

'Change of plan.' Craig told him. 'He's going to come down later. There's your authorisation.'

He passed it across and the orderly officer checked it. 'Fine. All in order.'

'All right, old boy, might as well get going,' Grant said and he and Craig went out and ran together through the rain to the Lysander.

It was nine-thirty, Arthur having been missed for his breakfast in the kitchen, when Baum went downstairs to see what was going on. He panicked then, sat in his study sweating with fear. It was ten o'clock before he plucked up courage and phoned through to the flat in Haston Place.

Munro had worked for most of the night, catching up on paper, was having a late breakfast when Carter joined him. The Captain stood looking out of the window, a cup of tea in his hand.

'What do you intend to do about Craig Osbourne, sir?'

'If the young fool won't see sense, I'll lock him up for the duration,' Munro said calmly as he buttered his toast. 'You don't like it, do you, Jack?'

'It's a dirty business, sir.'

The phone rang. 'Get that,' the Brigadier said.

Carter picked it up, listened, then held the phone to his chest, the slightest trace of a smile on his face. 'Baum, sir. It would appear our Craig was more than a match for Arthur. He's on the loose.'

'Dear God, that boy's worse than Houdini.'

'What do we do, sir?'

Munro flung down his napkin. 'Just tell Baum I'll handle it.' Carter did as he was told and Munro got up. 'One thing is clear. We can't have a fuss. That would never do.'

'No, sir.'

'Get the car, Jack. I'll change and we'll go round to Baker Street.'

*

The canteen at Baker Street served an excellent breakfast, Wallace was still in the building and going down the stairs as Munro and Carter were coming up.

'Morning, sir,' he said. 'Change of plans?'

'What on earth are you talking about?' Munro demanded.

So Wallace told him.

Joe Edge stood outside the hangar at Cold Harbour and watched the Lysander lift off into the fog that was rolling in from the sea as Grant began the return journey to Croydon. The telephone started to ring in the small glass office in the hangar.

Edge called to the mechanics, 'I'll get it,' went in and lifted the receiver. 'Yes?'

'Is that you, Edge? Munro here.'

'Yes, Brigadier.'

'Any sign of Osbourne?'

'Yes, sir, landed half an hour ago. Grant's just taken off on the return leg to Croydon.'

'Where's Osbourne now?'

Edge scented trouble, said eagerly, 'Hare picked him up in one of the jeeps. Julie was with him. They went down to the pub.'

'Now listen carefully, Edge,' Munro said. 'I think Osbourne may have some wild idea of persuading Hare to make an unauthorised trip to France. You must prevent that.'

'How, sir?'

'Good God, man, any way you know how. Use your initiative. As soon as Grant's back and refuelled, we'll be down there.'

He rang off. Edge replaced the receiver, a smile on his face, not a nice smile, then he opened a drawer, took out his Luftwaffe issue belt and holster with the Walther inside. He went out quickly, got into his jeep and drove down through the village stopping some fifty yards from the pub. He went into the back yard and peered through the kitchen window. It was empty. He opened the door quietly and went in.

The crew of the *Lili Marlene* leaned against the bar listening to what Hare was saying.

'You've heard the facts. All you need to know. Miss Trevaunce is in about as bad a spot as she could be, and it's all Munro's doing. Now the Major and I intend to do something about that, but I've no authorisation. If any man here feels he can't come, say so now. I won't hold it against you.'

'For God's sake, guvnor, what are we wasting time for?' Schmidt said. 'We've got to get ready.'

'He's right, Herr Kapitän,' Langsdorff said stolidly. 'If we leave at noon, we'll be at Grosnez by six if you should wish to use the pier again.'

Craig and Julie sat behind the bar, watching. In the kitchen, Edge could hear everything clearly.

Hare said, 'A daylight crossing. That's always hazardous.'

'We've done it before,' Langsdorff reminded him.

Schmidt grinned. 'To the gallant lads of the Kriegsmarine, anything is possible.'

Hare turned to Craig. 'There you go then.'

Craig said, 'I'll take Julie up to the house. I need some things from costume and she can arrange a radio message to Grand Pierre.'

Edge was already out of the back and running to his jeep. He got behind the wheel and drove away quickly as the crew emerged from The Hanged Man.

As Craig and Julie got into the other jeep Hare smiled wryly. 'Oh well, there goes my career.'

'What career?' Craig asked with a grin and drove away.

*

From Julie's costume store, he selected the black dress uniform of a Standartenführer in the Charlemagne Brigade of the Waffen-SS.

Julie came in. 'There's the SS identity card you wanted. I've made it out to Henri Legrande. Just for luck.'

Craig folded the uniform. 'I prefer the black when the going gets rough,' he told her. 'It always puts the fear of God into everyone.'

'What shall I say to Grand Pierre?'

'He must be at the pier at Grosnez by six and he must provide me with the right kind of military transport. A Kubelwagen – something like that.'

'All right. I'll take care of it.'

Craig smiled at her. 'You realise Munro will have you shot or something when he gets here.'

'To hell with Munro.'

The door creaked and as they turned, Edge appeared, the Walther at the ready. 'Actually, old son, you aren't going anywhere. I've just had Brigadier Munro on the phone and he gave me strict orders to hang on to you.'

'Is that a fact?' Craig said and swung the SS tunic on his hand, smothering the Walther. He smashed Edge's arm against the wall so that he dropped the weapon and at the same time punched him very hard on the side of the jaw.

The pilot doubled over, Craig got him by the collar and dragged him across to the big work table. 'Pass me a pair of those handcuffs, Julie.' She did so and he handcuffed Edge's arms around one of the legs. 'Leave him there until Munro and Jack Carter get here.'

She leaned up and kissed him. 'Take care, Craig.'

'Don't I always?'

He went out then, the door slammed and a moment later she heard the jeep start up. She sighed, left Edge where he was and went off to the Communication Room.

It was half an hour later that she went out to the end of the garden from where she could see all the way down to the village. Fog rolled in from the sea. It was going to be a dirty crossing. As she watched, the *Lili Marlene* left harbour, the scarlet and black Kriegsmarine ensign on her jackstaff, vivid as she was swallowed by the mist like a ghost.

Fourteen

As the *Lili Marlene* left Cold Harbour, Field Marshal Erwin Rommel was arriving at Château de Voincourt and Genevieve waited at the top of the steps to welcome him with her aunt and Ziemke and his staff, Max Priem among them.

The convoy was surprisingly small considering the importance of the visitor. Three cars and four military policemen on motor cycles. Rommel was in an open Mercedes, a short, stocky man in leather greatcoat, a white scarf loosely knotted at his neck, the famous desert goggles he affected, pushed up above the peak of his cap. Genevieve watched him salute and shake hands with General Ziemke and Seilheimer, the SS Brigadier, and then Ziemke introduced her aunt. A moment later it was Genevieve's turn.

His French was excellent. 'An honour, Mademoiselle.' He looked straight into her eyes as if sizing her up and she was conscious of the power, the enormous drive. He inclined his head, raised her hand to his lips.

They moved into the hall. Hortense said to Ziemke, 'We'll leave you now, General. You have important matters to discuss, I don't doubt. Field Marshal – we meet again this evening, I believe?'

'I look forward to it, Countess.' Rommel saluted courteously.

As they went up the stairs, Genevieve said, 'In 1942, certain sections of the great British public were asked to name their choice as the most outstanding General around. Most of them chose our friend down there.'

'Now you know why,' Hortense said. 'I want to talk to you, but not inside. The old summerhouse in fifteen minutes.'

She went to her room. When Genevieve opened her door, Maresa was just finishing making the bed. 'I'm going for a walk,' Genevieve said. 'Find me something warm to wear. There's a nip in the air.'

Maresa went to the wardrobe and produced a hunting jacket with a fur collar. 'Will this do, Mamselle?'

'I think so.' The girl was very pale, her eyes sunk into their sockets a little. Genevieve said, 'You don't look well. Are you all right?'

'Oh, Mamselle, I'm so frightened.'

'So am I,' Genevieve told her, 'but I will do what I have to and so will you.'

She held her firmly by the shoulders for a moment. Maresa nodded wearily. 'Yes, Mamselle.'

'Good,' Genevieve said. 'You can lay out the white evening dress. I'll wear that tonight.'

She left her there, looking thoroughly miserable, and went out.

It was pleasant in the garden with a hint of spring in the air, green grass under the trees, the sun filtering through in odd patterns, turning the leaves to gold. An unexpected moment of peace. She went through an archway in the grey stone wall and found Hortense sitting on the edge of the fountain, the white summerhouse behind her. There was green moss on its walls, a couple of windows were broken.

'I used to be happy here,' Genevieve said. 'When we were very small you would give us tea in the summerhouse.'

'Everything passes.'

'I know. It's very sad.'

'Give me a cigarette,' Hortense said. 'I think I prefer it in decay. That moss, for instance. Dark green on white. It creates an atmosphere that wasn't here before. A sense of things lost.'

'Philosophy in your old age?'

There was a gleam of amusement in her aunt's eyes. 'Stop me if it happens again.' One of the prowler guards passed a few yards away, a machine pistol slung from his shoulder, an Alsatian straining on a steel chain. 'You heard what happened last night?'

'I saw it.'

'A bad business. Philippe Gamelin from the village. He's been poaching the estate for years. I asked Ziemke to go easy on him, but he insists they must make an example in the interests of future security.'

'What will they do to him?'

'Oh, he'll be sentenced to some labour camp, I suppose.' She shivered in distaste. 'Life becomes daily more unpleasant. I wish to God the Allies would hurry up and make this landing we've all been promised for so long. Still – what about tonight? You know exactly what you are about?'

'I think so.'

'Not think, child. You must know.' Hortense shaded her eyes and looked up to the front of the house and the Rose Room. 'From your balcony to the terrace is what? Twenty feet? You are certain you can manage it?'

'Since I was ten years of age,' Genevieve assured her. 'And in the dark. The brickwork beside the pillar stands out like the steps in a ladder.'

'Very well. The ball is supposed to commence at seven. They don't want to be too late as Rommel is driving to Paris overnight. I shall come down just before eight. I suggest you slip away to your room as soon after that as you can.'

'Maresa has arranged to meet Eric here in the summerhouse at eight.'

'Well, whatever her charms, I wouldn't count on her holding him for more than twenty minutes,' Hortense said. 'Chantal will be waiting in your room to give you any assistance you need.'

'If everything works, I should be in the library, take my pictures and out again inside ten minutes,' Genevieve said. 'Back downstairs at the ball by eight-thirty, the safe locked behind me and nothing missing and no one will know a thing about it.'

'Except us,' Hortense said with a cold smile, 'and that, my love, I find eminently satisfying.'

It was just before six, the light fading as the *Lili Marlene* sailed boldly in towards the deserted pier at Grosnez. There was a slight mist, but the sea was calm and the Kriegsmarine ensign hung limply from the jackstaff. Langsdorff was at the wheel and Hare checked the shore with glasses.

'Yes, there they are.' He laughed softly. 'Now there's cheek for you. He's brought two vehicles. Looks like a Kubelwagen and a black sedan and they're in uniform.'

He passed the glasses to Craig who focused them on the pier. There were three men in German Army uniforms standing by the Kubelwagen. Grand Pierre leaned against it, smoking a cigarette.

'He's got style, this one, you have to admit that,' Craig said. 'I'd better go below and change.'

He left the wheelhouse and Hare said to Langsdorff, 'Dead slow.'

He went down to the deck where the crew were already at battle stations, all guns manned, and went below. When he went into the tiny cabin, Craig was buttoning the tunic of the Waffen-SS uniform.

Hare lit a cigarette. 'You feel okay about this?'

Craig said, 'In all those books I read in my teens, the hero always went back for the girl. It kind of programmed my thinking. Doesn't really leave me with much choice.' He was ready now, a belted Walther at his waist, the silver SS buckle gleaming. He put on his cap. 'Will I do?'

'Who in the hell from a military policeman on the road to a gate guard is going to query you in uniform like that?' Hare said and led the way out.

As they coasted in to the lower jetty, Grand Pierre came down the steps to meet them, as disreputable as usual. He smiled, 'Good heavens, takes me back to costume parties when I was at Oxford. You do look dashing, Osbourne.'

'I want to make one thing clear,' Craig said. 'This one's a private affair. We've come for the girl on our own initiative.'

'Save it, old son. Julie Legrande managed to put me in the picture. To be honest, my people weren't too keen to get involved. I mean, the life of one young woman, British agent or otherwise, is of little importance to them. They're used to a rather high body count that includes their own families on occasion. Still I do have certain powers of persuasion. I've got you a rather nice Mercedes and a Kubelwagen with three of my lads in uniform to escort you. Nice touch that. They'll peel off when you get to the Château.'

Craig said, 'You're going to hang around?'

'Why, yes, up there in the woods with some of my rascals. Does the boat stay?'

Hare turned to Langsdorff. 'Some sort of engine repair, I think?'

Langsdorff nodded. 'Dark soon, anyway, Herr Kapitän.'

'God knows when we'll get back,' Craig said.

'We'll be here.' Hare smiled.

The crew waited silently. Craig gave them a punctilious salute. 'Men,' he said in English. 'It's been an honour to serve with you.'

Those on deck sprang to attention. Only Schmidt replied. 'Good luck, guvnor. Walk all over the bastards.'

They went up the steps to the upper level and approached the cars. Grand Pierre said in French to the three in German Army uniform, 'Right, you rogues, look after him. If you cock it up, don't come back.'

They grinned and got in the Kubelwagen. Craig slid behind the wheel of the Mercedes.

Grand Pierre said, 'Take care now. Off you go. It's a ball they're having tonight, by the way. Sounds fun. Wish I could join you, but I don't have my dinner jacket with me.'

The Kubelwagen moved away and Craig switched on the ignition of the Mercedes and followed, Grand Pierre growing smaller in the driving mirror, disappearing altogether as he started up the hill.

The dress was really beautiful, some sort of white silk jersey material that was more than flattering. Maresa helped Genevieve into it then placed a towel round her shoulders as she sat down to finish making-up.

'Have you seen René today?' Genevieve asked her casually.

'I don't think so, Mamselle. He wasn't in the servants' hall for his evening meal. Shall I send someone to look for him?'

'No, it's not important. You've got enough to think about. You know what you have to do? You're sure?'

'Meet Eric in the summerhouse at nine and keep him there as long as I can.'

'Which means at least twenty minutes,' Genevieve said. 'Anything less is no good.' She patted the girl's cheek. 'Don't look so worried, Maresa. A joke we're playing on the General, that's all.'

The girl didn't believe it, Genevieve could see, not that it mattered. She picked up her evening bag, smiled reassuringly and went out.

*

The ball was being held in the Long Gallery and they had really made an effort, there was no doubt about that. When Genevieve went in, everyone seemed to be there already. The chandeliers gleamed, there were flowers and a small orchestra played a Strauss waltz. There was no sign of Rommel, but General Ziemke was standing with Seilheimer and his wife. When he saw Genevieve, he excused himself and crossed the floor, the dancers moving out of his way.

'Your aunt?' he said anxiously. 'She is coming down? There is nothing wrong?'

'Not as far as I know. What about the Field Marshal?'

'He was here a moment ago, but was called away for a phone call from Berlin. The Führer himself, apparently.' He wiped sweat from his forehead with a handkerchief. 'We have many people here that you know. The Comboults for instance.'

There they were on the opposite side of the room. Maurice Comboult, Papa Comboult to his workers, with his wife and daughter. Five vineyards, two canning factories and another manufacturing agricultural machinery. The richest man in the district, growing even richer out of collaborating with the Germans. Genevieve barely swallowed her anger.

Field Marshal Rommel appeared in the doorway, Priem beside him and Ziemke said, 'Excuse me for a moment.'

The young Lieutenant of the night before, the one who was such an excellent dancer, approached, and asked her for the next waltz. He was as good as ever and when the music stopped, offered to fetch her a glass of champagne.

She stood by a pillar, waiting for Hortense to appear and Priem said from behind, 'I would not have thought any improvement possible, but you look especially beautiful tonight.'

'That's nice,' she said and found that she meant it.

The band began to play another waltz, he took her in his arms without a word and they started to dance. Behind him, she could see her Lieutenant watching reproachfully, a glass of champagne in each hand.

The music seemed to go on for ever and there was an air of total unreality to everything, sounds muted as if under water. There was just the two of them, the rest clockwork figures only. The waltz came to an end finally, there was some sporadic clapping. No sign of Rommel now, but Ziemke was there and beckoned to Priem who excused himself and left.

It was at that moment that Hortense chose to make her entrance. Her face was like sculptured marble, her beautiful red-gold hair piled high on her head. Her gown of midnight blue velvet swept the floor, a perfect contrast to that live hair and those liquid eyes.

Conversation died as people turned to look and Ziemke hurried along the length of the gallery to meet her, bowing over her hand. Then he gave her his arm and escorted her to the far end where a group of Louis Quatorze chairs had been strategically placed.

Genevieve glanced at her watch. It was exactly five minutes to eight and as the orchestra struck up again, she moved back through the crowd, opened the door to the music room, and slipped inside.

She had intended it as a short cut to the hall and instead, received the shock of her life for Field Marshal Erwin Rommel was seated in a chair by the piano smoking a cigar.

'Ah, it is you, Mademoiselle.' He stood up. 'Had enough already?'

'A headache only,' she said, her heart pounding and unthinkingly ran a hand across the piano keys.

'Ah, you play, how charming,' Rommel said.

'Only a little.'

She sat down, because it seemed the natural thing to do and started to play 'Claire de Lune'. It made her think of Craig, that evening at Cold Harbour. Rommel leaned back in the chair, a look of intense pleasure on his face.

It was fate that saved her, for suddenly the door opened and Max Priem appeared. 'Oh, there you are, sir. The telephone again, I'm afraid, Paris this time.'

'You see, Mamselle? They will not leave me in peace.' Rommel smiled charmingly. 'Later, perhaps, we may continue?'

'Of course,' Genevieve told him.

He went out. Priem smiled briefly at her and went after him. She hurried across to the other door, let herself out into the hall and went up the great stairway quickly.

Chantal was waiting when she entered the bedroom, black sweater and a pair of dark slacks laid out on the bed. 'You're late,' she scolded.

'Never mind that now. Just get me out of this dress.'

She got the zip down, that magnificent white creation slipped to the floor and Genevieve stepped into the slacks and pulled the sweater over her head. She slipped the silver and onyx cigarette case into one pocket with the key, a torch in the other, and turned.

'Into battle, then.'

Chantal kissed her roughly on the cheek. 'Go on, be off with you and get it done, Genevieve Trevaunce.'

Genevieve stared at her. 'How long have you known?'

'I'm a fool, is that what you and the Countess think? Silly, stupid old Chantal? I was changing your nappies before you were a year old, my girl. You think I can't tell the difference between you and her by now?'

But there was no time for this, of course. Genevieve smiled, slipped out through the curtains to the darkness of the balcony. It seemed very quiet standing there, the sound of the music far away. She was twelve years old again and sneaking out by night with Anne-Marie to go riding in the dark because she'd dared her to. She climbed over the balcony, got a firm hold on the brickwork and descended quickly.

*

216

When she peered round the corner, the terrace lay quiet and deserted. She moved silently along to the third french window, placed a hand on the centre where the doors met and pushed. There was a certain amount of resistance, there always had been, but it gave in the end and parted the curtains.

The library was quite dark, the sound of music a little louder here. She switched on her torch and found the portrait of Elizabeth, the eleventh Countess de Voincourt. She stared down at her coldly, remarkably like Hortense. Genevieve swung the portrait back on its hinges revealing the safe behind. The key turned smoothly in the lock, the door swung open.

It was stuffed with papers as she might have expected. Her heart sank as she gave way to genuine panic and then she saw the leather briefcase with the single inscription *Rommel* stamped on the flap in gold leaf.

She opened it quickly, hands shaking. It contained only a single folder and when she opened that, the photos of gun emplacements and beach defences alone told her that she had found what she had come for.

She put the briefcase back in the safe for the moment, laid the folder on Priem's desk and switched on the desk lamp. Then she took out her cigarette case. In the same moment she heard Priem's voice quite distinctly outside the door.

She had never moved faster in her life. She got the safe door closed although there was no time to lock it, pushing the painting back into position. Then she switched off the desk lamp and picked up her torch and the folder.

As the key started to turn in the lock she was already on her way, slipping through the curtains and pulling the windows together as the door opened and the light was switched on. She peered in through a crack in the curtains and saw Priem enter the room.

She stood there in the darkness of the terrace, thinking

about it, but by then she simply didn't have any other choice. She slipped round the corner and climbed back up to her balcony.

Chantal drew the curtains together behind her. 'What's happened?' she demanded. 'Did something go wrong?'

'Priem turned up. Almost caught me in the act. It means I haven't had a chance to take my pictures. I'll see to that now.'

She laid the file down on her dressing table and brought the bedside lamp across for extra light.

'Then what will you do?'

'Go down again. Hope that he's gone back to the ball so I can return this before it's missed.'

'And Eric?'

'We'll just have to put all our faith in Maresa's powers of persuasion.'

She picked up the silver case, opened the flap and started to take pictures, exactly as Craig Osbourne had shown her, Chantal turning the pages. Twenty exposures, that's what he had told her and there were more pages than that. Still, it would have to do.

As she finished, there was a knock at the door. They froze. Chantal whispered, 'I locked it.'

The knock came again, the door knob rattled. Genevieve knew she had to answer. 'Who is it?' she called.

There was no reply. She pushed Chantel towards the bathroom. 'Get in there and stay quiet.'

She did as she was told. Genevieve slipped the Rommel file into the nearest drawer and turned to reach for her dressing gown. A key rattled in the lock, pushing the one on the inside out, the door opened and Max Priem walked in.

*

He sat on the edge of the table swinging one leg, regarding her gravely, then held out his hand. 'Give it to me.'

'What on earth are you talking about?'

'The file you have just taken from Field Marshal Rommel's briefcase. I can have the room searched, but it has to be you. There is no one else. Add to that your interesting change in dress . . .'

'All right!' she cut in on him sharply, opened the drawer and took out the file.

He placed it on the table beside him. 'I'm sorry it worked out this way.'

'Then you really are in the wrong business.' She picked up her cigarette case and selected a Gitane.

'I didn't choose it, but one thing we'd better get straight from now on, *Miss* Trevaunce. I know who you are.'

She took a deep lungful of smoke to steady herself. 'I don't follow you.'

'It's in the eyes, Genevieve,' he said softly. 'You can never get away from that. Exactly the same colour as hers and yet the light inside, totally different. Like everything else about you two, the same and yet not the same at all.'

She could not think of a single thing worth saying, stood there waiting for the axe to fall.

'They taught you everything about her,' he said. 'Is this not so? Provided our friend Dissard as guide and mentor and in the end, left out one essential fact – the most important of all. The one that told me from the first that you could not be Anne-Marie Trevaunce.'

In spite of herself, caught now, Genevieve asked entirely the wrong question. 'And what would that be?'

'Why, that she was working for me,' he said simply.

She sat down, curiously calm considering the circumstances, perfectly in control, or so she told herself. He parted the curtains and rain tapped against the window with ghostly fingers as if Anne-Marie was out there trying to get in. He continued to speak without turning around.

'Another thing which hardly helped your case was that I was tipped off about your true identity even before you got here by one of our agents in London, a mole we've had working for SOE for some considerable time.'

She was truly shocked. 'I don't believe you.'

'True, I assure you, but we'll come to that later. Let's talk about your sister.' He turned. 'When we first set up house here, we knew we would attract more than a little attention, so I decided to provide London with an agent and who more suitable than Anne-Marie Trevaunce?'

'Who in exchange could continue to live in the manner to which she was accustomed, is that what you're trying to say?'

He closed the curtains and turned. 'Not quite. She was never cheap, whatever else she was.'

'What then?'

He didn't answer, simply carried on in that calm voice. 'She gave the people at SOE enough information to keep everyone happy, most of it relatively unimportant, of course. She used a man we knew perfectly well was Resistance and we let him alone. I even allowed her to draw in Dissard to complete the picture. Then London found out about a rather important conference and took an unprecedented step. They sent for her and I said she must go.'

'And she always did what you told her?'

'But of course. We had Hortense, you see. Anne-Marie's one weakness, her only link with you, I think, is this love for her aunt.' Genevieve stared at him blankly. 'Her only reason from the beginning, don't you see that?' He shook his head. 'I don't think you ever knew her at all, this sister of yours.'

The rain tapped more insistently than ever. Genevieve sat there, unable to speak, so great was her emotion.

'Knowing you were playing games with me, it seemed prudent to have words with Dissard.'

'René?' she whispered.

'Yes, the message that took him away so urgently. I arranged that. When he reached his destination, Reichslinger and his men were waiting.'

'Where is he now? What have you done with him?'

'He shot himself,' Priem said, 'very quickly, in the head before they could disarm him. To protect you, I should imagine. He must have known he wouldn't last long in Reichslinger's hands. Every man has his breaking point, sooner or later. Not that it mattered. Our man in London had provided all the necessary information. Our mole at SOE. A certain Dr Baum who I think you know. The only problem with that was that I've known for some time he was working for the other side. I have a more reliable source in London, you see.'

'You're lying,' Genevieve said.

'Your sister is at this very moment in the cellar of a house at 101 Raglan Lane in Hampstead. She is, I am given to understand, quite mad, but then, you are aware of this?'

Her reply came boiling out of her, instinctive, hot with rage. 'And you swine made her like that. Your own agent and yet it was an SS patrol that picked her up. They ruined her, those animals. Did you know that?'

'Not true,' he said and there was something close to pity in his eyes now. 'It was your own people – no one else.'

The room was very quiet and she was horribly frightened. 'What do you mean?' she whispered. 'What are you trying to say?'

'My poor Genevieve,' he said. 'I think you'd better listen to me.'

What he told her, although she did not know it, was substantially what Baum had told Craig Osbourne. The truth, the real truth about her sister, the good doctor, Rosedene Nursing Home and Munro.

When he was finished, she sat there gripping the arms of her chair for a while then she reached for the cigarette case and got a Gitane. Surprising how much the damn things helped. She went to the french windows, opened them and looked out at the rain. Priem followed her.

She turned to face him. 'Why should I believe you? How could you know all this?'

'The British operate double agents and so do we. A game we play. As I've said, when the Jewish underground told Baum his daughter was dead, he went to Munro. To make his dealings normal with us meant they couldn't afford to pull in Mrs Fitzgerald, his contact. She also was given a choice. To work as a double or face execution in your Tower of London. Naturally she chose the sensible course or appeared to.'

'Appeared to?'

'Mrs Fitzgerald is Dutch South African and does not like the English. Her dead husband was an Irishman who disliked them even more and served with the IRA under Michael Collins in 1921. She had done what Munro wanted, yes, but what the good Brigadier did not realise was that she has contacts with the IRA in London and they are more than sympathetic to us. She warned us, through them, of Baum's defection months ago which means we've been very well aware that he works totally for the other side now. He tells us only what they want us to know, which means, in this case, that they wanted us to know about you. Any information he didn't tell us, Mrs Fitzgerald passed on to our IRA friends.'

'What nonsense,' Genevieve said and yet, with some horror, saw the terrible truth.

'What was the purpose of your mission? Field Marshal Rommel's conference? Plans for the Atlantic Wall?' He shook his head. 'It couldn't have been. They sent you here to be betrayed by Baum whose word they still think we believe.'

'But why would they do that?'

'The Reichslingers of this world can be very persuasive. They expected you to break, your people. Wanted you to. They've told you something, let something slip, something you can't even remember yourself for the moment. Something that would apparently be of supreme importance.'

She remembered Craig Osbourne on the *Lili Marlene*, felt again the grip of his hand on hers and struggled wildly not to believe and then she recalled Munro in his study at Cold Harbour, the map on the desk that he had so quickly put away after allowing her to glimpse the D-Day landing areas.

Priem had been watching her intently. Now, he smiled. 'You've got it, I see?'

She nodded, suddenly very tired. 'Yes, would you like to know?'

'Would you tell me?'

'I'd try not to, just in case I'm wrong. You've proved very effectively that there are people on my side as rotten and unscrupulous as you are, but I'd still rather see my side win. There are some very nice people where I come from and I'd hate to see the SS in St Martin.'

'Good,' he said. 'Exactly what I would have expected of you.'

She took a deep breath. 'What happens now?'

'You will change back into your gown and return to the ball.'

She was beginning to feel just a little light-headed by then. 'You can't be serious?'

'Oh, but I am. Field Marshal Rommel will leave with his escort in one hour. He drives to Paris overnight. You will be among those who will smile and wish him well. You will exchange a few words. All good stuff for the photographers. He will drive safely away into the night and you, my dear Genevieve, will continue dancing.'

'The life and soul of the party?'

'But of course. It could be argued that you might seize some chance, however slight, to slip away, but that would mean leaving the Countess in our hands, which would be unfortunate. You follow my thinking?'

'Completely.'

'Perfect trust between us then.' He kissed her hand. 'I've fallen in love with you a little I think. Just a little. You were never her, Genevieve. Always yourself alone.'

'You'll get over it.'

'Of course.' He paused, a hand on the ornate handle of the door. 'One gets over everything in time. But this, you will discover for yourself.'

He started to open the door. Genevieve said, 'You really thought you knew her, didn't you?'

He turned, slightly surprised. 'Anne-Marie? As well as anyone, I think.'

Her anger was so great now that she could not contain herself. 'Does the name Grand Pierre mean anything to you?'

He went very still. 'Why do you ask?'

'A very important Resistance leader, am I right? I'm sure you'd give a great deal to get your hands on him. Would it surprise you to know that my sister actually had dealings with him?'

His face was quite pale now. 'Yes, to be perfectly frank, it would.'

'You failed to catch General Dietrich's assassin. You know why?'

'No, but I have a feeling you are about to tell me.'

'Anne-Marie spirited him away from under the noses of your precious SS hidden under the rear seat of her Rolls-Royce.' She smiled fiercely, enjoying her small triumph. 'So you see, Colonel Priem, she was never completely what you thought she was at all.'

He looked at her for a long moment, turned and went out, closing the door softly. She took a deep breath, hurried across to the bathroom door and said, 'Stay in there until I've gone.'

'All right,' Chantal whispered.

The rain drifted against the window and she stood there, listening. So, this was how the world ended, just like the poet said. No great bang. There was, as Priem had pointed out, Hortense to consider. Out of her hands now, all of it, and no way out. Worst of all, no desire. In the end, the greatest irony of all was that with the gloves off, Max Priem was Craig Osbourne and Craig Osbourne was Max Priem.

So . . . she took a deep breath and started to dress.

Fifteen

She drifted down the great stairs on Priem's arm as if in a dream. He nodded pleasantly to an officer who passed them. She laughed out loud in spite of herself and Priem turned in surprise, his hand tightening on her arm. 'Are you all right?'

'Never better.'

'Good.' They crossed the hall and paused at the door. 'Prepare to make your entrance now – and smile, always that. People expect it of you.'

An orderly opened the door and they passed inside. For the moment, the orchestra had stopped playing, but there was laughter and raised voices, a general air of well-being, pretty women and uniforms everywhere reflected in the great mirrors in the walls.

Hortense was sitting in one of the gold chairs on the opposite side of the room, an infantry Colonel leaning attentively over her. She was laughing at something he'd just said and then her eyes met Genevieve's. There was a pause, only fractionally, and then she smiled brightly again and looked up at her Colonel.

'May I speak to my aunt?' Genevieve asked Priem.

'Certainly. It will be to everyone's advantage, after all, that she should know the state of the game. I'm sure that you would not attempt to deny that she knows the difference between Anne-Marie and Genevieve.'

Genevieve walked unhurriedly through the crowd. As she arrived, Hortense smiled, raised her cheek for her to kiss. 'Having a nice time, *chérie*?'

'But of course,' Genevieve perched on the arm of the gold chair.

Hortense handed her empty glass to the Colonel. 'Would you mind, and do try to get them to make it just a little drier this time.' He clicked his heels obediently and moved away. She selected a cigarette from her niece's case and said casually as Genevieve flicked her lighter. 'Something's wrong. I can see it in your eyes. What happened?'

'Priem arrived at the wrong moment. He knows everything.'

Hortense smiled gaily, waving to someone on the other side of the room. 'That you are not Anne-Marie?'

Genevieve was aware of the Colonel, a glass in each hand, on his way back across the floor. She said softly, the smile fixed firmly on her face, 'I was sent here by Munro to be betrayed. The purpose of the exercise. I've just learned that from Priem. A rotten business from the beginning. René is dead, by the way.'

That got through to Hortense as nothing else had, wiping the smile away instantly. Genevieve gripped her hand. 'Hang on, my love, very tightly. It's going to be a long, long night.'

The Colonel was beside them, gallantly offering her her drink. Genevieve patted her aunt's cheek. 'Now behave yourself,' she told her, laughing and turned away.

She reached automatically for a glass of champagne from a tray carried by a passing waiter and almost immediately, it was taken from her and placed on one of the small marble tables.

'No, I don't think so, Genevieve,' Priem said. 'A clear head is what you need tonight.'

She didn't bother to turn, simply confronted him in the mirror. He really did look very handsome, immaculate as always, decorations gleaming, the Knight's Cross at his throat.

He was waiting for some kind of response, a quiet, grave smile on his face. There was an intimacy between them again and that wasn't right at all.

'So, no indulgences?' she asked.

The music started again at that moment, a waltz, and he inclined his head, bowing slightly. 'A turn around the floor, perhaps?'

'Why not?'

He held her lightly as they circled. She remembered to smile at the General as they passed, noticed Field Marshal Rommel talking politely with her aunt and above, from the shadows, the portraits of long forgotten, obscure ancestors peered down.

'Strauss,' she said. 'A far cry from Al Bowlly. Were you playing with me or warning me – or did you just like the song?'

'And now, we are on dangerous ground,' he said gravely. 'For both of us, I think.'

'If you say so.'

'But I do, so for the moment, we will stick to the essentials. At the end of the evening, when the Field Marshal has departed, you will be escorted to your rooms, you and your aunt, as normal. The only essential difference will be that I will post a guard outside your doors.'

'Naturally.'

Out of the corner of her eye she seemed to catch sight of a shadowy figure on the fringe of things like an elusive memory that wouldn't go away, the tilt of a head as someone lit a cigarette that was somehow horribly familiar. But that was impossible – totally impossible.

She saw him clearly now, leaning against the wall, a haze of smoke around his head, cigarette in hand. He smiled delightedly as if seeing her for the first time, then started across the dance floor. Craig Osbourne, immaculate in the black dress uniform of a Colonel in the French Charlemagne Brigade of the Waffen-SS.

*

Which didn't make any kind of sense for if what Max Priem had told her was true, there was no reason on this earth why Craig Osbourne should be here like this. They stopped dancing as he arrived, Priem frowning slightly.

'Anne-Marie, how marvellous. I hoped you might be here.' His French was perfect. 'This really is quite delightful.' He turned to Priem. 'You will excuse me, if I cut in. Mademoiselle Trevaunce and I are old friends.' He took her hand and kissed it lightly. 'July of '39. The long hot summer a thousand years ago.'

Priem's expression had changed to one of sardonic amusement and she realised he must imagine her truly caught now, playing Anne-Marie with an old friend whose name she couldn't possibly know.

'Henri Legrande,' Craig said smoothly. 'Colonel . . . ?'

Priem clicked his heels. 'Priem. At your orders, Standartenführer.'

He withdrew. Craig took her firmly in his arms and they commenced to dance. 'Do you come here often?' he asked.

Strange, considering what she knew about the whole thing now and yet her immediate concern was only for him. 'You must be mad.'

'I know. My mother used to say that all the time. Don't look so worried. Keep that dazzling smile of yours firmly in place.' His arm tightened across her back. 'Daniel in the Lion's Den, that's me. Power of the Lord. I'll get out of here all right and you'll be coming with me. That's why I'm here. It was a set-up, angel. Munro put your head in the noose like a sacrificial goat. Try anything and they'll be waiting for you.'

'Old news,' she said. 'I tried this evening and I was caught. Priem knows, Craig. Told me everything. Baum, Anne-Marie, the whole rotten affair. I'm only out now on a leash, don't you realise? He knows I'll do exactly as I'm told because of Hortense. He's watching every move I make.'

He stopped dancing and slipped her arm through his. 'Let's

give him something to think about then,' and he guided her firmly through the crowd and out through the french windows.

There was a slight chill to the air and they stayed under the colonnade because of the rain. 'Nice and normal and the occasional laugh would be a good idea,' he said, 'and a cigarette would help.'

She glanced up as the match flared in his cupped hands, illuminating the strong face. 'Why, Craig? Why?'

He said, 'What did Priem tell you?'

'That Anne-Marie worked for him.'

He whistled softly. 'Now that *is* something to shake Munro. That means you didn't stand a chance, not from the start, even if Baum hadn't turned you in.'

'Are you trying to tell me that you didn't know? I can't believe that. You used me, Craig, just like you used Anne-Marie. I know the truth about that now. Know what you did to her.'

'I see. And René?'

'Dead. Shot himself to protect me because they were on to him.'

There was silence. Rain drifted in a fine spray through the light from the open French windows. He said, 'Now you believe me, or you don't, but this is how it was. The business with the drug and your sister was an accident; a new gimmick they were going to try on every agent fresh in from the field, only it went wrong. I only found that out from Baum last night. The story they sold you, the SS atrocity thing, was Munro's idea. Good of the cause, and all that, just to give you the urge to do your bit. I was told the same yarn.'

'And Baum?'

'I didn't know the first thing about him or his connection with German Intelligence until last night. What you were told, I was told. That you were coming here for one reason only —

to attempt to fill your sister's place and get hold of any information you could on Rommel's Atlantic Wall conference.'

'If that's true, then why has Munro allowed you to come here now like this?'

'He hasn't. I'm here strictly on my own account. Right now he must be madder than hell.'

And suddenly, with a tremendous feeling of relief, she believed him. Believed him completely.

'It was poor old Baum who spilled the beans by getting drunk and admitting his daughter only died six months ago.'

'I know,' Genevieve said. 'Priem told me.'

'Munro confirmed everything. Told me to grow up. War is hell and all that. Then had me locked up for the night to think things over. I managed to break out and got myself down to Cold Harbour. Martin Hare and his boys brought me over on the E-boat. Julie radioed Grand Pierre to meet us. The boat's waiting at Grosnez now. Getting in here was no problem, not in a uniform like this. I've an uncomfortable feeling it suits me.'

'You fool,' she said.

'I told you I was a Yale man, didn't I? Now, tell me exactly what the situation is here.'

She covered that side of things in a few brief sentences. As she finished, there were footsteps on the terrace and her young Lieutenant paused casually at the balustrade and peered out at the rain. She laughed gaily, accepting the cigarette Craig offered, leaning over as he gave her a light.

'They're watching me every second now. Just go, Craig, while you can.'

'Not on your life. Do you think I could leave you to that lot in there? To the cellars at Gestapo Headquarters in Rue Saussaies? I've been there, and what they do to people like us isn't nice. We go together, or not at all.'

'Not possible. I wouldn't leave Hortense, even if I could. You've still got a chance. Take it.'

He said urgently, 'What in the hell do you think I'm doing here? Were you really so blind back there at Cold Harbour? Did you think it was her I saw every time I looked at you?'

Which left Genevieve only one way out, for his sake now, not her own. She took it, pulling herself free, turning and going back through the french windows before he realised what was happening.

Priem was standing by the fire, smoking a cigar. He tossed it into the flames and came forward. 'Abandoned the poor Colonel already?' And then his eyes narrowed slightly. 'Anything wrong?'

'You might say that. An old lover of my sister's who still has the urge. My memory, you may be interested to know, was all that got him through Russia.'

'These French,' he said, 'are so romantic. The Field Marshal, by the way, is leaving soon. He was asking after you. You are all right now?'

'Of course.'

He smiled briefly. 'You are a remarkable woman, Genevieve.'

'I know and in other circumstances . . .'

'This is beginning to sound like a bad play.'

'Life very frequently is. And now, I think I've earned a glass of champagne, don't you?'

So, Field Marshal Erwin Rommel left Château de Voincourt and Genevieve stood with Hortense and smiled and wished him well, as Priem had told her she would. No sign of Craig Osbourne any longer, which was something. The chill on her deepened. She didn't want to go back to her sister's room ever again.

The crowd started to fade and Priem turned to her and Hortense. 'Time to retire, ladies. A long night.'

'So thoughtful, isn't he?' Hortense said.

Genevieve gave her an arm, they started up the stairs followed by Priem and the Lieutenant, who now, she noticed, carried a Schmeisser machine pistol.

'At the first opportunity you will get out of here, do you understand me?' Hortense murmured.

'And leave you?' Genevieve said. 'Do you imagine for one moment that I can do that?'

They reached the top corridor, Priem nodded and the young Lieutenant brought a chair forward which he positioned where he could watch the doors of both bedroom suites. He looked different, harder somehow. Pale and determined.

'You really are concerned about our welfare tonight, Colonel,' Hortense observed.

'Lieutenant Vogel is merely on call, Countess, should you need him, as is the man Captain Reichslinger has stationed under your balcony. I wish you a peaceful night.' She hesitated, glanced at her niece once and went in.

He turned to face Genevieve. 'It went well, I think,' he said. 'The Field Marshal enjoyed himself. Of course, if he had been aware that a certain file had disappeared from his briefcase, however temporarily, he would not have been so pleased. But that, I think, we can keep to ourselves.'

'Naturally. It wouldn't look too good for you, would it? May I go in now?'

He opened her door. 'Goodnight, Miss Trevaunce,' he said formally.

She could have told him to go to hell, but there would have been little point. So, she simply went in, closed the door and leaned against it. She heard the murmur of voices, the sound of footsteps receding. Her key was missing and a closer inspection of the door revealed that the bolt had been removed also. And, of course, the gun with which she'd so carefully practised was gone.

So she took off her dress, changed into slacks and sweater again, then stepped out on to the balcony. It was still raining and quite dark. She listened for sounds of the guard down below and after a few moments heard a cough. So that was that, and the ledge round the corner to her aunt's balcony was so narrow that only a skilled rock climber could have hoped to negotiate it.

She returned to the bedroom, picked up the silver case and flicked it open. Not a single cigarette left, only the spool of film in its secret compartment and useless now. She felt tired and cold and put on Anne-Marie's hunting jacket and slipped the cigarette case into the pocket.

She got the quilt from the bed, wrapped it around herself and settled in the chair by the window, leaving the light on like a little girl afraid of the dark.

She dozed off for a while, came to, stiff and miserable and saw the curtains stir. They parted and Craig Osbourne moved into the room, a Walther in his right hand. He was still in SS uniform. He raised a finger to silence her.

'We'll take your aunt as well. Satisfied?'

Genevieve was filled with sudden cold excitement. 'How did you get here?'

'Climbed up to your balcony.'

'I thought they had a man down there?'

'Not any more.' He padded across to the door and listened. 'What have they got outside?'

'A young Lieutenant with a machine pistol.'

'Get him in here. Tell him you've heard something suspicious on the balcony – anything.'

He holstered the Walther and took something from his pocket. There was a sharp click, a blade gleamed dully in the light. She stared, fascinated and he gave her a little push. She moved to the door, knocked lightly, then opened it. Vogel was across the corridor in an instant, the machine pistol ready in his hands.

'What is it?' he demanded in bad French. 'What do you want?'

Her throat was so dry that she could hardly speak and yet forced herself, turning and pointing towards the curtains that lifted in the slight breeze. 'Out there, on the balcony. I think I heard something.'

He hesitated, then came forward. Craig Osbourne moved too, an arm around the throat, knee up into the spine, arching Vogel backwards like a bow. Genevieve never saw the knife slide home, heard only the faintest of groans as she turned away, remembering how well he had danced, sick to her stomach. There was the scraping of feet across the floor as Craig dragged the body to the bathroom. When he returned, he was holding the Schmeisser.

'All right?'

'Yes.' She took a deep breath. 'Yes, of course I am.'

'Let's go, then.'

Hortense was sitting up in bed, a shawl about her shoulders, reading a book. She showed no surprise at all as always completely in control.

'So, you would appear to have made a friend, Genevieve.'

'But not quite what he seems.'

'Major Osbourne, ma'am.'

'You've come for my niece, I presume?'

'You too, ma'am. She won't leave without you.'

She got a Gitane from the box on the bedside cabinet and lit it with her silver lighter. Genevieve took out her empty cigarette case and filled it from the box quickly.

'You are familiar with the work of the English novelist, Charles Dickens, Major Osbourne?' Hortense asked. '*A Tale of Two Cities* in which a Mr Sidney Carton, in a glorious act of self-sacrifice, goes to the guillotine in another man's place? By tradition, we have always believed that incident concerned a member of my own family.' She blew out smoke in a long plume. 'But the de Voincourts were always over-enamoured of the grand gesture.' She turned to Genevieve now. 'However misplaced.'

'We're rather short on time, ma'am,' Craig said patiently.

'Then I suggest you go, Major, while you still can. Both of you.'

Genevieve filled with panic, reached forward to pull the bedclothes back. Hortense grasped her wrist with surprising strength. 'Listen to me.' There was iron in her voice now. 'You once told me you knew I had a bad heart?'

'But that wasn't true. Just another lie they fed me to induce me to come here.'

'Anne-Marie believed it. An invention of my own to explain certain dizzy spells I've become increasingly subject to. I kept the truth to myself. One has one's pride.'

The room was so quiet that Genevieve could hear the clock ticking. 'And what is the truth?' she whispered.

'A month now, perhaps two, and it will be painful. Already is. Dr Marais didn't pretend. He's too old a friend for that.'

'Not true.' Genevieve was angry now. 'Not any of it.'

'Did you ever wonder where you got your eyes from, *chérie*?' She had both of Genevieve's hands now. 'Look at me.'

Green and amber, flecked with golden light and filled with love, more love than Genevieve could ever have believed existed and she was telling the truth, she knew that. Her childhood seemed to slip away from her. She experienced a feeling of utter desolation that was almost unbearable.

'For me, Genevieve.' She kissed her on both cheeks gently. 'Do this for me. Always you have given me your love, total, unselfish. The most precious thing in my life, I can tell you this now. Would you deny me the right to give less?'

Genevieve backed away, hands shaking, unable to reply. Hortense said, 'You'll leave me one of your guns, Major?' It was a command, not a request and Craig took out his Walther and placed it beside her on the bed.

'Hortense?'

Genevieve reached out, but Craig caught her by the arm. 'Go now,' her aunt said. 'Very quickly, please.'

Craig got the door open, started to pull Genevieve through. Her eyes were hot. No tears would come. The last view she had of her aunt was of her sitting up in bed, one hand on the Walther and she was smiling.

They moved silently down the great staircase. The hall was a place of shadows. Nothing stirred.

'Where would Priem be?' Craig whispered.

'In his office in the library. He sleeps there too.'

A light showed under the door. He paused, the Schmeisser ready, turned the handle very gently and they went in.

Priem was still in uniform, seated by the fire, working on some papers in the light of a desk lamp, totally absorbed in what he was doing. He glanced up, but showed no surprise, calm, totally in control as always.

'Ah, the lover. Not quite what he seemed.'

'Get his pistol,' Craig told her in English.

'American?' Priem nodded. 'Of course a burst from that Schmeisser would arouse the whole household.'

'Leaving you very dead indeed.'

'Yes, that thought had occurred to me.'

He stood up, hands on the desk. Genevieve moved behind him and took the Walther from its holster.

'And now,' Craig said, 'the papers. The Atlantic Wall material. In that safe behind you, perhaps?'

'And there, I'm afraid, you really are wasting your time.' Priem smiled. 'When I last saw them, they were in Field Marshal Erwin Rommel's briefcase. Half way to Paris by now, I should imagine. You're welcome to check, naturally.'

'No need, Craig.' Genevieve took the cigarette case from her pocket and held it up. 'I had those documents for five minutes in my room earlier tonight as the Colonel well knows. I used this to good effect, just as you taught me. All twenty exposures.'

'Now that really is beautiful,' Craig said. 'Wouldn't you agree, Colonel?'

Priem sighed. 'I said you were a remarkable woman, Genevieve, did I not? So . . .' He came round the desk. 'What happens now?'

'We leave by the side door,' Craig told him. 'The cloakroom entrance. Then we take a little walk down to the back courtyard. I noticed the General's Mercedes there earlier. That should do very nicely.'

Priem ignored him, addressing himself to Genevieve. 'You'll never get away with it. Reichslinger is on duty himself tonight at the gate.'

'You'll tell him the Field Marshal left important papers,' Craig said. 'Anything goes wrong, I'll kill you and if I don't, she will. She'll be down in back of us.'

Priem looked faintly amused. 'You think you could, Genevieve? Now that I doubt.'

No more than she did. Her flesh crawled at the very idea, her fingers, wrapped around the butt of the Walther trembled, her palm already damp with sweat.

'No more talk,' Craig said. 'Now put on your cap, nice and regimental and let's get out of here.'

And then they were somehow outside and walking through the rain across the cobbles of the rear courtyard. It was amazingly still, the Château black and empty. Nothing stirred and she tightened her grip on the Walther in the right-hand pocket of her hunting jacket.

They reached the Mercedes. She opened the rear door and crouched down in the darkness between the seats holding the Walther ready. Priem got behind the wheel, Craig beside him. There was not a word spoken. The engine roared into life, they moved away. It wasn't long, of course, before they started to slow, then rolled to a halt. She heard the sentry's challenge, the click of his heels as he sprang to attention.

'Your pardon, Standartenführer.'

Priem hadn't needed to say a word. There was a slight creaking as the barrier was raised and then, quite suddenly, another voice, calling sharply from the guardhouse. *Reichslinger*.

Genevieve held her breath as his feet crunched across the gravel. Perhaps he hadn't recognised Priem at first for there was only the diffused light of the guardhouse lantern. He leaned down, saying something in German she couldn't understand.

Priem spoke to him. The only word she recognised was Rommel, so he was playing Craig's game after all. Reichslinger replied. There was a slight pause, his boots crunched in the gravel again, and, imagining him to be walking away, she glanced up cautiously. To her horror, she saw his face above, peering in at her through the side window.

As he jumped back, tugging at his pistol, Craig raised the Schmeisser and fired straight through the window, showering her with glass, driving Reichslinger back in a mad dance, then he had the barrel hard against Priem's neck.

They surged forward into the night, Priem working the wheel, swerving furiously as the sentry behind started to fire. And then the darkness swallowed them up and they were away.

*

'You okay back there?' Craig asked.

There was blood on her right cheek, sliced by a sliver of flying glass. She wiped it away casually with the back of her left hand, no pain, only the air, cold on her face and the rain drifting in through the shattered window.

'Yes, I'm fine.'

'Good girl.'

They passed through Dauvigne, quiet as the grave and took the mountain road. 'A pointless exercise,' Priem said. 'Already every command post for miles will have been alerted by radio. Within an hour there will be a roadblock at every conceivable point.'

'Long enough for our purposes,' Craig told him. 'Just keep driving and do as you're told.

Hortense de Voincourt lay there in bed, propped against the pillows, aware of the pandemonium in the grounds outside that had followed upon the sounds of firing down at the main gate. There was shouting in the hall below, footsteps a moment later pounding along the corridor and then a thunderous knocking. She took a Gitane from the silver box and as she lit it, the door was flung open and Ziemke appeared, a pistol in his hand, an SS corporal standing behind him holding a Schmeisser.

'Why, Carl,' she said. 'You do look agitated.'

'What's going on,' he demanded. 'I've been informed that Anne-Marie, Priem and that French Standartenführer just drove out of the main gate. Reichslinger's dead. That damned Frenchman shot him. The guard saw it from the hut.'

'The best news I've heard in ages,' she informed him. 'I never did like Reichslinger.'

He went very still, a slight frown on his face. 'Hortense? What are you saying?'

'That the party's over, Carl. That it's time I acted like a

de Voincourt and remembered that you and your kind are occupying my country.'

'Hortense?' He looked totally bemused.

'You're a nice man, Carl, but that isn't enough. You see, you're also the enemy.' Her hand came out from under the bedclothes. 'Goodbye, my dear.'

She fired the Walther twice, catching him in the heart, driving him out into the ante-room. The SS corporal ducked out of sight, poked the barrel of the Schmeisser round the door and fired in return on full automatic, emptying the magazine. For Hortense de Voincourt, the darkness was instant and merciful.

St Maurice was quiet as the grave as they drove through. Twenty minutes further on at the speed at which Priem was driving and they reached the coast road and Leon. The moon came out from behind a cloud at that moment as they reached the wood on the cliffs above Grosnez.

Craig tapped Priem on the shoulder. 'Stop here.'

The German braked to a halt, switched off the engine. 'What now? A bullet in the head?'

'Nothing so easy.' Craig smiled. 'You're coming to England with us. There's someone I'd like you to meet. I'm sure he'll find you a mine of information.'

He got out of the car. 'Grand Pierre?' he called.

There were men up there, moving down out of the wood in sheepskin jacket and beret. Some with shotguns, others with rifles. They paused, looking down, and Grand Pierre moved forward.

'Hello there!' he called cheerfully.

Priem had a slight fixed smile on his face as he looked at Genevieve in the mirror. 'There's blood on your cheek.'

'It's nothing. Just a cut.'

'I'm glad.'

Craig opened the driver's door and Priem reached under the dashboard of the car. His hand came out clutching a Luger and she reacted instinctively in blind panic, ramming the Walther against his spine, pulling the trigger twice.

His body jerked, there was the smell of burning, the stench of cordite in her nostrils. Very slowly, he pushed himself up and half turned, surprise in his eyes more than anything and then blood erupted from the corner of his mouth and he slumped across the wheel.

Craig reached for her as she scrambled out and she pushed him away. 'No, leave me alone!'

He stood there, staring at her, his face dark, then unbuttoned the black SS tunic and tossed it into the Mercedes. Grand Pierre threw him a sheepskin coat, turned and nodded to one of his men who leaned across Priem's body and released the handbrake. It didn't take much of a push to send the Mercedes rolling over the edge of the cliff, crashing down into the sea below.

She realised that she was still clutching the Walther, shuddered and put it in her pocket. 'He never thought I could do it,' she whispered. 'And when it comes right down to it, neither did I.'

'So, now you know what it feels like,' Craig said. 'Welcome to the club.'

His men stayed on the upper level while Grand Pierre went down the steps to the lower jetty with Craig and Genevieve to where the *Lili Marlene* waited.

Schmidt called, 'Bleeding hell, he's done it. He's got her with him.'

There was an excited murmur from the crew and Hare called down from the bridge, 'Congratulations. Now let's move it.'

The engines rumbled into life. Craig stepped over the rail, turned to give Genevieve a hand.

She said to Grand Pierre, 'Thank you for everything.'

'Crumpled rose leaves, Miss Trevaunce, I warned you.'

'Will I ever get over what I just did?'

'Everything passes. Now off you go.'

She reached for Craig's hand. As she touched the deck, the lines were cast off and the *Lili Marlene* slipped out to sea through the darkness.

Sixteen

Himmler frequently spent the night in a small study adjacent to his office at Prinz Albrechtstrasse. It was four o'clock in the morning when Hauptsturmführer Rossman approached the door with some trepidation, hesitated, then knocked. When he went in the Reichsführer had turned on a small lamp and was already sitting up in the narrow camp bed.

'What is it, Rossman?'

'Bad news, I'm afraid, Reichsführer.' Rossman held up a signal. 'This Château de Voincourt business.'

Himmler reached for his glasses, adjusted them and held out his hand. 'Let me see.'

He read the signal quickly, then handed it back. 'A nest of traitors, this place. I was right, you see, Rossman. All was not as it seemed. And Priem has completely disappeared?'

'So it would appear, Reichsführer.'

'For good, I fear. This French terrorist movement, Rossman. Animals who will stop at nothing.'

Rossman said, 'But what does it all mean? What was it about?'

'I should have thought that was obvious. Rommel was their target. A great coup from their point of view, but according to the report on his movements you showed me before I retired, he left the ball early and travelled overnight to Paris. They got their timing wrong, that's all.'

'Of course, Reichsführer. I see that now. All troops are on full alert in the area. The countryside is being turned upside-down. Are there any other orders?'

'Yes, hostages. One hundred, I think, taken from every village in the area. Executions at noon. We really must teach these people a lesson.' He removed his glasses and put them on the sidetable.

'At your orders, Reichsführer.'

'Wake me at six,' Heinrich Himmler said calmly, and switched out the light.

It was still dark as Dougal Munro walked down from the Abbey to Cold Harbour. He had his umbrella raised, an old tweed hat pushed down firmly over his head, his free hand holding the collar of his cavalry coat closed against his throat. Light showed through the drawn curtains of The Hanged Man, the sign swinging to and fro in the wind, creaking eerily.

When he opened the door and went in he found Julie Legrande sitting by the fire, a glass in her hand.

'Ah, there you are,' he said, shaking rain from his umbrella and putting it in the corner. 'Can't sleep, eh, just like me?'

'Any news?' she asked.

'Not so far. Jack's standing by in the radio room.' He took off his coat and hat and held his hands out to the fire. 'What are you drinking?'

'Whisky,' she said. 'A little lemon, some sugar and boiling water. When I was a child it was a remedy my grandmother employed against the flu. Now it's just a remedy.'

'Little early in the day.'

'For a lot of things, Brigadier.'

'Now don't let's start all that again, Julie. I've already expressed my willingness to forget your part in this wretched affair. No recriminations, please. Let's leave it at that. Any chance of a cup of tea?'

'Certainly. You'll find a kettle on the stove in the kitchen, a tea caddy and a pint of milk beside it.'

'Oh, dear, like that, is it?'

He went behind the bar and into the kitchen. Julie stirred the fire then moved to the window, pulled the curtain and peered out. There was a perceptible lightening outside. Not much, but a hint of dawn to come. She closed the curtain, went back to the fire and Munro came in, stirring a cup of tea with a spoon. In the same moment there was the sound of a vehicle drawing up outside. The door opened, a gust of wind blowing in followed by Jack Carter and Edge.

Edge got the door shut with some difficulty and Munro said, 'Well?'

Carter was smiling, a kind of awe on his face. 'He did it, sir. Craig actually pulled it off. Got her out of there.'

Julie leapt to her feet. 'You're certain?'

'Absolutely.' Carter unbuttoned his wet trenchcoat. 'We had a message from Grand Pierre fifteen minutes ago. Hare waited with the *Lili Marlene* at Grosnez while Craig went to the Château. They left Grosnez just after midnight. With any luck they could be here in an hour and a half.'

Julie flung her arms around his neck and Munro said, 'I always did say he was Houdini come back to trouble us, that boy.'

Edge was wearing a black military trenchcoat over his Luftwaffe uniform. He unbuttoned it slowly, went behind the bar and poured himself a large gin. His face was quite composed, but the anger showed in the eyes, touched by more than a bit of madness.

'Isn't it marvellous, sir?' Carter said to Munro.

'Highly dramatic, Jack, but very counter-productive,' the Brigadier told him.

Julie laughed harshly. 'Craig spoiled your rotten little scheme, didn't he? It would have suited you far more if he hadn't managed to get back at all? If none of them had?'

'It's a thought, I suppose, but a slightly hysterical one.'
Munro picked up his Burberry and put it on. 'I've things to
do. You can run me up to the house.' He turned to Edge.
'You want a lift?'

'No, thanks, sir. I'll walk back. I need the air.'

They went out. Julie, still angry, paced up and down. 'That
man – that damned man.'

'You certainly told him.' Edge took a bottle of gin from
behind the bar and put it in his pocket. 'Anyway, I'm for a
little shut-eye. It's been a long night.'

When he let himself out, the wind was freshening. He went
to the edge of the quay and looked out to sea. He uncorked
the bottle of gin and drank deeply.

'Damn you, Osbourne,' he said softly. 'Damn you and your
bitch to hell! Damn the whole lot of you!'

He replaced the bottle in his pocket, turned and started up
the cobbled street through the village.

The sea was lifting into whitecaps, rain driving in as the *Lili
Marlene* raced onwards to the Cornish coast like a greyhound
unleashed. Dawn was staining the sky in the east and when
Genevieve peered out of one of the small portholes from the
tiny ward room, she looked across a desolate wasteland.

Craig sat opposite, still wearing the sheepskin jacket and
Schmidt came in from the galley with tea. 'England, home
and beauty. Not long now.' He was wearing a lifejacket over
his yellow oilskin.

'What's all this?' Craig demanded.

'Skipper's orders. He thinks it's going to get a bit nasty.'
Schmidt put the mugs on the table. 'You'll find yours in the
locker under the bench.'

He went out, Genevieve swung her legs out of the way and
Craig opened the locker and produced a couple of Kriegsmarine lifejackets. He helped her into one then pulled on the

other himself. He sat down opposite her again and drank his tea.

She offered him a Gitane. 'I suppose I should take care with this.' She held up the silver and onyx case. 'It wouldn't do to get water in and ruin the film.'

'No chance,' he said. 'Designed by a genius, that thing.'

They sat there in silence for a moment. She said, 'What happens now, Craig?'

'Who knows? The situation's changed somewhat. You actually brought it off. Filmed those Atlantic Wall plans and, what's more important, the Germans don't know. They won't change a thing.'

'So?'

'Makes you something of a heroine, doesn't it? And if Martin and I hadn't gone for you . . .' He shrugged. 'Munro will have to like it and lump it. In any case, he'll have his own moment of glory. Ike's going to think he's a magician when he sees those pretty pictures.'

'And afterwards?'

'One step at a time.' He patted his hand. 'Let's go topside and get some air.'

Water cascaded beneath the canvas screens of the rail as they negotiated the deck. Both the 20mm anti-aircraft gun in the foredeck and the Bofors on the afterdeck were manned, two ratings on each wearing yellow oilskins and sou'westers. Genevieve went up the ladder to the bridge, Craig behind her and went into the wheelhouse. Langsdorff was at the helm while Hare was plotting the final approach.

'How are we doing?' Craig demanded.

'Fine. An hour at the most. Maybe less. The sea's behind us.' He looked out. 'Going to get worse before it gets better, but we'll get there.'

Craig put an arm around her. 'I've had a really great idea. Dinner at the Savoy, champagne, dancing.'

Before she could reply, Martin Hare said, 'I've had an even

better one.' He searched his pocket and found half-a-crown. 'I'll flip you to see who gets the first dance.'

By five-thirty it was raining hard at Cold Harbour. Joe Edge sat by his window at the Abbey drinking gin from a tin mug and staring out into the grey dawn morosely. More than half the bottle was gone and he was drunk in an angry, excited way. Not long now and the *Lili Marlene* would be entering harbour. The heroes return, Hare and that stupid Trevaunce bitch and then he thought of Craig and the way the American had humiliated him and his rage boiled over. He poured another shot of gin into the mug. As he raised it to his lips he paused because suddenly he saw the absolutely perfect way to pay them back. All of them.

'My God, it's beautiful.' He laughed drunkenly. 'I'll put the fear of God into the bastards.'

He picked up the phone and called his chief mechanic, Sergeant Henderson, who was billeted with the rest of his ground crew in the Nissen huts at the back of the hangar. It rang for a long time before the receiver was lifted at the other end and Henderson said sleepily, 'Yes, who is it.'

'Me, you fool,' Edge told him. 'You've got ten minutes to get the Ju wound up for me.'

'What is it, sir, an emergency?' Henderson was suddenly alert.

'You could say that. I'll see you there.' Edge put down the phone, got his flying boots and jacket from the wardrobe and dressed quickly, let himself out and went downstairs.

Expecting the *Lili Marlene* in before very long, Munro hadn't gone to bed. He was in the library working on some papers when he heard the front door bang. He got up and went to the window in time to see Edge drive away in one of the jeeps.

249

The door opened behind and Carter limped in, a tray in one hand.

'Tea, sir?'

Munro returned. 'Edge has just driven off. I wonder what he's up to?'

'He'll have gone down to The Hanged Man, sir. They should be in soon.'

'You're right,' Munro said. 'We'd better get a move on ourselves so pour the tea, Jack.'

Sergeant Henderson still had his pyjamas on under his overall. He had already moved the Junkers out of the hangar, was just emerging from the plane as Edge drove up in the jeep. Edge pulled on his flying helmet and goggles and adjusted the chin strap as he walked forward, swaying slightly.

'Everything all right, sergeant?'

'All ready to go, sir.'

Edge staggered and Henderson reached out to steady him. 'You okay, sir?' In the same moment he got a whiff of the gin, pungent on the morning air.

'Of course I'm okay, you idiot,' Edge told him. 'Going to have some fun. I'm going to teach an E-boat a lesson.' He laughed. 'By the time I've finished, Hare and Osbourne will know who the hero is around here. And won't Munro just be properly grateful?'

He turned to the plane and Henderson grabbed his arm. 'Just a minute, sir. I don't really think you should be flying.'

Edge pushed him away violently and drew his Walther from his service holster. 'Get away from me!'

He fired wildly into the ground at the sergeant's feet and Henderson ran, ducking under the belly of the Junkers, taking cover on the other side. He heard the door clang shut in the fuselage. A moment later, the twin BMW radial engines rumbled into life. The aircraft started to move. Henderson ran inside the hangar and made for the office and the telephone.

At the Abbey, Munro and Jack Carter were just finishing their tea when there was a roaring overhead. 'Good God, what was that?' the Brigadier said.

He moved to the french window, opened it and stepped on to the terrace in time to see the Ju88 sweep low over the harbour and start to climb into the grey morning.

'What in the hell is going on, Jack?' he demanded.

The library phone started to ring. Carter answered it. Munro watched the aircraft go, aware of the murmur of conversation behind him. He turned and saw Carter replacing the phone, face troubled.

'What is it, Jack.'

'That was Sergeant Henderson, sir. It seems Joe Edge got him out of bed a little while ago to get the Ju ready for take-off. Said it was an emergency.'

'An emergency? What bloody emergency?'

'He said he was going to teach an E-boat a lesson, sir. Said that by the time he has finished Hare and Osbourne would know who the real hero was and that *you'd* be properly grateful.'

Munro was astonished. 'He must be mad.'

'Also drunk, sir. So drunk that he fired his pistol into the ground at Henderson's feet when he tried to restrain him.'

'Dear God, Jack.' Munro's face was white. 'What are we going to do?'

'Nothing we can do, sir. The *Lili* never uses her ship to shore radio. That's always been a strict rule. You didn't want the Royal Navy or the Coastguard listening in and wondering what was going on. Impossible to warn her. One thing we can do. If we drive up to the headland we can see the approach.'

'Then let's get moving, Jack.'

Munro struggled into his Burberry and hurried out.

As they approached The Hanged Man in the other jeep, Carter at the wheel, Julie came out. Carter slowed down and she said, 'What's going on? What's Joe up to?'

'Get in!' Munro ordered.

She scrambled into the rear and as Carter drove away, he said, 'Edge appears to have blown his top.'

'We don't really know, that, Jack,' Munro said. 'He's had a few drinks and he's playing silly buggers, that's all. It's all going to be all right.'

'What is?' Julie demanded, so Carter explained as he drove up the track to the headland. When he was finished, Julie said, 'He always was a little mad, now he's gone over the top.'

They breasted the hill and bumped over the grass towards the edge of the cliff. Carter braked to a halt. 'There's a pair of binoculars here. Put them there myself.' He fumbled around under the dash. 'Yes, here they are.'

They got out of the jeep and went forward. It was a strange sort of morning. The clouds were very low and black, stretching in a straight line to the horizon. There was some mist at sea level, but the wind kept blowing great gaps in it. It was rough now, the waves in on the beach below.

Suddenly Julie pointed. 'There they are.'

The *Lili Marlene* came out of the grey morning about a mile away, moving towards Cold Harbour at speed, the Kriegsmarine ensign standing out vividly and then the Junkers simply swept out of the black cloud like some bird of prey and raced towards the E-boat at sea level. A moment later there was the sound of cannon fire.

*

Edge had fired wide of the *Lili Marlene* and banked to starboard. Craig and Genevieve had joined Hare in the wheelhouse for the final run to harbour.

'Jesus, it's Edge,' Craig said. 'What's he playing at?'

Hare turned to the radio which was normally never used, flicked on the loudspeaker and picked up the hand mike. 'Come in, Edge! Come in! What's going on?'

The Junkers had banked again, was coming straight for them, and again cannon shell churned up the sea on their port side.

'Bang, you're dead!' Edge's voice was clear over the loudspeaker and he was laughing hysterically. 'Can you hear me, Hare?' He lifted overhead. 'You've really given us a lot of problems. The poor old Brigadier was most concerned. Far better if you and Osbourne and that stupid little Trevaunce bitch hadn't come back at all.'

He banked again to starboard. Hare opened a locker, took out a bundled flag and pushed Langsdorff to one side. 'I think we could have real trouble here. Have one of the men haul down the ensign and put that in its place.'

The bows lifted as he increased speed and spun the wheel, turning to starboard as Langsdorff went out. The Obersteuermann called to Wagner who came up the ladder. Langsdorff gave him the flag and his orders then returned.

'Still there?' Edge's voice sounded again from the loudspeaker. 'Try again, shall we? See how close I can get.'

He banked again, closing on the stern no more than fifty feet above the water as Wagner hauled down the Kriegsmarine ensign on the jackstaff above the wheelhouse. A moment later and the Stars and Stripes streamed out bravely. The sight enflamed Edge even more.

'Bloody Yanks!' he screamed.

Edge was very close now, opened up with his machine gun this time and got it badly wrong, ripping up the afterdeck on the starboard side, killing Hardt and Schneider instantly, driving them both over the rail into the sea.

'Jesus, he's gone mad!' Craig said.

Already Wagner and Bauer were working the Bofors gun on the afterdeck, tracer streaming up in an arc, following the Junkers as it sped away and Wittig was hammering at it with the 20mm ack-ack gun in the foredeck well.

The Junkers staggered as cannon shell punched holes in the starboard wing. Edge cursed and flung the aircraft to port. 'All right, you bastards,' he cried. 'If that's the way you want it.'

He went down then, dangerously low and came in towards the stern again. Hare was giving the *Lili Marlene* everything she had, those tremendous Daimler-Benz engines responding at better than forty knots, criss-crossing from one side to the other. Edge had always been a great pilot, but the madness on him that morning seemed to give him the touch of genius for he closed at over four hundred miles an hour no more than thirty feet above the waves.

Craig grabbed Genevieve by the arm. 'Down!' he cried and flung himself on top of her.

Edge used his machine guns again, ripping up the afterdeck, mowing down both Wagner and Bauer at the Bofors gun, shattering the wheelhouse windows, catching Langsdorff in the back, driving him headfirst through the door.

Suddenly, the *Lili Marlene* was slowing in the water. Craig stood up and as Genevieve joined him, she saw Hare slumped forward, blood on his reefer jacket. Half the controls had been shot away, and down on the foredeck Wittig was hanging over the ack-ack gun, supported only by its shoulder rests.

'You're hurt, Martin.' She put a hand to his shoulder.

As he pushed her away the Junkers came in on the port side, raking the entire ship with cannon fire. The *Lili Marlene* was on fire now and below, through the smoke, she saw Schmidt clamber across the foredeck to pull Wittig away so that he could get at the gun.

Hare said, 'We've had it. Get Genevieve off.'

Craig pushed her ahead of him. There was already water slopping across the deck as Hare followed them. He and Craig wrestled to uncouple one of the rubber dinghies stowed on the afterdeck and got it over the rail.

Craig held the line. 'Go on, get in!' he told Genevieve.

She did as she was ordered, losing her balance, falling headfirst into the dingy and in the same moment, Edge came in towards the stern very low.

Hare said, 'I'm going to get that son of a bitch,' and he turned and plunged towards the Bofors gun.

Craig hesitated then suddenly released the line and before Genevieve knew what was happening there was ten yards between her and the E-boat. 'Craig!' she screamed but by then it was too late.

He was beside Hare at the Bofors, already knee-deep in water. 'Concentrate on his belly,' Craig shouted. 'Remember those nitrous oxide tanks.'

The Junkers came in hard, Edge giving them everything he had. The Bofors gun hammered in reply and Genevieve saw Martin Hare lifted up and blown back. And now Craig was at the gun, swinging to follow the Junkers as it passed overhead and started to climb.

The explosion, when it came, was the most catastrophic thing she had ever seen. The Junkers simply disintegrated into an enormous ball of fire as its nitrous oxide tanks exploded like a bomb, fragments of fuselage dropping into the sea all around.

A great wave pushed the dinghy up. She was already fifty yards away and moving fast. Genevieve saw the prow of the *Lili Marlene* lift high out of the water. There was no sign of Craig Osbourne or little Schmidt, no one in the water that she could see. The prow lifted even higher, the Stars and Stripes flowering for a moment and then the *Lili Marlene* went down by the stern and slid under the surface.

*

On the clifftop, Dougal Munro slowly lowered the binoculars, his face ashen. Julie Legrande was crying. Carter put an arm around her shoulder in some sort of comfort.

'What now, sir? I think I saw a dinghy down there.'

'Back to the village, Jack. Inform the coastguard. It won't take the lifeboat long to get here from Falmouth. There's always a chance.'

But he didn't sound as if he believed that, even to himself.

The dinghy was pitching violently. Genevieve had been sick so many times that there was nothing more to come. The sky was blacker than ever and it was raining heavily. Not that it mattered. With a foot of water in the dinghy she was soaked to the skin anyway and she just lay there, head pillowed on the side, as miserable as any human being could be.

It was perhaps three hours after the *Lili Marlene* had gone down that she heard the sound of an engine approaching. She pushed herself up and saw the Falmouth lifeboat bearing down on her. Five minutes later she was inside its cabin wrapped in blankets, one of the crew handing her a mug of coffee.

A man in oilskins came in, middle-aged with grey hair and a pleasant face. 'I'm the coxswain, Miss. Are you all right?'

'Yes,' she said.

'We haven't found anyone else.'

'I don't think you will,' she said dully.

'Well, we'll keep looking for another hour and then we'll take you into Cold Harbour. Those are my orders.' He hesitated. 'What went on out here, Miss? What was it all about?'

'I'm not sure,' she said. 'I think it was a game that went wrong. A sort of ultimate stupidity, just like the war.'

He frowned, not understanding, shrugged and went out. Genevieve wrapped her hands about the mug, seeking comfort from its warmth, and sat there, staring into space.

*

Carter in the dark room, Munro at his side, gently unrolled the film. 'Is it all right, Jack?' Munro asked. 'I mean, she was in the sea for a long time.'

'Looks perfect to me, sir. I thought it would be. Even the cigarettes were bone dry in that case.' He held the film up.

Munro said, 'And she maintains these are of the contents of Rommel's briefcase?'

'Apparently, sir. Said there was more, but she only had twenty exposures.'

'A miracle, Jack. One of the major intelligence coups of the war. Eisenhower and his planning staff at SHAEF will be over the moon when they see this.' He shook his head. 'She did it, Jack, a slip of a girl like her. A rank amateur. I was wrong.'

'Yes, but at what cost, sir?'

'The Luftwaffe raided London again last night, Jack. People died. Do you want me to go on?'

'No, sir. Point taken.'

Munro nodded. 'I've calls to make to London. I'll see you in the library in thirty minutes.'

'And Genevieve, sir?'

'Oh, bring her along by all means.'

Genevieve lay in the hot bath Julie had provided until the water started to cool. She got out and dried herself carefully. There were bruises all over her body, but she felt no pain. In fact, she didn't feel anything. Julie had left underwear on the bed for her, a heavy sweater, cord slacks and jacket. She dressed quickly, was just finishing when Julie entered.

'How are you, *chérie*?'

'Fine, nothing to worry about.' She hesitated and then said calmly, 'Any news?'

'I'm afraid not.'

'I didn't think there would be.'

'I've just seen Jack. He said the film turned out to be perfect. He asked me to give you this.'

She handed her the silver and onyx case. Genevieve smiled slightly and took it. 'An interesting souvenir. Do I get to keep it?'

'I don't know. Jack said Munro would like to see you in the library.'

'Good,' Genevieve said. 'As it happens, I'd like to see him.'

She started to walk to the door, stopped and picked up Anne-Marie's hunting jacket which lay in the corner with the other clothes she had taken off. She felt in the pocket and took out the Walther.

'Another interesting souvenir,' she said, slipped it into her pocket, opened the door and went out.

Julie stood there for a moment, frowning anxiously, then she went after her.

Munro was sitting in the wing-backed chair by the fire sipping brandy from a crystal goblet. Carter was standing at the dresser, pouring a Scotch when Genevieve entered the library.

The Brigadier said, 'Ah, Genevieve, come in, let's have a look at you.' He nodded. 'Not too bad, I see. Good. You've heard the splendid news about the film. A major coup. You've shown a real talent for this kind of work. I can use you at SOE, my dear, very definitely. You should do well.'

'Like hell I will.'

'Oh, yes, Flight Officer Trevaunce. You hold the King's Commission. You'll obey orders and do exactly as you are told. The Lysander will be here in a while. You'll come back to London with us.'

'Just like that?'

'Naturally there will be some sort of decoration for you and well deserved. The French will probably give you the Legion of Honour. Some of our girls in the field have been awarded the MBE, but that decoration hardly seems appropriate in your case. I think we can manage a Military Cross. Unusual for a woman, but not unprecedented.'

'I know about my sister,' she said. 'Baum told Craig and Craig told me. Even Priem knew.'

'I'm sorry,' Munro said calmly. 'An accident of war.'

She said, 'You sit there calmly swilling brandy and yet you sold me out. Worse than that, you set me up quite cold-bloodedly from the beginning. And you know what's so funny about that, Brigadier?'

'No, but I'm sure you'll tell me.'

'You didn't need to have Baum sell me out. It seems Anne-Marie was working for the other side so I didn't stand a chance with Maz Priem from the beginning. I shot him dead, by the way. Twice in the back with this.' She took the Walther from her pocket.

Munro said, 'I'm sorry, my dear. I presume you didn't think you were capable.'

'No.'

'But you were, you see? I said you had an aptitude for this work. You're certain about Anne-Marie?'

'Oh, yes, and there was something else.' She frowned, finding it difficult to concentrate. 'This Fitzgerald woman at Romney who you've been running as a double. Did you know her husband worked with Michael Collins in the IRA during the Irish Troubles?'

Munro went very still. 'No, I don't think we did know that. Why?'

'She's fooled you. She still works for German Intelligence using IRA contacts in London.'

'Does she indeed?' Munro's eyes sparked as he glanced at Carter. 'Get on to Special Branch at Scotland Yard as soon as we get back. The Irish Section. With any luck we'll bag the lot.' He turned to her. 'Ike will be delighted about this. Copies of Rommel's Atlantic Wall plans and the beauty of it is, Rommel doesn't know.'

'Wonderful,' she said. 'Do you get a cigar?'

He said calmly, 'All right, so I'm a bastard – the kind who wins wars.'

'Using people like me?'

'If that is what it takes.'

She walked to the table, turned, leaning against it, the Walther heavy in her hand. 'You know, I was going to make a speech. All about standards and honour and how if you didn't have rules, even in a bloody stupid game like this, you're as bad as the people we're trying to beat.'

'What changed your mind?' Munro asked.

'Oh, I thought about all those bodies stretching from Cold Harbour to Château de Voincourt. René Dissard, Max Priem, Martin Hare and the crew of the *Lili Marlene*, Craig Osbourne. All the brave young men asleep in the deep, isn't that how the poet puts it. And for what?'

'My dear Genevieve,' he said calmly. 'Time is limited. What exactly are you trying to say?'

'That as you're as bad as the Gestapo, maybe I should treat you like the Gestapo.'

The Walther swung up in her hand. Munro didn't flinch, and it was Julie, hidden in the shadows at the back of the library, who cried, 'No, Genevieve, he isn't worth it!

Genevieve stood there, very pale, the Walther steady in her hand. 'Well, get on with it,' Munro said impatiently. 'Make your mind up, girl.'

'Damn you, Brigadier!' She sighed and put the Walther down on the table beside her.'

Jack Carter came forward and placed a tumbler of whisky in her hand. He picked up the Walther and put it in his pocket.

Munro said, 'Very sensible. I'd drink that if I were you. You're going to need it.'

'More bad news and it isn't noon yet? Come on now, Brigadier. I don't think you're really trying today.'

He said, 'Your sister died last night.'

She closed her eyes and then there was only the dark and Carter's anxious voice. 'Are you all right?'

She opened her eyes again. 'How?'

'I ordered a post-mortem. It was the heart.'

'Another side-effect of that drug of yours?'

'Very probably.'

'Where is she? I want to see her.'

'I don't really think that's going to be possible.'

'The Official Secrets Act? You're going to start throwing that at me?'

'No need,' he said. 'Not with your father still around. If you go stirring things up, it would all come out, amongst all the other little unpleasantnesses, that his favourite daughter had been a Nazi agent. That should just about finish him off, wouldn't you say?'

Genevieve said, 'I did bring you those photos. I think you owe me something for that at least.'

'All right, you win.' Munro sighed. 'She'll be buried in a pauper's grave, unmarked, naturally. Six a.m., the day after tomorrow. Highgate Cemetery.'

'Where is she now?'

'An undertaker in Camberwell handles these things for us. Jack can take you.'

She said, 'What about Herr Baum?'

'He was only doing his job like the rest of us.'

The phone rang and Carter answered it. He turned. 'The Lysander just landed, sir.'

'Good.' Munro stood up. 'We'll be off then.'

'But there still might be a chance,' Genevieve said. 'Craig – the others.'

'Yesterday's news,' Munro said, 'so let's get going.'

Seventeen

On the afternoon of the following day, Jack Carter delivered her to the undertakers in Camberwell. He waited outside while she went in. It was pleasant enough, a small, oak-panelled waiting room smelling of beeswax polish and candles, a sheaf of white lilies in a brass container by the door. The man who attended was very old, probably someone who had stayed on because of the war, his hair snow white, a perceptible shake to his hands.

'Ah, yes,' he said. 'I did have a telephone call about you, Miss. The party in number three. There is just one small difficulty. There's a gentleman in there already.'

She brushed past him and entered the small corridor beyond. There was a sealed coffin in the first cubicle, the second was empty but a green baize curtain was drawn across the third. A voice murmured softly the Prayers for the Dead in Hebrew. She's heard them often enough in the casualty wards at Bart's during the Blitz.

She pulled the curtain aside and Baum swung to face her clutching a prayer book, a small round capel on his head. Tears coursed down his cheeks.

'I'm sorry – so sorry. As God is my witness, I never meant for such a thing.'

Beyond him she could see Anne-Marie, hands folded across her breast, the face, her own face, framed in the shroud, peaceful now in the candlelight. She took his hand in hers and held it tightly, saying nothing, for there was nothing to say.

It was a grey morning, fog in the air and Highgate Cemetery was not the best place in the world at that time of day. She was delivered to the gate, once again by Carter in a green Humber limousine.

'No need to wait,' she told him. 'I'll find my own way back.'

Strangely enough, he didn't argue, but drove away and she walked up through the cemetery, hands pushed deep into the pockets of her jacket. She didn't need to search for the plot number, she saw them up in the far corner soon enough. The old man from the undertaker's in black overcoat, hair very white in the grey morning, bowler hat in hand, two grave-diggers leaning on their spades while a minister in black cassock worked his way through the burial service.

She waited until he'd finished, turned and walked away with the undertaker, approaching herself only as the gravediggers started to shovel in earth. They glanced up, old men, long since past the age for military service.

One of them paused. 'Anything I can do for you, Miss? Someone you knew?'

She glanced down at the plain deal coffin partially covered with dirt. 'I thought I did once. Now, I'm not so sure.' It started to rain and she looked up. 'I wonder if God ever intended mornings like these?'

They glanced at each other in some alarm. 'You all right, Miss?'

'Perfectly, thank you.' Genevieve said.

She turned and found Craig Osbourne standing a few yards away watching her.

*

He was in uniform. Forage cap and trenchcoat and when he took it off, she saw that he wore olive drab battledress underneath, his pants tucked into jump boots. His medal ribbons made a brave show in the grey morning as did the double wings on his right sleeve.

'I like it better than the last one,' she said. 'The uniform, I mean.'

He slipped the trenchcoat over her shoulders without a word. They walked down the path between the gravestones and fog swirled in spite of the rain, shrinking the world until it encompassed only the two of them. The rain intensified into a solid downpour and they ran together, making for a small shelter with benches by the fountain and all she could think of was another graveyard in the rain and Max Priem.

She sat down, he took out a pack of cigarettes and offered her one. 'I'm sorry,' he said. 'About Anne-Marie. Munro only told me last night.'

'They didn't tell me you were safe. Even Jack didn't mention it.'

'It was after midnight when I got in. They told me you'd be here this morning.' He shrugged. 'I asked Jack not to say anything. I wanted to tell you myself.'

'What happened to you?' she asked.

'I drifted away when the *Lili* went down. Same thing happened to Schmidt. We held hands for a long, long time. Finally washed up on a beach near Lizard Point.'

'And Martin?'

'Gone, Genevieve. They're all gone.'

She nodded, took out her case and selected a Gitane. 'What's going to happen to you now. Munro can't have been too pleased.'

'At first he was madder than hell. Said he was shipping me out to China. There's an OSS project starting out there to train Chinese commandos in hit-and-run tactics, parachute jumping, that sort of thing.'

'And then?'

'The Supreme Commander took a look at the blow-ups of those photos of yours.'

'And everything changed?'

'That's about the size of it. It's coming soon now, Genevieve – the big day. It's been decided to drop in SAS and OSS units far behind German lines in France when the time comes, link up with the Maquis and cause as much disruption as possible.'

'In other words, Munro finds he needs you again?' she asked. 'What for, Major? Another oak leaf cluster to your DSC?'

He didn't reply to that, simply said, 'Jack tells me the old bastard wants you for SOE?'

'So it would appear.'

'Damn him to hell!' He put his hands on her shoulders. 'You were always yourself alone, never her. Remember that.'

Priem had said that to her. Amazing how alike they had been. She nodded. 'I will.'

He stood there, looking at her. 'That's it, then?'

'I suppose so.'

He walked away suddenly, the greyness swallowed him and that was no good, no good at all. There was a war on. You lived for today and took what there was. It was as simple as that.

She ran forward, calling his name. 'Craig!'

He turned, hands in the pockets of the trenchcoat. 'Yes?'

'Didn't you say something about dinner at the Savoy?'